WELCOME TO SENIOR SHORT STORIES

Here are 54 stories of various lengths, from one page to ten pages, covering many ages, from pre-history to years in the future. Stories using both imagination and reality that, hopefully, will not only entertain you, but also stimulate your mind and put a smile on your face.

Stories written between age 68 and 88 by a man who has enjoyed the blessings of life, has seen and/or participated in some of the big events of the twentieth century, has traveled in many foreign lands, and wants to share his thoughts with a busy world before he says goodbye.

Once you read the stories, here are some questions you might ask yourself:

Does imagination fade with age?
Or does it bloom and flower?
If you look inside and read every page,
will you enjoy each minute and hour?

L. Macon Epps

PREFACE:

I don't remember when I first started creating fictional short stories. I suppose most everyone has the ability to do so since we all learn to tell a fib at an early age. To me, a fib is a child's way of trying to get out of trouble by making up a fictional story. It requires two things: <u>Imagination</u> and <u>Inspiration</u>. We all have imaginations, some more vivid than others, and getting out of trouble is an inspiration we develop at an early age.

As we get older, we learn that one can make up a fictional story that is not a fib, because the storyteller <u>labels</u> it fiction. Furthermore, it is told to entertain others, not deceive them. Therefore, fictional stories, be they short stories, novelettes, or full novels, are widely accepted. Since I have labeled all of the short stories in this book as fiction, they are all examples of my imagination.

As to the things that inspired me, they are many and varied. Sometimes a remark of a friend inspired a story. Sometimes stories were inspired by dreams, both the night and day type. Sometimes a news item, or an event that I actually witnessed was the inspiration. In any event, something inspired each one, and I usually didn't pay much attention to its source. You see, I was eager to write my story down for my own entertainment, or perhaps for family and friends.

I have chosen short stories for three reasons. First, in today's busy world, time is precious, and short stories can entertain, and perhaps inspire readers, without taking a lot of reading time. Furthermore, unlike a novelette or novel, a short story can achieve its goals in one short reading session, not multiple sessions that are extended for days. My second reason is my age. (I was born 1-16-1920). Tackling a novel is a big endeavor that requires time and energy, which gets in short supply as you age, especially the energy part. My third reason is the time and energy required for my other creative activities, which include writing poems, essays, memoirs, true experiences, letters to political leaders, and inventing new products. Of course, I also have the regular activities of life, such as daily life with family and friends, plus club, community and church events, and tennis four times a week. If that sounds like I have a lot of energy, you should see me when I take my afternoon nap.

With this book, I hope to reach a much larger audience than family or friends, and I hope that you will like my <u>imagination</u> and find at least some of my stories <u>entertaining</u>.

L. Macon Epps   9-18-08

P. S. Feel free to make limited copies of stories you especially like for family, friends and students. However, if you want to use them commercially, please honor my copyright and get my permission by writing to me at 17236 Village 17, Camarillo, CA, 93012, or by telephone at 805/389-9478.

INTRODUCTION

As you can see by the table of contents, this collection of short stories has lots of variety. For example, there are stories involving: Ghosts interacting with people; political satire and fantasy; extra-terrestrial beings; everyday people and everyday problems; marital relations; pre-historic people; musicians and music; psychiatrists and their patients; an ancient great philosopher; mysteries; stories inspired by dreams; religious characters and events; talking inanimate objects; stories inspired by my youth that are partly true, but greatly embellished; natural events; world affairs, etc. Some are basically meant to be humorous, and I have tried to sprinkle a bit of humor in most of them.

I have chosen my titles carefully, and in the table of contents I placed a lead-in sentence before the title. This was done so you can get an inkling as to what the story is about, and, hopefully, be persuaded to read it.

I realize that some stories may be better than others, but no one bats a thousand. I also realize that people have different tastes, so perhaps a story that get a low mark by one person may get a high mark by another. I would appreciate some feedback, either pro or con, from readers that feel inclined to do so. (See preface for my address and tel. #).

Speaking of printing, this one was limited to 50 books because I paid for them myself. If you like my book, please lend it to friends, or have them order it directly from me or from: Amazon.com

I would like to thank friends from my New Hampshire and California Writers' Clubs for their past help, support, and inspiration. Their comments, both pro and con, have always been appreciated. I especially thank Gerry Kaplan for his computer help and Beatrice Epstein, from the California Club, for proofreading my typed manuscript. She is the only person (other than my wife of 63 years) who has read all of my stories. Here's hoping many more readers will join her!

Finally, I would like to emphasize that my motive in getting this book published isn't money, but to make sure that some of my writings aren't lost forever. If anyone sees commercial possibilities by using any of my stories via another method or medium, please contact me via the information in the preface, and if successful, I will give a standard agent's fee of 10%.

Although I have been responsible for three other published books, this is the first one that I have done solo. I have at least four others that need finishing touches, and if this one goes well I might be tempted to do it again. Wish me luck!

L. Macon Epps   9/22/08 (rev. 2/18/09)

TABLE OF CONTENTS:	PAGE

A BAD RAP

(By Ghost Ezra, as told to medium L. Macon Epps)

You living mortals don't understand us ghosts. You listen to the spooky tales and legends, and conclude that <u>all</u> of us are evil, scary, mischievous, mean, terrifying, and even worse things. The bad actions of a few ghosts tarnish the reputation of us good ghosts. In your lingo, we think we're getting a BAD "RAP"!

The truth is, most ghosts are quite decent and just want to be left alone so they can serve their time for the evil deeds they did when alive. Occasionally, we do enjoy encounters with living people as a relief from our lonely existence. However, the encounters are usually fun, or at least exciting, for both the haunters and the hauntees.

I know that many of you are skeptical about our existence, so the fact that we have a good sense of humor and have fun-filled encounters, probably stretches your latent belief to the breaking point. To help you overcome your disbelief, let me tell you about an encounter I had in 1906, one hundred years ago.

The occupant of my house at that time was a scientist from the University of New Hampshire. His name was Dr. Steven Hamilton, and the house was in Lee, a small town near the University and in a sparsely settled area. Dr. Hamilton bought the house even though there were strong rumors that a ghost (me) resided there. Like most scientific types, he was a "Doubting Thomas" when it came to ghosts, so his disbelief posed a challenge to me. To respond, I dipped into my bag of tricks so he would become a believer. Since I am a gentle ghost, I decided to use humor; I didn't want to frighten him too much, because his type might go over the edge.

One night, when he was alone in the house working on next day's lecture, I made a loud rapping noise in the cellar. Naturally, he came down to investigate it. I stopped it soon after he started looking, and moved it up near the front door. Incidentally, I got the idea from Edgar Allen Poe's famous poem, *The Raven.* Remember these lines:

'Once upon a midnight, dreary,
While I pondered, weak and weary,
Over a quaint and curious
volume of forgotten lore.

As I nodded, nearly napping
Softly, still I heard a tapping,
As of someone gently rapping,
Rapping at my chamber door.
This I heard, and nothing more."

I guess he too had read *The Raven,* because he bounded up the cellar stairs and went to his front door. There was no one there; he looked around and even shouted, "Is anyone there" several times. He was annoyed, curious, and a bit frightened, so he picked up a baseball bat-- just in case. I then moved the rapping sound to different rooms on that floor, diminishing its volume each time he entered the room.

After he had searched each room thoroughly, I moved the rapping to the second floor. By then he was determined to find the source of the noise, even though he was both puzzled and perplexed. I heard him swearing, muttering to himself, and vowing to find out "What the hell is going on here?"

Finally, I moved the noise to the attic, but this time I concentrated it in an old chest of drawers, starting with the top one. When he opened the first drawer, he had the bat raised over his head so he could konk the critter that emerged. Nothing did-- the drawer was empty and silent.

I moved the noise to the second drawer, and he repeated his motions. Again, the drawer was empty and silent. I then moved it to the bottom drawer and increased its volume and frequency so he would think he'd finally solve the puzzle. As he slowly opened it, I stopped the rapping noise, and he gazed dumbfounded at the drawer's contents-- a large roll of wrapping paper!

He was stunned, but slowly a big grin came on his face, he lowered his bat and started chuckling. He knew that I had played a humorous trick on him, especially once I made the wrapping paper bounce around and then slowly rise up to the rafters. I even partially materialized myself, so he could see my ghostly shape and big smile.

At first he gasped, but eventually he said, "OK, Ok, I was wrong about ghosts. Not only do you exist, but you have a damn good sense of humor and some awesome powers--can we be friends?

"Of course," I replied. We then had a long discourse, mostly concerning his questions about my life in the sixteen-hundreds, the world of the departed, and the meaning of life.

It was a very successful night for me. Not only did I convert a doubting scientist into a believer, but I made a good friend with whom I could talk during lonely evenings. He would not tell his friends about our encounter because of his faculty position, but he did get local fame as the originator of the joke about the ghost and the wrapping paper.

Before we parted that night, he insisted that we make a pact. As he put it, If you don't give me a bad rap, I won't give you a bad RAP!

ACTIVE PASSIVISTS

Congress and the President were impressed by the sincerity and persuasiveness of the delegation from Passive Voices United. (PVU) They were especially impressed with the careful research and the logic of the group's conclusions, which were confirmed by government researchers, statisticians, and independent pollsters.

While they agreed that the nation was being endangered by the excessive behavior of many activists, it seemed like political suicide to curb them because of their widespread publicity and the first amendment's support of free speech. The nation was forced to give in, much too often, to the foolish demands of a small minority of excessive activists. When they took to the streets to loudly, and frequently violently, raise their active voices, It became a problem that caused all politicians many headaches!

The activist minority referred to above had little to do with race or ethnicity, but was simply a tiny percentage of the population. The vast majority was passive on many issues and therefore considered un-newsworthy; so the news media focused on the actions of the active few and usually ignored the opinion of the passive many. Naturally, the politicians were overly influenced by the news media, plus the many calls, letters, and personal button- holing of the activists.

The politicians finally decided to support PVU's solution: Whenever activists raised their voice in excessive protest, or in demand of really stupid actions, PVU would be asked for its opinion. This alerted PVU so it could mount demonstrations that called for fact-finding, careful and objective analysis, and clear thinking on how to resolve the conflict using latest information and techniques. (Can't you just see the signs they used?)

The results amazed the politicians. First, the media was responsive to the demands of the passive majority for equal coverage. In fact, events where people acted rationally, instead of emotionally and violently, were considered by many editors as newsworthy. Next, facts were gathered, analyses were made by clear thinkers and validated by honest experts, and the media and the politicians were forced by self-interest to cooperate and lead the general public to accept rational and workable solutions.

The passive majority was so pleased that it not only re-elected supportive politicians, but actually honored them. Supportive media become richer and more respected, because the public saw the error of the extremist's ways. The few in each group who clung to the emotional, violent, and irrational behavior soon found themselves out of office or out of business.

Activists leaders were especially displeased when the comedians started making jokes and performing funny skits that depicted them as stupid, semi-morons. Their behavior soon changed for the better, because few people want to continue to be public laughing stock. The good old U.S.A. became a much better place, and it wasn't long before other nations started emulating us. By the year 2020, the world's vision was also 20-20!

With that sort of vision great things were accomplished: wars were abolished; population growth was controlled; resources were conserved and brought into balance with sustainable growth; education was universally effective; crime was rare; prosperity was widespread; and human rights, the arts and creativity flourished.

Yes, things sure changed for the better when all the passive voices were mustered to out demonstrate, out think, and out do all the loud mouthed, illogical active voices!

To cap it all, a photo of mother earth was taken by a cosmos-astronaut during a Russo-American trip to Mars that became world famous. Some said the unusual feature in the photo was caused by changes in vegetation-- others attributed it to shadows on existing geological formations; but everyone agreed on one thing:

Our sad old planet finally had a BIG SMILE on its face

Note: This story about human potential was inspired by a class assignment to write in the passive voice. I hope today's fantasy will become tomorrows reality! L.M.E.

Future news item?

AMAZING VISITORS COME TO LEISURE VILLAGE
By: Jason Argon, Staff Reporter (2001 words)

Camarillo, CA-- May 6, 2008. An elderly couple in the active retirement community of Leisure Village were visited by two unusual guests on April 25, 2008. Macon and Elizabeth Epps were the hosts, and their guests, Paul and Pauline Parsons, were amazing guests because they brought four gifts that could only be classified as extremely unusual. The guests had been sent there by Mr. Epps' nephew, Dr. Stephen Greer, a Virginia resident, who had told them, "The Parsons are the most gifted and intelligent people I have ever encountered. I'm sure you will find them amazing!"

The following report was obtained via an interview with Macon and Elizabeth, after the guests had left:

The first gift, given to Elizabeth by Pauline, was a bottle containing an elixir of unknown content. According to Elizabeth, who followed the bottles directions, one drop placed in a gallon of bottled water made it change color to that of a beautiful, multicolored rose. Furthermore, its scent was like the most fragrant rose she had ever inhaled. When she and her husband tasted a teaspoon of the colored water, they immediately felt a strong wave of energy flow through them. In fact, it was so strong that Macon placed a dance CD in his Hi-Fidelity system, and the couple began dancing vigorously to very lively tunes from the forties, when they were in their twenties. Their guests were delighted, and applauded after each tune.

Sometime later, Pauline suggested they look in a mirror. Upon doing so, the couple found that their hair had turned back to the color it was in the forties--medium brown for him, auburn red for her. Furthermore, all the wrinkles in their faces had disappeared, their complexion was flawless, and both were trim and muscular. Both of them wanted to know what was in the elixir bottle, but all Pauline would say was: "Oh, it's just one of the standard products we produce. We can bring you some more when that one is used up, but, as you might guess, it should last a decade or longer since you need take only a teaspoon each month."

Macon wanted to know if it was available commercially, but Paul said, "Sorry, but it's not. It's too special for commercial use, but we will give it away to people recommended by Dr. Greer. We can leave an extra bottle for your children if you like."

Elizabeth wanted to know about their relationship with Dr. Greer, and Pauline said, "Oh, Steve and his wife, Emily, were the first persons to be kind to us when we arrived in your country. In addition, Steve was doing research that made us very attracted to him, since we felt we could be of help, and repay him for his kindness."

Paul then handed each the second gifts, both of which were in large boxes. Upon opening them, they found classy garments that made both of them ooh and ah, and protest that they were too nice! "Not for relatives of Steve, Pauline responded.

They then left to change into the new garments, and, upon returning, Paul said, "Now slowly raise one of your thumbs."

Once they did so, they both slowly rose to the semi-cathedral ceiling in their home. Macon was delighted, but Elizabeth wanted to know how to get down. "Just slowly move your thumb the other way," Paul replied.

Once down, Elizabeth tried to coax Macon down, but he was so overjoyed, he wanted to stay longer. "Now tilt your body slightly and you will be able to move in that direction," Paul advised.

This Macon did, and started whooping and hollering as he moved back and forth. After several minutes, he came down, saying, "Wow! That was great. Can we do it outdoors, and are there any restrictions?"

Paul said, "Yes, you can do it outdoors, and the only restriction is stay below 60,000 feet. You can go any speed you like, up to Mach 3, by inclining your bodies at a steeper angle. Maximum speed is when you are horizontal."

"What would happen if we ran into an airplane while going fast, or even going slow? And could we stand the aerodynamic pressure and elevated temperature at high speeds?"

"You will be perfectly safe because the garments have permanent force fields that will automatically cause you to deviate from a collision course with an airplane, or any other object. In fact, even if someone shot at you with a high-powered rifle, the force field would cause the bullet to drop to the ground at your feet. More powerful weapons that couldn't be stopped by the field would deviate around you and save your lives. You should also know that high air speed doesn't put any aerodynamic pressure on your bodies, because the force field sends the onrushing air around you, but keeps enough air within the field to keep you breathing normally. As to temperature, the field is a good insulator, so your bodies stay warm no matter what."

"But how can we breathe at high altitudes? I suppose we must go pretty fast to have the onrushing air provide the proper pressure."

"You are absolutely correct. In fact your body will automatically incline to get the speed you need to keep breathing normally!"

"Gosh, you folks have thought of everything," Macon replied, "And your technology is more advanced than any I have ever heard of. Have you contacted NASA? I worked on their Manned Lunar Landing Program in the sixties for Grumman Aerospace."

Paul said, "No we haven't contacted NASA yet, and Steve told us about your Lunar landing experience. That's one of the reasons we contacted you."

Pauline then spoke to Elizabeth. "There's another feature which you both may find useful. If you cross your arms, or even your fingers, you can become invisible, and escape from dangerous or unpleasant situations. Even if you are in a massive building, you can go through the walls or ceilings without harm when you are invisible."

Elizabeth was speechless, but Macon said, "That's truly amazing, and I'll try it very soon. I have another question: What will happen if we keep the garments on all the time, even at bedtime? Can we sleep in zero gravity, or near it, and will we need cover for warmth?"

"We recommend keeping them on most of the time, except when you need to have them off for personal reasons. You do not need cover or anything else, since they automatically keep your body at normal temperature, even in sub-zero weather. As you might suspect, you do not need to have your home heating and A/C system operative, except when you have regular visitors or for personal reasons. As to sleeping at zero gravity, we recommend it. It is not only the most comfortable way, but lets you sleep most anywhere in your home. You can even sleep in a public place by using your invisibility and floating to the ceiling, where people will not see or bump into you."

Elizabeth then asked, "Can we put something over them to change their looks? Although they are very attractive, our friends will wonder why we wear the same garments all the time, and even I may eventually get tired of the same outfit."

"Of course you can change them," Pauline replied. "The color, pattern and shape can easily be changed by rubbing the left or right shoulder until you find one you like; there are thousands of combinations!"

Elizabeth was so impressed that she rubbed her shoulder several times to check it out. "It's wonderful," she said, "but I might have a problem making up my mind with so many choices."

The third gift, given by Pauline to Elizabeth, was a metallic box about the size of a large dictionary. When Elizabeth opened it, she and Macon were awe struck, because they saw hundreds of precious jewels. Both protested that the jewels were much too expensive, saying that the other gifts were really more than they should accept, and were wonderful beyond their imagination. Paul and Pauline both said, "Please accept them. You will not only please Steve and Emily, but us. You see, we have an almost unlimited supply of these gifts, and we got great happiness by giving them to Steve, Emily, and Steve's research associates. We plan to give them to their children and siblings soon, but Steve thought we should give them to you early on because of your age. Besides, they are part of an experiment we are running to see what wonderful things will be developed by mature recipients. You will be doing us a great favor to accept all of them."

Elizabeth then said, "Well, if you put it that way, I suppose we can accept them. And I know I speak for both of us when I say that we'll use them when possible to help the human race overcome its many problems."

Macon said, "Amen!"

The fourth gift was in a very small box. When Paul handed it to Macon and he opened it, there was a small, gold-colored device in it. "Is that a flash drive?"

"Yes", replied Paul, "and it is the most important gift of all. It is special knowledge, which our civilization has developed to help those who receive our gifts do wonderful things. Read the information together every night on your computer and it will guide you to accomplish your goal to help solve the world's problems. You are the tenth couple we have given them to, and we hope you will work with the Greer's and Steve's associates, to make big changes to the earth."

Once both recovered from the impact of Paul's words, Elizabeth said, "You mentioned your civilization, almost as if it were out of this world. Is it?"

"You are very perceptive, my dear," Pauline said. "Yes, we are from another planet, called 581 c by your astronomers. It is the one they discovered last year. We met Dr. Greer during his investigations of extra-terrestrial Intelligence. We are now working with him and his associates on most of his projects, and now you two are included. The elixir will keep you young and energetic for many decades; the garments will not only help you with your work, but will be both protective and very enjoyable; the jewels will provide you with plenty of money, both for your own needs and for your new work; and the flash drive will provide the advanced knowledge needed to make important changes. We both wish you much success and happiness in your new life and work!"

"I have one more question," Macon said. "How can we protect these wonderful gifts from evil people? As you know the world is full of them, and some are extremely clever."

Paul's reply was both comforting and amazing. "All of them have been coded so that only you and Elizabeth can use them. And they are invisible and untouchable to all others."

The next morning after breakfast, Paul and Pauline said goodbye. They then became invisible and left the house through the cathedral ceiling.

The great physical change in both Elizabeth and Macon was the talk of Leisure Village, and soon it became known to the community. It was then that I, your reporter, interviewed them. Once my interview ended and we were outside, they said they were going to start on their first mission. Of course I found their story unbelievable, and figured that some young look-alikes had moved into their home and were involved in some sort of wild publicity stunt. That is until they both rose 50 feet into the air and disappeared from sight!

Note: My nephew, Dr. Steven Greer, is one of the major investigators of Extra-terrestrial intelligence. He has written two highly informative books on the subject and been interviewed on TV. This fictional story is dedicated to him and his associates.

ARE GHOSTS REAL?

This question has been raised so often, that I, Ezra Dobson, ghost for the last 300 years, decided to give it a firm answer by writing this piece. Being an up to date ghost, I have written it on the computer of an elderly man who recently lived in New Hampshire. I'm sure he'll show it to his family and writing groups, so a few people will find that we are not only real, but may learn something about us. Hopefully, he will get it published so a lot of people will be better informed. Here goes:
You living mortals don't truly believe we are real, and you certainly don't understand us. You listen to all the spooky tales and legends, and conclude that if by some odd chance we _are_ real, we are evil, mischievous, mean, horrible, scary terrifying, and maybe even a few things worse than those.
The truth is, most of us want to be left alone and undisturbed. Oh, sometimes we like encounters with live people as a diversion from our lonely routine; but usually, we wont bother you if you don't bother us.
Of course, many of you don't believe we exist. That not only displeases us, but also perplexes us. Why? Because many of you have a religious faith that deals with a spiritual hereafter, but somehow you can't imagine that we ghosts are part of it. Well, you are wrong, and let me tell you why.
All living mortals are a mixture of good and evil, and once you die your spirit must be cleansed before you can enter the eternal presence of OUF. OUF is an acronym used in the spirit world for the Omnipotent Universal Force. We use that term because you mortals have so many names for OUF-- God, Jehovah, Allah, the Great Spirit, etc. I was raised as a Christian in New Hampshire, so I am aware that a true believer's sins are forgiven by Christ's sacrifice on the cross. But, as I will show, most departed souls, be

they non-believers or believers, must be cleansed.

As part of the cleansing process, you must spend a small part of eternity confined to a limited area on earth. The size of the area and the time you must spend depends on the amount of cleansing you need. I hasten to add that this process is not punishment, but is done so you will be able to enter OUF's magnificent presence with a pure heart, instead of a guilty one.

To illustrate, let me use my wife, Emily, and myself as examples:

I was born in 1635 and died in 1706. Emily was born in 1636 and died in 1715. After our deaths, I was confined to the boundaries of my farm for 300 years. Emily was free to roam anywhere in New Hampshire for 25 years. Now most of my life I was a good person. My evil side was limited to a few lies; minor cheating; a quick temper; and the usual lascivious thoughts. I probably could have been cleansed in 50 years, except for one big evil-- I killed my neighbor, Zophar!

Oh, I felt justified at the time because the s.o.b. was trying to rape my wife while I was out hunting for our Thanksgiving turkey. Fortunately, I found a big turkey very quickly, so I returned home earlier than usual. As I entered the house, I was shocked at what I saw. Zophar had tied Emily to our bed, gagged and partially disrobed her, and was about to force his way on her. He immediately stood up, started to flee and reached the back door. Unfortunately, my quick temper was red hot and I had reloaded my gun in case I spotted some other game. I lifted my musket and shot him dead. My aim was perfect, because the musket ball hit him right between the eyes as he was looking back to see if I was following him. I untied Emily, who was grateful to be saved, but horrified by the method I had used. After I had calmed both of us down, I wished I hadn't killed him. Maybe a sound beating and having him arrested would have done the trick.

The judge at my trial was pretty lenient, and ruled it was justifiable homicide. He did make me pay Zophar's widow a yearly stipend until she re-married. But OUF deals with Eternity, hence the 300 year term. Zophar was confined to his barn for 800 years. It seems that Emily wasn't his only prey; he was successful with five other rapes, and the wives were too ashamed to tell anyone. One had a baby by him, and that caused a lot of explaining to her husband, who wasn't very bright and bought her story after a bit of persuading. Zophar also had some very crooked business dealings and other evil ways, so 800 years seemed pretty lenient to me.

I was very lonesome until Emily's ghost joined me. During that 25 years, we didn't contact any living people. Mostly, we stayed in our barn and only materialized ourselves when it was night and everyone was asleep. During the day, Emily roamed to other places in NH and she told me about her travels when she returned. Our eldest son had inherited the farm, and we weren't about to bother him or his family. Sometimes we used our ghostly powers in a helpful way, and occasionally we entered his dreams, but that was all.

When a heavy-drinking stranger cheated my son out of the farm in 1748, I decided to take the sort of action that is proper for ghosts. What is proper action? Well, it is OK to get rid of evil undesirables, provided we use decent means.

For example, we can make a fire sputter, burn poorly; and send sparks to land on an undesirable person; we can hide things they need, and then create highly localized sickening odors before they approach their hiding place; we can make all sorts of sounds, from a muffled sob to loud bumps in the night; we can levitate an object as large as a mule and change its size; we can make a portion of any room or hallway chillingly cold; we can make candles flicker, grow dim, and go out, and we can even do the same thing with your new-fangled electric lights and TV sets; finally, we can materialize, walk through solid walls, and disassemble our body parts.

Here's what I did to the stubborn oaf who cheated my son: Initially, I used the first three of the above actions, but he wasn't about to leave my prosperous farm for a few unexplained tricks. I then materialized so he could see the front door through me. I made sure the door was bolted, and when he approached me I walked through the closed door and de-materialized. When he unbolted it to find me, he was perplexed, and then became visibly frightened. I added to his fright by re-materializing behind him and whispering: "Get out, and NEVER come back!

He rushed out into the yard, ran toward his bedroom and told his wife, "Start packing, because we're moving as soon as possible."

He never came into the house again, and in a few days he had sold the house back to my son and moved his family to Maine. That was fitting, because people in Maine are jokingly called "maniacs." In his case, it was true, because he never got over the frightening experience

Once my son and his family moved back in, I did all I could to make their life pleasant. Partially-aged wood would burn brightly and last longer than the best aged wood; candles and lamps were brighter and so long-lasting that they marveled at their endurance; lost objects were placed in conspicuous places and the house filled with pleasant odors; the wind played musical sounds in the eaves and nooks and crannies; rodents and other pests were kept away from the house, the barn, and even the fields. Naturally, I got a lot of pleasure in helping my son and his family, and I continued my help even when the last heir died and the farm was sold.

I especially enjoyed seeing all the kids play and grow into good men and women, Sometimes I would materialize and talk to the kids, but I made them think I was a stranger who occasionally visited the area. I explained that I once lived on their farm, and told them tales about life there in the early days. One of them, who later became a history teacher, jotted down some of my stories and told them to his classes. I also taught them many other things, and even helped them with their homework until it got too difficult for my eighth grade education.

I marveled at the new equipment and farming methods that were developed through the years. The crop yields they obtained each year were many times greater that the farmers of my day, and one of their farms could provide food for many families. The nation became more and more industrialized. I guess that's where those new tractors and other equipment came from, and was one of the reasons part of my 200 acres became a sub-division once the nearby town started expanding.

Well, it is now 2006, and my 300 years are almost up. I guess I won't need to frighten any more undesirables, but neither will I be able to help any good ones. I'll sure miss talking with the kids and watching the world progress, even though some of the progress is a bit frightening for mankind's future. From what I hear from Emily's communications with me, I'll be going to a wonderful, spiritual place and be reunited with my family, old friends, and make new friends.

Best of all, I will be in OUF's marvelous presence with all my guilty feelings cleansed!

Author's Note: When I turned my computer on this morning, the above story appeared on the screen. I recently cancelled my Internet service, so it couldn't come from there. My wife doesn't use a computer so that let's that source out. I keep my doors locked, so I doubt if an intruder came in and typed the story instead of stealing my few valuables. I am 86 years old and belong to two writing groups, so I qualify as the elderly man in the story. I will read it to both groups, send family and close friends copies, and may even try to get it published. I have never seen a ghost, except in my dreams, but this story has removed some of my doubt and given me a better insight into a ghost's stay on earth. I hope readers will soften their doubt and get a better understanding of ghosts, or at least find Ezra's story entertaining.

BARELY BELIEVABLE

"I'm going to the dry cleaners tomorrow--want me to take anything for you?"

Thus spoke my wife, Betty, in late May 1955. That was over 40 years ago, so skeptical readers may ask: "How can you recall such a small detail that far back—are you putting us on?"

My answer is simple—the above quote was the start of an incredible story, and the whole sequence of events made such an impression on me that it has a permanent place in my memory. As to the "putting on" question, I'll let the story speak for itself.

My reply to her question and the subsequent conversation went something like this:

"No thanks, dear, but what are you taking to the cleaners at this time of year?"

"Oh just a few things for our White Mountain trip next week, " she replied. " Things like my heavy wool sweater and pull-over cap."

"Well, I 'm taking some wool clothes too-- probably need 'em once we get to the higher altitudes— but I'm not going to clean 'em until we return and avoid double cleaning. I hoped she'd get my point.

Ignoring my thrift hint, she replied: "Yes, dear, but don't you want to look your best on the trail?"

"Have you seen how hikers look on the trail lately? They aren't the epitome of elegance, you know—in fact, most of them look kind of grungy —and some of them look like tramps." (My thoughts flashed back to my first White Mountain trip when my buddies and I were mistaken for tramps because of a five days' growth of whiskers.)

"Well, I think we should set a good example. After all, we are now in our mid-thirties and the young folks expect it." Her mother's instinct was in full display, even though friends were going to take care of our two kids while we were away.

I knew it was useless to argue with her, so I dropped the subject. In fact, It disappeared from my mind until the subsequent events of this story revealed its importance.

When we arrived at Pinkham Notch, our bunk assignments were in order, thanks to Betty's writing far in advance for a reservation. We had stayed at Pinkham notch several times before and had met the genial manager, Joe Dodge, also known as the Mayor of Porky Gulch. It hadn't taken me long to learn that his gruff manner concealed the proverbial 'heart of gold'. In fact, I enjoyed his good-natured banter—not only with me but also with some of his other guests. I'm sure some of the newcomers found it shocking, because Joe didn't mince words, but spoke his mind directly; and his vocabulary was very colorful and sometimes punctuated with 'cuss' words for emphasis.

Joe and I would tease each other about our growing girth, and he never failed to notice my graying hair, nor I his thinning hair. And once he found out that I lived near New York City, a "cesspool of crime and corruption," to use his terms, some of the others looked shocked and offended. But that was Joe, a man who loved his mountains and the natural beauty and purity that abounded there. It was clear that he wanted to stay far away from any large city.

Although I knew that Joe was a major figure in the region, and had a reputation as a natural born manager whose solutions to problems and crises were 'Immediate, informal and effective,' I didn't know that he was already becoming a legend. Nor did I know that his fame would increase in the coming years, growing after his retirement from his job with the Appalachian Mountain Club. I'm thankful for my ignorance; otherwise I would have been less flippant and missed-out on some good exchanges.

We got to sit at Joe's table that night, and enjoyed a simple but hearty meal. We also enjoyed conversing with Joe, fellow hikers and two rock climbers. Toward the end of the meal, Joe said, "If any of you are headed for Lion's Head, watch out for bears. Two hikers had a close encounter last weekend. Fortunately, they heeded my standard advice and stood still—can't outrun a bear, you know—and dumped all their food while they carefully backed away. Now I'm not saying' you'll see any bears there or anywhere else, but if you do, remember my advice and you'll make it back to supper here, instead of becoming the bear's supper!"

We all laughed at his last bit of humor, and I then said, "Joe, I've heard that you don't have to outrun a bear--just your trail mates."

The other tablemates laughed at my little joke, but Joe didn't find it amusing. Joe was dead serious when he said, "I want all my guests to make it back for supper, and don't any of you ever think otherwise I"

One of the others said, "Aren't bears a rarity in New Hampshire, Joe?"

"Yup," he replied. Ever since the state put a bounty on them, they've been as scarce as hen's teeth!"

One of the rock climbers asked Joe to tell the story about the time he found a dead bear and collected a bounty four times, but Joe declined. He did tell about the stuffed bear some of his hut boys found, and the fun they had putting it in the ladies' latrine now and then. Joe was full of fascinating tales if you could ever get him started, and his memory for details was simply amazing.

I told Joe that Betty and I decided to heed his warning and cancel our plans to go to Lion's Head; we were going to hike to Huntington Ravine instead. Not to climb it-- that's for rock climbers, but to look at its sheer cliffs close up-- from the bottom!

We left after breakfast the next morning with our backpacks loaded with trail lunches from Joe's kitchen crew, plus emergency stuff-- warm clothes; ponchos in case of rain; flashlights and candles in case we were caught overnight; etc. My hunting knife and hatchet were on my belt, and both of us carried canteens full of fresh water. Betty pointed out her newly dry-cleaned clothes in their sealed-for-summer plastic bags, complete with mothballs.

"It's the way they came from the cleaners," she said, "so I figured I'd leave them that way. If I don't need them I'll store them for summer and save money too! See how neatly they fit in my backpack?" She was obviously proud that her foresight was working out so well, but was kind enough not to chide me.

"Yeah," I replied/ "but why do you have them on top?"

"So they'll provide insulation for my lunch!" She gave me her "I'm not as dumb as you think" look! Or was it her "men are so stupid" look? Sometimes it's hard to tell.

I stopped the incipient argument by saying, "Good Thinking!"

When we got to the trail, we were virtually alone. About half way up the trail, some of the morning coffee wanted out, so I headed for nearby bushes. I was rudely interrupted by Betty's soft call:

"Come back at once—there's a bear coming down the trail!"

I made my way back as quietly and quickly as possible, considering the circumstances. When I reached her side, she had slowly removed some items from her backpack. Naturally, the sealed garments preceded her lunch as she carefully backed down the trail. First the wool sweater, then the wool pull-over cap, then the lunch bag-- each looking like strange rocks spread out uniformly on the trail.

"Good work," I whispered excitedly. "Now let's keep backing down and see what he does."

Joe's advice was working. The bear looked at the first plastic bag and figured it was discarded garbage and thus easily entered, as he had done on many other feast occasions. He ripped it open to devour its contents, but the quick release of pent-up gases made him recoil. His look of surprise would have been downright funny, except for the danger still confronting us.

While the loud 'poof of the gases startled him, the strong odor of residual cleaning fluid and mothballs gave him second thoughts about the whole situation. He sneezed several times, scratched his nose, and started ambling back up the trail.

"Let's beat it!" I whispered.

"How about my clothes and lunch?" Her voice was insistent.

I waited until I was sure the bear was going to stay away before saying, "Oh well, I guess it's the least I can do since you did such a good job remaining cool and chasing friend bear away." The sweater was undamaged and the other bags still unopened.

Our visit to Huntington Ravine was delayed until there were more hikers on the trail. We arrived back at Pinkham around one p.m., having eaten a hasty lunch at a clearing near the bottom of the trail-- where there was a zero chance to encounter another bear!

Joe Dodge was surprised to see us back so soon, and said:
"Did you folks set a new record?--or did you poop out?"

"Neither," Betty responded. "We met a big black bear-- and thanks to your advice we came back early. Didn't want to miss supper. We decided to disappoint the bear instead of you!"

Joe chuckled, but was all ears as we told him the details of our adventure. When we concluded, he said, "Well, that's certainly one for the book—dry cleaning and moth ball odors, you say? Maybe I'll throw some mothballs in all the lunches we pack!" As he walked away to do his duties, we heard him muttering-- " I wonder if that damn bear was the same one as on Lion's Head; if not, maybe 'Cow Hampshire' should up the bounty."

I don't know whether he made it a general practice or not, but every time we got a lunch from his kitchen there was a small plastic bag filled with mothballs! To this day, we both keep his unopened mothball packets on our closet shelves—in memory of the surprised bear and our life-saving friend, Joe!

Author's note: While the bear-on-the-trail incident and most of the story is pure fiction, I do have a cool-headed wife named "Betty" and I did meet Joe Dodge several times during my stays at Pinkham Notch; not with Betty, but with a hiking buddy, who knew him real well and gave me insights into his unforgettable character. The book, Joe Dodge, by William Putnam, is recommended reading and is where I learned about the bear bounty, stuffed bear and other things. Although Joe is now long dead and I 'm in my mid seventies, I can still see his face and hear his New Hampshire accent in my memory; I hope my portrayal of Joe is on the mark and that my story will renew fond memories of him to the countless hikers, climbers, skiers, hut managers, kitchen help, trail people, and any one else who knew and appreciated this New Hampshire original—Joe Dodge. May their tribes increase!

THE BIG BOO-BOO

"Why did you say that?" Evelyn asked.

"Why did I say what?" Tom replied.

"You know perfectly well what I mean." There was ice in her voice.

"No I don't, damn it," he insisted. "Why can't you be clearer—I can't read your mind, you know."

"You're exasperating!" she said sharply.

"Me?" he said huffily. "What do you think you are when you won't even tell me what you mean?"

"Well, I think you're mean, or obtuse, or something for not knowing that you just insulted me." She said, modulating her voice a bit.

"You're driving me daffy." he said in a loud voice.

"Lower your voice, you brute. People are starting to look this way. After all, it's a party and we should be having fun."

"Some fun," he said in a subdued voice. He faked a smile and patted her arm so the others would "tune out' of their private argument. He thought a minute and suddenly caught on.

"Do you mean my comment about how much I liked Florence's new dress? That was five minutes ago!"

"Of course," she said indignantly, "and it was only two minutes ago!"

"Five."

"Three and a half."

"O.K."

"What's wrong with my complimenting her—not jealous, are you?"

"Of course not, you oaf, but when will you ever learn?" There was despair in her voice and hurt on her face.

"Learn what?" There was a puzzled look on his face.

"That your wife comes first, you big ape." Don't you know the dress I'm wearing is <u>brand new?</u> Why did you effuse over Florence's new dress and not even notice mine?" Her voice was plaintive and a bit angry.

"Oh," he said, "I understand now. I'm sorry honey. I guess I made a boo-boo. Say, your dress is very nice—how much did it cost?"

There was frustration, annoyance, anger, disdain, disappointment, sadness, hurt and a few other negative emotions that she managed to blend into the one little word that closed the argument: "MEN!"

He walked away in silence to freshen his drink. Women are so sensitive, he thought. But it was dumb of me not to notice her new dress and dumber still to ask the price. I guess I've spoiled my plans for later on. Next time I'll be sure and compliment her first—or at least wait until she's out of earshot before I compliment another woman. I can't believe I made two boo-boos in one night. That adds up to one Big Boo-Boo—only big boobs do that—the male kind!

THE BIG OOH-OOH!

"What a nice thing to say," Marilyn said sweetly.

"What do you mean, dear?" David inquired.

"That nice compliment you just gave Florence on her new dress." Her voice was warm and loving.

"Well, it was pretty and it seemed to be made just for her," he responded. "But between you and me it's not nearly as nice as your new dress."

"You're sweet dear," she said. " And I really appreciate your quick reaction and compliments when I came down the stairs at home."

"I meant every word, sweetheart. You know that don't you?" His voice was soft and sincere.

"Of course, of course," she replied. Tears welled up in her eyes and she patted his arm gently.

"As a matter of fact," he continued, "as pretty as your dress is it can't compare with your own loveliness. You're certainly the belle of the ball tonight!"

"Oh darling," she said, as she planted a big kiss on his willing lips.

"People are starting to stare, honey. Maybe we should save that for later. I might lose control—you know how easily you turn me on."

"Like an incandescent light bulb powered by an Ever-Ready battery." She laughed merrily because she had used that simile many times in the past. "But let them stare - this is a party and we're supposed to have fun."

"Right on," he replied. "But the real fun will come later. As far as I'm concerned, this is just the overture—the opera starts when we get home!"

"Oh, listen, they're playing our song." There was excitement in her face, her voice and her body.

"Shall we dance?" He took her in his arms and they "tripped the light fantastic" oblivious of all others....

"Wasn't that a grand party?" she said, as he inserted the key in their door.

"Sure was—and I was real proud of you tonight. I think a lot of the other men thought you were the "belle of the ball' too!" A sudden impulse hit him. He opened the door, picked her up and carried her across the threshold.

"How romantic," she said. "Does this mean we're starting a new honey-moon?"

"The tenth, I think." His voice was uncertain.

"The eleventh, dear. The tenth was last fall in Hawaii."

"Of course—I didn't forget it," he replied, "I just lost track of the number."

"I have a surprise for you," she said. "Make yourself comfortable on the sofa and give me five minutes."

"I'm waiting breathlessly." He started panting rapidly.

"Still my little puppy dog?" She patted his head and stroked his hair gently.

"Woof, woof!" His smile was as mischievous as a small boy's. He took off his jacket and shoes, sat on the sofa and waited impatiently....

"Wow!" he said. "What a gorgeous negligee."

"I thought you'd like it," she replied. "I got it at the same sale as the dress—both were 50% off."

"I don't care if they were 50% on—the dress was lovely but this is—uh—uh—stunning! What a wife—she's beautiful, has great taste and saves money to boot—I'm a lucky guy!"

She sat beside him and threw her arms around him. There was tenderness, excitement, joy, pride, love, affection and a few other positive emotions that she managed to blend into the two little words that ended the conversation and started the action. It wasn't long before he heard the familiar "OOH, OOH!"

His last clear thought, before his senses started reeling, was that its better to hear a big ooh-ooh, than to make a big boo-boo, like some husbands do. That way, the only big boobs encountered are female ones!

THE BIRTH OF MUSIC

PROLOGUE:

I was fortunate to have two very good friends in college, Dave Strong and Dan Bowen. I was doubly fortunate that we ended up in the same region of the country, and thus could see each other often. I was triply fortunate that Dave and Dan were absolute geniuses in their chosen field -- Dave in microbiology and genetics, Dan in computer science and programming. But the most fortunate thing of all was their invitation to accompany them on a fantastic voyage to the distant past-- Mission: To discover "The Birth of Music!"

I know it may seem incredible, but they found a way to use DNA, in combination with very advanced computer technology and virtual-reality goggles to explore the past. Don't ask me how it works, because I couldn't really grasp it even though I have a master's degree in Aeronautical Engineering and they explained it several times. About the closest I can come is that DNA, having been coded for eons to produce certain results, can be interpreted, via electron microscopes, to reveal past history in great detail, provided it is coupled with a computer program and advanced technology so that it becomes feasible. Yes, they found a way to "surf" the past from one generation of genes to the previous generation ad infinitum.

As a starting point, they used DNA from Bach, Beethoven and Mozart, three of the greatest musical geniuses that ever lived. They also used DNA from some lesser musical geniuses as back up. Other researchers had obtained DNA samples from various famous people's grave sites, and Dave got permission to use the famous musician samples for three months. During that time, my two genius friends got enough data to send to Dan's computer programs to get the project underway. The DNA samples were the key to their eventual success, and both agreed they were well worth the $10,000 rental fee.

Dan's computations, using probability theory, indicated that the odds were very good that we would not only find the original creator of music, but would discover when, how and why it happened. Needless to say, I was excited about the voyage, even though we did all our traveling back in time in Dan's computer lab.

They had selected me as the third voyager, not only because of our long friendship, but also because of my writing ability, at least compared to theirs. I had helped both in college with English Composition and Technical Writing, and while they both became proficient, they looked up to me when it came to putting great events down on paper. I was happy that they appreciated my modest skills, because it gave me a first class seat on the greatest adventure of my life.

After several months of surfing back in time, and innumerable false leads, we finally arrived at our destination. It was the year 103,642 B.C., according to Dan's computer program. He found the first inklings of music later in that year, and then ran the computer back in time to earlier in that year. It was May 6 of that year that we were able to witness the birth of music in the mind and musings of a teen-age boy named Glork.

With inputs from the three of us using visual observations to support vocal messages from the people of that era, Dan's computer program was able to convert their primitive speech into its English equivalent. Not only were we able to understand everything he and other tribal people said, but the speech conversion was so good that it made these primitive, but smart people sound like the well educated people of today. As to their gestures and body language, they were easy to interpret without the aid of a computer. We could fast forward and back at will, so we were able to avoid the days and weeks when nothing creative or interesting was happening, or go back to get greater detail.

While we all watched intently at the unfolding scenes, Dan tried to record it on digital video, but it was too blurry for commercial use, so I wrote it up in narrative form for the world to read. We felt the written word would be a good forerunner, because if it made a big splash there, we could follow it up by releasing the video once Dan works out the technical problems. We are all financially well off early retirees, so making a huge personal fortune is not our motive. We will use the proceeds to fund similar projects in other fields--medicine, art, writing, law, engineering, science, writing--you name it, and we believe it is possible to find their roots and evolution, provided we can find the right DNA and there is sufficient dough. The importance of money was something we all agreed about, since Dave and Dan spent over $400K of their own cash, not to mention thousands of hours of research and development time. I even kicked in $50K when they needed more equipment to complete the first prototype. I guess that was another reason they selected me. Incidentally, they have filed a number of patent applications to protect their inventions, and only they and their sons and daughters know some of the more esoteric secrets.

What follows is my summary account, as revealed by DNA that goes back to a young cave boy, named "Glork". Although he was sometimes in great danger, we were never at risk since we experienced virtual reality, not the real thing. We did share some anxious moments with our new friend, which almost matched his own anxiety.

So here is what we saw, heard, felt, tasted and smelled through Dan's advanced virtual-reality goggles. Yes, he had added the other three senses to the sight and sound ability of most goggles. I told you that he and Dave were absolute geniuses!

CHAPTER 1: GLORK AND HIS TRIBE

Glork woke up with a big yawn, looked toward the mouth of the cave and saw that daylight had come. He glanced around the dimly lit interior and discerned other signs of life-- women nursing their infants, other women poking up the fire at the entrance and adding more wood -- mustn't let it go out because restarting was too difficult and would arouse the wrath of Chief Bomba. Fortunately, the chief was still sleeping and snoring gently.

Everyone hoped he would be in a good mood after last night's feast on a large animal. Bomba wasn't a man of moderation and usually gorged himself to excess on such occasions. When that happened, he usually woke up in a foul and abusive mood and struck at the nearest person. The medicine men of that era had not discovered antacids, which might have quelled Bomba's fierce temper.

Glork rolled up his animal skin bed and stowed it in the usual niche. He put on his foot covering, grabbed his club and hastened outside, hoping to be well out of range when Bomba woke up. Alas, Bomba woke up just as he was moving softly past him and grabbed his ankle. Fortunately for Glork, Bomba was distracted when he reached for his club and would have hit him hard. Glork wiggled free just in time, taking care to avoid showing his face to Bomba. He barely made it out of the cave before he heard Bomba's roar, followed by the screams of those who received his cruel blows.

Glork quickly grabbed some nuts as he left, so he could break the long fast of the night. As an adolescent boy, he wasn't allowed to gorge during a feast, nor was he allowed to have any of the leftover morning meat at that time-- that was reserved for Bomba first, followed by his father, Glorko. When his father died, Glork would add the "o" to his name in accordance with tribal tradition. Only the male elders could have two syllable names. Once Bomba and Glorko had grabbed their food, the other men could eat. They pushed, shoved and grunted in their quest for nourishment.

Glorko was the smartest man in the tribe, having invented the spear and the bow and arrow. He also discovered which plants were edible and how to track game. These talents had earned him the number two position and chief advisor to Bomba, but being chief wasn't possible; that exalted position went to the strongest, meanest and best fighter, and Bomba had the scars to prove he had earned his chiefdom.

Next came Bomba's mates, followed by Glork's mother and then the other women. The mothers fed their small children, but the larger ones were last and scrambled for their share of the remains. The women smiled softly as they took turns, keeping their long-held secret. (They always turned the meat over so the best portions were on the bottom, knowing that the men would be too hasty to notice.)

After eating, the tribe went about its usual tasks: The men went hunting for fresh meat, the women gathered edible plants, fruit and nuts in season, wood for the fire and slender limbs to use as spits for cooking the meat. Everything else was consumed raw. Small children accompanied their mothers, including infants who were carried in animal-skin pouches on their mothers' backs.

Glork and the other adolescents were expected to bring back small game, or fruit and nuts. Glork usually went with his three best friends, Teeg, Zod, and Drang. He and Drang had learned to use a bow and arrow, and the others were good at tracking, spear throwing, and clubbing. They were all about sixteen years old and still developing. Sometimes they were allowed to go with the men so they could learn large animal hunting skills, and most fathers taught their sons other necessary knowledge around the campfire at dusk.

They also learned a lot from the storytellers, especially when they told about wars with other tribes and fights with ferocious beasts. Once it grew dark, everyone went into the cave to sleep, leaving the fire at the entrance to discourage wild nocturnal beasts. They didn't worry about other tribes, because who would be foolish enough to venture forth in the dark?

Glork was about five feet five, with broad shoulders and a narrow waist; his eyes were alert, even penetrating when he concentrated, and he was a quick learner. He had long brown hair with a hint of curls, and the first signs of a beard. He was the tallest and smartest of the group and a natural born leader. Teeg was the shortest and Zod and Drang were an inch or two shorter than Glork. They were the best of the adolescent teams in bringing back food and were both admired and envied by the other youths.

CHAPTER 2: BIRDS, GIRLS, AND EMBRYONIC MUSIC

Around mid-morning, they stopped at a small stream for a drink. Glork heard two birds and liked the sounds they made, especially when they seemed to be conversing. In fact, he was so enthralled that he persuaded the others to follow the birds down stream, even though it was beyond their usual territory. The stream became swifter and swifter, and soon they heard a loud roar. They had to climb among the rocks and cliffs that formed the gorge, and near the top Glork slipped and nearly fell to his death, but Teeg grabbed him just in time. Glork grunted his appreciation, since "Thank You" had not entered their primitive vocabulary.

The four friends persevered until they saw an amazing sight: a large waterfall. We could see from their astonished faces that they were thrilled to make such a discovery. As they looked at the large pool below it, they discovered the water had become more peaceful. As their gaze went to the opposite shore, they saw something even more thrilling: four nude, teen-aged girls bathing in the placid waters.

(Dave, Dan and I chuckled at their reaction, and Dave said, "I guess some things don't change, even if a hundred thousand years of civilization has gone by!")

Glork was immediately attracted to one of them. She was slender and shapely, moved quickly and gracefully, and had long dark hair that glistened in the sun. Previously, he had thought he was too young to have a mate, but the girl below made him think again; maybe it WAS time, so he vowed to come back alone with his club and drag her back to his tribe, as was the custom. He glanced around the waterfall to spot a way to safely descend once the right time came.

As he and his friends returned to their cave home with their small game, Glork had two images in his mind: the lovely girl and the sweet sounds of the birds. Somehow, the two seemed to go well together. That night, as he slept under his animal skins, his active, stimulated mind had a brilliant idea. Here's what we heard as he muttered to himself in the darkness: "I'll get ten of the other boys, and using the birds as a model, we'll create some sweet sounds of our own. First I'll convince my friends that I have a secret idea which might elevate all of us in the tribe's esteem, thereby leading to a better choice of food and other privileges." (Secrets and greater choices were as appealing to these early youth as they are today's youth, so the plan was bound to work.) "Next, I'll use the nearby box canyon as our secret meeting place, and select a time when the adults are busy elsewhere."

But how to create the sweet sounds was more difficult, so he racked his brain well into the night. Finally, inspiration came and I could hear him mumbling to himself: "I'll place the boys in a row, with each one saying his name in his natural voice. Then I'll arrange them in order, with the lowest voices to my left, and the highest ones to my right. Then I'll point one finger at an individual, two fingers to a pair, three to a trio, etc, so I can coax some pleasing sounds from them." He grew excited as he considered the possibility of jumping around to get the right combination of sounds. "I'll go fast or slow by moving my arms fast or slow; I'll make the sounds loud or soft by cupping my hands around my mouth -- wide apart for loud, finger to my lips for soft, and in-between positions for other levels."

Sleep finally came, and with the new dawn Glork started to work his plan. Everything went well until he tried to coax some pleasing sounds from the group, because they weren't as pleasing as he had expected. It was then that he started to innovate. First, he said his own name in a natural tone, and made each boy modulate his tone until it sounded good. He didn't realize it, but he had just discovered the importance of being in the same key. He was then able to go up and down the scale in pitch, and by trial and error he was able to get some pleasing combinations by pointing first at one boy, and then another. His first music sounded something like this: do do do; re so so; fa fa fa fa; mi mi re; do do do! Both he and the group were amazed at what they had accomplished, but Glork wasn't satisfied.

After a week of practicing on his ten-boy "keyboard", Glork decided to imitate the birds by having each boy go the next few sounds higher and lower than their basic ones, calling for them by raising or lowering his hands accordingly. This took several weeks to perfect, and most of he boys were ready to quit, but Glork reminded them of the potential rewards and all but two stayed. Strictly by chance, the first octave was formed, and the higher and lower sounds helped form extended scales.

Then, by starting with different basic sounds and a little fine-tuning, Glork was able to invent a few different keys. Thus armed with these basics, Glork used his fertile mind to create six different compositions, and with repeated rehearsals the entire group committed them to memory.

CHAPTER 3: THE FIRST CONCERT-- AND THE INVENTION OF INSTRUMENTS

Next came the acid test-- a live performance for Bomba and the tribe. Naturally, Glork let his dad hear the group sing before springing it on the tribe, and got his advice on the best way to handle his amazing discovery. So after a big tribal feast on a large animal, when Bomba and the tribe were in a mellow and receptive mood, Glorko arose, assembled his son and the boys, and announced that they had prepared something to honor their great chief and his brave tribe. (Glorko had learned the importance of flattery from his deceased father, had become a master at it and drilled it into his own son.)

Glork then started conducting his first composition, which was a strong, masculine one which he hoped would please Bomba. After a few notes, Bomba grabbed his club and was about to rise to punish Glork and the group-- after all, he wasn't sure about new things and his imagination was limited. Some of the men grabbed Glork so he couldn't run away, and the other boys bowed down to submit to their leader's wrath. Fortunately, Glorko sensed his reaction, brought Bomba another tasty morsel, and convinced him to listen further to show the tribe how great he was. Glorko's words and Bomba's laziness let the boys continue, and the tribe didn't protest once the two top men seemed to agree.

Dave, Dan and I breathed an audible sigh of relief when Glork was released and continued with the music.

The group performed each composition while Glorko supplied Bomba with food and drink. Seeing their chief happy and contented, the tribe showed their appreciation after each composition with the customary foot stomping. (Further research by our team showed that it was many millennia later before hand clapping was invented, although there are still a few foot stompers in our midst today.)

Glorko, in his usual diplomatic fashion, rose at the end and praised Bomba thusly: "Hail to our great chief, Bomba! He is the exalted leader of a brave tribe, one that has good youth to praise and serve his greatness." Bomba was so pleased that he offered the group more food!

The success of the first performance started a new tradition, and the group was commanded by Bomba to perform after each large animal feast. The boys soon became the toast of the tribe, and the two boys who had dropped out wanted back in.' Glork told them they would have to come with an idea other than voice sounds, so they searched for some more pleasant sounds. One of them discovered several hollow tree limbs that made nice sounds when he hit them with his club. That was the start of drums and rhythm, although some experts think they came first. Anyway, Glork welcomed him to his ensemble, and the new beats were a big hit with Bomba and the tribe. In fact, some rose to do their foot stomping, and with rhythmic music just born, dance quickly followed.

Some months later the second boy found an animal horn which, when blown in the small end, produced sounds out of the other end. Furthermore, different lip shapes could vary the sounds, so Glork not only added the horn boy and his discovery to his group but also came up with a new invention of his own. He discovered that his bowstring made a nice twanging sound when plucked by a finger. Then he wondered what would happen if he added more strings of shorter length. The result, after a bit of trial and error, was the first harp. Glork had now added instruments to his male chorus, and his status in the tribe grew and grew until he was allowed to eat right after the other men, with his group following him. That of course pleased the boys and their mothers, but not the other women who complained a bit.

CHAPTER 4: THE MATING GAME CHANGES

Life looked very rosy to Glork, and would have been perfect if he could capture the girl at the pool and make her his mate. To realize his dream, he enlisted the aid of his father. Glorko was eager to help his son, so he convinced him that clubbing was the wrong way. He then approached Bomba, saying, "Mighty Chief, you have often said that the tribe near the waterfall has some fire-starting secrets that we could use. With your permission, we can send our new musical group to perform for the neighboring tribe and if they like it, as I think they will, we can learn their fire starting secrets."

Bomba thought a minute, then said, " I approve. However, I think I will hide myself and some of my warriors to protect the boys. Their chief may not be as smart as I am, and attack our boys." Glorko was pleasantly surprised at Bomba's wisdom, made more praising remarks and withdrew.

Bomba's precautions were wise but unnecessary, because once Glorko made the necessary arrangements and the boys performed, the neighboring tribe was enthralled, and stomped their feet vigorously. Their chief invited the group to share the leftovers from the feast they had just finished.

Dan then remarked, "Wasn't that smart of Glorko to wait until the other tribe had finished their feast and they were in a mellow and lazy mood? Otherwise Bomba's prediction may have come true. Dave and I nodded in agreement.

Glork spotted the girl from the pool in the audience and noticed that she seemed impressed, and perhaps interested in him. So he asked the chief her name (it was Oool), and if he could talk with her. She was the daughter of the number three man in the tribe, so the chief first got his permission. I guess he figured there was no point in arousing trouble with one so high up and almost as strong as he was. Both men felt that Glork had so much talent and good looks that it would be proper for him to visit the daughter according to their customs.

Glork and Oool had to stay within the confines of the fire, so their meeting was limited to conversation. But that was enough to convince both that something was "brewing". Glork set a date for a meeting at the waterfall pool, and told her to bring three friends. "I will have a pleasant surprise for you," he promised.

When the day arrived, Glork and his three best friends made their way to the pool and waited out of sight until the girls appeared. The girls waded into the cool water to make their feet tingle, but an even better tingle happened when Glork and his friends sang a new composition. It was the first male quartet, and this art form still exists today. The composition was soft and sweet, and the girls' reaction was exactly what they hoped for. When the boys appeared from their hiding place, the girls laughed and invited them to share some food they had brought. It was Oool's surprise for Glork and just happened to be the first picnic, as further research proved.

The other boys were ready to club their girls and drag them back to the tribe's cave, but Glork had a better idea -- follow his father's advice and get their tribe's permission and thus avoid a war. Fortunately, they were all successful and even started a new custom, which most of the girls liked. Some masochistic women among the tribe still liked the conking-on-the-head tradition-- "it is more manly" they said.

The two tribes didn't merge, but they formed a mutual defense pact and enjoyed all the new things Glork, his friends and their mates had created: picnics, no-club mating, quartet singing, male choruses with instrumental support and dancing. Oool's tribe came up with the idea to tell stories, with Glork's music as emphasis. Both Dan and Dave think that was the start of opera, but I make no such claim.

The two tribes even spread the customs among other tribes, and the region enjoyed the best relations ever. There were only a few minor clashes, and most of the tribes even used the "no-club mating system. Of course there were some who hated change in something so basic, but they accepted music and picnics, which were new ideas with no taboos against them.

The old adage, "Music has the power to soothe the savage breast!" is certainly true, as those event proved. However, I would add this:, "It also has the power to lift the human spirit to new heights and depths, and in my book music is the greatest art form ever invented -- thanks to Glork and his friends!

EPILOGUE:
Dave thinks Glork and his dad sired Mozart's genes, since they also

made many innovations in one short lifetime. Both father and son outlived the other tribal men, but died in their forties. Glork's music spread quickly among other tribes, and by 50,000 BCE it was well established in the human race. Today it provides much pleasure and unity among mankind. Here's hoping it keeps evolving until all of mankind's "savage breasts" are soothed so much that violence becomes an extremely rare commodity!

CHARISMA

Ask the average person, and probably they will give you the "second" definition for charisma—that is, the gift of leadership, with very persuasive powers and dedicated followers. Franklin D. Roosevelt and Ronald Reagan were such leaders, but much to the world's misfortune, so were Adolph Hitler and Benito Mussolini! Charismatic leaders can do much good or tremendous harm, so the second definition is a mixed bag.

On the other hand, the first definition is almost always good, because it comes from the Greek word "divine gift", such as the gift of prophesy, healing, teaching, miracles, etc. If it is a truly divine gift, it stands to reason that it will be very good.

This story is about the first definition. It started one fall day when my wife was visiting her out of state sister and I explored some New Hampshire back roads in my Geo Metro. Now when I say back roads, I include the little-traveled paved roads and even the single lane unpaved roads. Since my Geo is not a four-wheel drive vehicle, I try to avoid the steep, very bumpy roads.

Anyway, I was enjoying the pristine countryside and the gorgeous fall colors, marveling at the "charisma" of it all. What a beautiful place is the earth, I mused, and what a divine gift it is when we take time out from our busy lives and go exploring.

Soon it was after twelve p.m. I decide to seek out a small village to get a bite to eat. Hunger pains made me realize that good food itself is a divine gift, even though I know how much human effort goes into producing it. Still, I thought, for a few measly bucks, I could satisfy those hunger pains and continue satisfying my thirst for natural beauty.

The road I was on had become a grassy path, but the two worn lanes indicated that farm vehicles, such as wagons and tractors, used it. There were no signs saying "keep out-- loaded shot gun!', as I had once seen in Arizona, so I forged ahead. I did pass a few isolated farmhouses, but no one was around to challenge me, or even wave to me. I wondered what it would be like to live in such a remote location, especially when the snows of winter piled higher and deeper, and an emergency arose. 'What hardy people', I thought with deep admiration.

Eventually, the grassy path led to a dirt road, which led to a two lane paved one, which led to a charming village. Before I could find a place to eat, my eye caught an unusual building-- a large church with cathedral qualities. What made it unique, at least to me, was its construction--- stainless steel welded together with almost invisible seams, interspersed with Gothic, stained-glass windows. The total effect was striking!

It was a three story structure, with a broad steeple that added four more stories. I wondered how such a disproportionate edifice was created in such a small population center, so I parked my car and walked closer to it.

The sign in front said the church was erected by five Desmaris brothers who had struck it rich in Australia's opal country. They decided to use their skills as iron workers, acquired in Bath, Maine, to build a "Cathedral to the glory of God Almighty!" They never married; instead they devoted thirty-nine years to their calling. Each brother was able to receive Holy Communion in it before they passed away, all in the same year. Again, I thought of the word " charisma" and marveled at the divine gift bestowed on the brothers, and the divine gift they bequeathed to the village.

Somehow, the cathedral piqued my interest so much that all thought of food left my mind. I just had to go inside and explore this marvel further. The interior was even more startling, and revealed the brothers skill in using metal to create religious scenes; statues; a large pipe organ; and other works of art. The floor was New Hampshire granite, supplied and installed by a local company, and the pews, altar, etc. were finely carved wood, which the elder and younger brother had crafted.

As I stood in awe at the lifetime accomplishments of the dedicated Desmaris men, a priest was showing a Protestant minister its features. Both men of the cloth were accompanied by some of their followers. Strangely enough, they were discussing "charisma" and each one was explaining how they demonstrated the term to their followers. The priest took everyone up to the top of the steeple, which had a small outside walk-around platform. I tagged along.

"Watch this", he said. He then waved his arms to his followers, and they jumped up to the narrow railing and walked around the periphery. Each one had perfect balance and absolutely no fear.

"There is my demonstration of 'charisma' my friend. They have the divine gift to overcome their natural fear of falling and walk where only angels could safely tread. Even a circus performer could not duplicate their fearless feat." The priest smiled broadly, and I detected a hint of "top that if you can!"

The minister apparently felt the same challenge, so he turned to his followers and said: "Let us show our friends how deep our faith in God's awesome power is. Let us show them how His holy love can overcome gravity itself!"

With surprising agility and utmost confidence, he leapt to the railing, walked a few feet, and then said "Behold, the leap of faith!"

We all gasped in horror as he threw himself out into thin air, but the gasps soon turned into oh's and ah's of admiration. You see, he did not fall, but stayed suspended in air as if a mighty, invisible hand were holding him up. He smiled and moved his arms such that he flew; first farther away then closer. Still smiling, he then invited anyone who truly had faith to join him. The priest jumped up on the railing, but once he saw the paved streets below and the gathering crowd, he lost his nerve and returned to the safety of the platform.

Two of the minister's followers hopped on the railing, then leapt toward him. One had the faith to sustain himself, but the other one had to be saved by the minister. It reminded me of the time when Christ walked on water and one of his disciples, who tried, it had to be saved.

The minister sensed my thoughts, so he said, "How about you sir? You seem to have the age and wisdom to understand the power of faith. Come join me so that we may make a powerful testimony to the gathering crowd!

It was an invitation I could not resist, especially in view of my previous thoughts on "charisma". I didn't even bother to climb the railing, but with one mighty leap I soared past the minister, stayed up, and then paddled my way through the air like a small boy swimming at a Sunday School Picnic.

The crowd below roared its approval, and it wasn't long before the priest and his followers joined us. He then yelled down to them, "Come, all ye faithful, and join us. Let God and your faith bring you up to us."

About half of them rose in the air from the street; some, who tried, faltered on the way up, but fluttered like a maple leaf, safely back to earth. The rest were either too timid or too awed to attempt it. After a while we all descended safely to ground level, and the priest invited everyone inside to praise God and his wonderful, divine gifts. He shared the pulpit with the minister, and both gave excellent homilies on their demonstration and the ancient Greek word, "CHARISMA1"

After I finally got some food, I thought I would record this event to provide spiritual food for a world that sorely needs it! Anyone interested?

Author's note: If you think this story is far-fetched and unbelievable, you should join me in some of my other dreams and imaginings!

THE CRIMINAL MIND

I was shocked to see two friends leaving the Durham Police Station. I was driving on route 108 toward Dover when I first spotted them, and I glanced twice to see if my eyes had deceived me; but no, there they were, Don and Dorothy, headed for the same car.

My imagination kicked into high gear and I wondered what crime they had committed. My first thought was, 'Aha, some one caught them having an affair!' But then reason prevailed: 'Don is in his late eighties, and Dorothy is a minister's wife. Besides, affairs are hardly a crime in this era of loose morality.' I wavered a bit when I recalled the sayings: "Hope springs eternal," and "Age is just in the mind," but I then moved on.

'Maybe they're guilty of speeding or reckless driving.' This idea seemed more plausible for a time, but, when I considered their positions in life, both seemed unlikely. I put them in my reserve file in case I couldn't come up with a better reason.

Shoplifting was my next thought, since I recently read an article that said many decent, normally law-abiding people, can be cursed with that addiction. After a bit of "noodling," I also placed it in my reserve file.

Then I asked myself, 'Do you suppose they have joined forces to engage in some sort of senior citizen scam?' The papers are full of such crime, and it occurred to me that the two of them would look so trustworthy that they could con other seniors to part with some dough. I knew they were both clever enough to concoct a foolproof scheme, so I put this one on a front burner.

Then I had a terrible thought: 'Maybe they've read too many mystery novels and decided to act out a good one by murdering some scoundrel. After all, these are crazy times and it is possible for really nice people to go off the deep end and do something terrible in anger, or even for a good cause. In fact, the media is full of such cases, so maybe this one will prove true. Although I have never seen either one angry or militant about a cause, my contact with them has been limited. Perhaps they have Dr. Jekyl and Mr. Hyde personalities which they keep secret.' Upon sober reflection, I decided they were much too nice, so I put that one in the bottom of my file.

Finally, I hit on a more realistic explanation. 'They witnessed a crime or accident and were at the Police Station to give testimony.' I sort of liked that one, but it wasn't nearly as provocative as the others. I opened my file to review all candidates, and maybe invent a new one. In fact, I did invent a new one but it is too terrible to print.

During my thought process I was stopped at a traffic light in Dover. When it turned green I started to move, but my attention was diverted by a disheveled, evil-looking young punk in a hippy-type car running a red light. 'Now there's a criminal type for sure; probably a drug dealer, or thief, at best. Hey, he makes three I've observed in the last few minutes, so it sure looks like there are many people who have criminal minds. I suppose even nice folks like Don and Dot aren't exempt.'

A few days later, I learned that they belong to a senior group that meets at the Police Station, and since they both come from Exeter, they car pool. It was then that an embarrassing truth dawned on me. 'If anyone has a criminal mind it may be little old me. After all, I'm the one who concocted all these criminal scenarios for Don, Dot, and that car driver!'

DANGEROUS DREAMS

Sergei A. Petrovich, age 53, was the most famous psychiatrist in New York City, probably the country. His associates were carefully selected, and their credentials were outstanding. The firm's patients were either rich or famous, usually both, with Dr. Petrovich treating the richest and most famous.

Now this is pure speculation, but some people think the rich and famous need psychiatric help much more than ordinary folks. Why? Because they feel guilty about taking advantage of others to get rich, or the lying and cheating they did to become famous. Besides, they can afford it and it probably seems a good way to spend some of their ill-gotten dough.

Ambitious and money-hungry young psychiatrists were eager to become one of Dr. Petrovich's associates. Since Dr. P. believed in expanding his practice, there were usually 2 or 3 openings per year with several hundred applicants. That's why Dr. Adam P. Englehardt, age 26, felt extremely fortunate to be one of the two new junior associates selected in 1976.

Most of Dr. P's associates were ambitious, but none more so than Adam. Not only was he brighter and more devious than the others, but his ultimate dream was to take Dr. P.'s lofty and lucrative position. The other ambitious doctors hoped to rise in rank, perhaps become one of Dr. P.'s three senior associates.

Adam was smart, very good looking and personable. His rich baritone voice could be soothing, authoritative, or persuasive, and he knew when to use the proper one. It wasn't long before some of the richest and most famous ladies were his patients, but he never went beyond his professional limits, which were a bit flexible.

By May 1981, Adam became the youngest senior associate in the firm's 28-year history, and Dr. P's favorite. He advanced so quickly because of his winning personality, his in-depth knowledge, and, most importantly, because his high fees enriched Dr P. more than the next two highest doctors. Adam was making lots of dough himself, lived in an upscale apartment, and had several interesting and beautiful girl friends, but remained single.

Although Dr P. was approaching retirement age, he had recently gone through his third divorce and pledged to stay single for the rest of his life. Adam knew this, and hoped Dr. P. would lose interest in his work and retire; but Dr. P.'s troubles only made him more dedicated, with retirement far away. It was then that Adam's deviousness went into overdrive.

It was Adam's custom to discuss puzzling cases with Dr. P., so late one afternoon he stopped by the chief's office. In his rich baritone voice he said, "May I have a few words with you, sir? I have a patient who is so unusual that I need your advice."

"Of course," Dr. P. replied. "Come in and have a seat. You know I enjoy discussing your most challenging cases. Now tell me all about your current one."

Adam took his seat and said, "Well, one of my more frugal patients has a recurring dream, which is not only unusual, but possibly life threatening. I know that it is rare for dreams to be fatal, but this may be one of those rare ones. I would feel terrible if it happened and I'm also concerned about legal problems, especially if he should die when I am using hypnosis, which I do once a month."

"Well, Adam, you certainly should be concerned and I'm glad you want to discus it with me. Now tell me the dream."

"O.K.," Adam replied. "Here's what my patient told me in his own words, which I recorded and had typed:

I was walking along a mountain path headed for a small river. As I crossed a wooden footbridge, I heard a voice crying, "HELP ME, HELP ME!". It seemed to be coming from below the footbridge. When I looked, I saw a nearly dry stream with a three-foot fish flopping around trying to swallow enough water to breathe. It was the fish that was crying for help!

I decided to help the poor fish, so I climbed down, picked it up, and carried it to the river, which was about fifty feet away. After I tossed it in, it started breathing again and seemed safe. I started to walk away, but the fish called to me. "Wait, I want to reward you for your help. After all, you saved my life!"

My curiosity rose, so I replied, "What do you want me to do?"

"Come in and hold on to me, and I will swim you to an earthly paradise."

"What do you mean, 'earthly paradise'?"

"Well, beyond that mountain downstream, there is a beautiful castle overlooking splendid views. Behind the castle is the most productive land ever created, and all types of wonderful foods grow there without any human effort. Best of all, there are ten gorgeous young women who are eager to have a man join them, so everyone can be happy and fulfilled. How does that sound, John?"

Somehow it knew my name, so I said, "Like an earthly paradise. When do we start and how do we get there?"

"We can start immediately and we get there via a tunnel the river carved through the mountain. Hang on and we'll start."

I held on and the fish moved rapidly through the water, which was already flowing at around five mph. We went so fast that I could feel the wake my body made in the river, and it was an exciting experience. About a mile downstream, we entered the tunnel and the river flowed even faster.

The tunnel got very dark, but there was a strange glow that let me see where we were going. I started getting worried when it got smaller and smaller, but my friend, the fish, spoke again.

"We will have to swim underwater for a minute or two. Just hold your breath, and we will soon reach the end of the tunnel. You will then see the earthly paradise."

"O.K.", I said. Friend fish then dove down so I wouldn't hit the top of the tunnel, which was now completely filled with water. The minute drifted into two, and was headed for three, and we were still underwater. I didn't think I could hold my breath any longer and felt I was going to die.

I wondered if the fish had tricked me to get even for all the times humans had caught and killed its fellow fish, but concluded that it was too grateful to kill me. Besides, it could talk, and had a male personality that was almost human. The next thing I knew, I woke up in my bed gasping for breath. It took me at least five minutes to recover, but I didn't die.

Since that first dream, I have had the same one at least twice a week for the past year. I knew I got closer, because the proverbial 'light at the end of the tunnel' grew brighter and brighter. I even made it out of the tunnel twice and reached the earthly paradise.

It was even better than I had expected and I spent at least a week in dreamtime before I woke up. Even after I woke up, I was so happy and energetic that my life was the best ever. My second marriage had ended in a nasty divorce prior to my dreams, and I have become wary of women ever since. But the ten gorgeous women in E.P., as I called it, were absolutely wonderful. They were so happy and grateful to finally have a man that they showered me with everything any man could wish for: wonderful meals; melodious music; exciting dancing; exhilarating sport; unbelievable kindness; tender affection; and best of all, heavenly sex!

Since then, I could hardly wait to go back to sleep, hoping I would repeat my victorious dreams. Alas, they have been elusive, and although I have seen the light at the end of the tunnel several times, I haven't reached it for the last month. Worse yet, my gasping for breath is so extreme that I barely recover.

During one dream, I told friend fish about my plight. Here's what he said:

"Don't worry, my friend. If you wake up before you reach E.P., as you call it, you probably won't die. Even if you do die in your sleep, you will reach

E.P. as your first destination in heaven, and can stay or leave for other heavenly places whenever you like."

"On the other hand, if you persist, I promise that the number of dreams you need before you reach E.P. will grow fewer and fewer, and pretty soon you will make it every time you go to sleep. So my advice is to stop worrying. Not only can you not lose, but death might be better than living, because you will reach your heavenly goal sooner!"

When friend fish finished his talk, we dove down again, and by golly I reached E.P. again. It lasted two dream weeks, and made me realize that such a prize was worth trying for again and again.

"So what do you think, Doc? Should I continue dreaming, or do you have a remedy that will either make my dreams more successful, or let me wake up without gasping so long and painfully?" Adam then waited for his boss's answer.

Dr. Petrovich listened carefully during Adam's reading, and when he finished, he said: "That IS a very unusual case. Probably the most unusual and interesting one I have ever even heard. Tell me, what did you advise your patient?"

"I told him I needed to do more thinking, a bit more research, and seek an opinion from you. Naturally, I promised not to reveal his identity. My patient seemed pleased with my answer."

"I am pleased with your answer too, Adam. I agree it is too important and complex to make a hasty decision, so please leave your copy of the dream with me so I can do my own thinking and research. But first, tell me more about your patient."

"He is a famous actor who is well past his peak. He no longer gets major roles, and although he has plenty of money, he worries about his future. He had a very active love life when he was in his prime, and was married twice. One marriage ended in divorce, and one in which his wife was killed in an automobile accident. He misses women, but is afraid to start a new relationship because his confidence is so low. He has an active imagination, vivid dreams, and is fond of Disney Cartoons, which probably explains the talking fish."

"How about his childhood?"

"During hypnosis, he seemed exceptionally happy during his childhood. His parents and friends showered him with praise about his talents, which gave him the tremendous confidence needed for a successful acting career."

Dr. P. stroked his beard thoughtfully before he said, "Thank you Adam. Your description was very good, but it makes the case even more puzzling. As you know, many neuroses can be tracked to an unhappy childhood, or career failures, but his childhood and career were so trouble-free that we can't blame them, or even find remedies by exploring them. That is, unless you think there may be some problems you didn't uncover."

"I think I have been careful and thorough, but I am willing to probe deeper."

"That won't be necessary for the present." Dr. P. ended the conversation with: "Let me do more thinking and some research. I'll get back to you in two weeks."

True to his promise, Dr. P. called Adam to his office late one afternoon. He poured two glasses of wine, which he had done before on important occasions. He then said, "I'm going to give some advice for your patient, which I'm not willing to take myself. Tell him there are no known remedies for his problem, and that all you can offer is hypnosis once a week. Based on what you have said of his frugality and his enrapture with the dream, I suspect he will decline. Please let me know his decision, and thanks for contacting me on this fascinating case."

"Thanks very much, sir. I will do exactly as you advised. But I don't understand what you meant when you said you wouldn't follow the same advice yourself."

"Then let me explain. I read the copy of the dream many times looking for clues. In fact, I have had the dream several times myself. I found it so fascinating and intriguing that I want to see how it will play out in spite of the uncomfortable gasping when I wake up."

A week later, Adam told Dr. P. his patient's decision. As predicted, he declined further services, because the dream was much too wonderful and important to give up.

As for Dr. Petrovich, he reached earthly paradise during his dreams several times during the following weeks, and confided it to Adam shortly after. During their meeting, Dr. P. said, "Adam, I've been doing some serious thinking. I'm so happy with the dream and my life, even when I'm awake, that I plan to retire as soon as I can complete my plans. If you are agreeable, I will not only put you in charge, but will give you enough stock so you will be almost co-equal with me. Because of the happiness you have brought me, I will leave you more in my will, with the rest going to charity. As you know, I have no children or close kin, and none of my three ex-wives deserve a damn thing more than the courts gave them."

Adam put on his most sincere look as he replied, "Of course I accept your kind offer, and I will do my very best to keep the high standards and financial rewards you have so ably established." They shook hands and Adam parted with a huge smile on his face, which he erased once he approached office staff.

Once the papers were signed, Adam took charge and Dr P. retired to his Vermont home, where he died about six months later from a mysterious strangulation during his sleep. It was mysterious to the coroner, and even to the associate doctors once they heard about it, but not to Adam. You see, Adam had used a made-up patient and a highly imaginative dream to hook Dr. P. in order to realize his own dream of being top dog. He felt sure that the advice the fish gave about death being better than living could be fatal to a man like Dr. P., and it worked.

Adam was especially pleased when he had this thought:

I, Adam P. Englehardt, initials A.P.E., outwitted a distinguished psychiatrist, Sergei A. Petrovich, initials S.A.P. In other words, an APE made a SAP of his boss!

I told you that Adam was clever and devious, didn't I?

Epilogue:

Adam was never caught and apparently got away with pre-meditated murder. Some may say it was not murder, since Dr. P. was alone in a secured house and died in his sleep, supposedly from natural causes. Furthermore, Adam had retrieved the copy of his fake dream from Dr. P., and destroyed it and all other evidence involved. Naturally, the case never got to court, and even if it had there was absolutely no evidence to convict Adam. It was so cleverly planned and executed, that it should join the limited number of perfect murders.

Adam never got hooked on his imaginary dream, but realized his ambitious dream of becoming boss and owner. However, his fulfilled dream was nowhere near as satisfying as Dr. P.'s realized 'earthly paradise' dream. Adam never experienced anything close to earthly paradise, even after his marriage to a wealthy beauty. He died prematurely and with some remorse, as I later learned.

Adam and I had been roommates for three years in undergraduate school, and he told me this story on his deathbed in 2005. Whether or not it is true I cannot say, because Adam had a wild imagination. If it is true, I believe that Adam committed murder, however mysteriously.

I will leave it to a Higher Power to decide whether Adam will ever enter:
A HEAVENLY PARADISE!

Authors Note: The above story and epilogue are pure fiction, but they are based on a real dream. During the dream a large fish cried for help, and after I saved his life he wanted to reward me by taking me to an earthly paradise, as described. My trip down the river and through the tunnel, with the fish towing me, was part of my dream, including the frightening underwater adventure.

It was so real that the only way I could save myself was to wake up, which I did, gasping for breath. It was such a powerful dream, that it sparked my imagination to concoct a story about an ambitious psychiatrist who uses my dream to fulfill his own dream of success. Since my background is Aerospace Engineering, I asked my neighbor, a retired psychologist, to review my story for professional correctness and he found no faults. Thanks, Stan.

My title, "Dangerous Dreams," reminds me of some real life dreams that not only proved to be dangerous, but deadly on a large scale. Most of history's tyrants have ambitious dreams that have killed millions and caused great destruction. During my 86 years I have experienced: Hitler, Stalin, Tojo, Mussolini, and lesser tyrants, including the latest such as

Sadam Hussein, the North Korean dictator, etc. Compared to them, Adam was a bit player whose sins might be forgivable.

L. M. E.

DIALOGUE WITH ARISTOTLE

(Translated from the Greek by Morpheus)

"How goes the day, friend Aristotle?"

"Not well, friend Maconius. I am feeling frustrated and depressed."

"I'm sorry to hear that, and frankly I am both perplexed and saddened. "

"How so, my friend, for you have such a cheerful and optimistic nature?"

"Yes, oh perceptive one, but when someone as learned and wise as you is frustrated and depressed, it makes me wonder what hope there is for us lesser mortals. Even my natural optimism is strained to the breaking point."

"Now you have made me feel even more depressed; I have transferred my ills to you, and guilt hangs heavy on my mind. It just tightens the Gordian knot strung around my soul by the earlier ills."

"That certainly wasn't my intent, wise one; perhaps if we discuss the source and nature of your ills we can untie the awesome knot, or at least loosen it so you can wiggle free from its bonds."

"I thank you for your concern. Perhaps a bit of discourse would help both our souls. The source of my frustration lies in the stubbornness and foolishness of men. They call me 'wise one', as you just did, and they admire my logic and perception. Yet they act in foolish ways and seem to take great pleasure in giving just lip service to my advice. As to its nature, it is like a stormy day in my mind in which all sunshine is banished and ill winds continually devastate the landscape "

"I understand. Now tell me about your depression."

"Ah, that is even worse. Its source is my advanced age and the sad realization that I am in the winter of my life. If men do not listen to me now, while I am among them, what will happen when I am dead? And even more depressing, what will happen to my soul? I feel like I have the weight of the world on my shoulders; the burden is so great that it seems life is just an empty shell that can never be filled."

" I marvel at your words, good friend. Even when you are beset with great problems, your keen intellect can muster words that move me to the depth of my being. Please bear with me while I seek some potential solutions."

" I will be the epitome of patience, for I wish to be made whole again. "

" Then let us begin! As to the stubbornness and foolishness of men, it seems to me that we must view those ills in the perspective of time. Men have always had those characteristics, yet they have created great works. Look at the splendor of the amphitheaters and contemplate their architectural marvels and the genius and cooperation required to erect them. Think of the splendid dramas created and performed in them, and the talent and skill of those who perform. "

" True, my friend, they are certainly monuments to the great creative powers of men. But in time they too will crumble, and future civilizations will wonder what happened to our civilization. They may even surpass us, and do things we cannot even imagine today."

" Ah, you have just given me an idea! Permit me to prophesize about the future: I see your name enshrined in the hearts and minds of men as one of the great philosophers of all time. And not only in the minds of men, but in the minds of women; for someday they will be recognized as our mental equals, and perhaps our spiritual superiors."

" But how will people in the future know about me? You and my other followers are almost as ancient as am I. Will not our words and thoughts die with the last of us, or soon thereafter?"

" Not if we write them down and entrust them to our children. Even now, some of the others and I have started compiling your thoughts and dialogues on papyrus. And we plan to continue to do so as long as we are able. My two daughters have mastered the art of reading and writing, and even as I speak they are making duplicate copies and recording some of your recent words of wisdom, which I conveyed to them last week.

" I thank you, my friend, and also your clever daughters. Perhaps your prophesy about women will come true some day."

" I am certain of it. Our superior physical strength and great ego have kept women from realizing their true potential. Someday, machines and powerful weapons will negate the physical advantage of men, and women will compete with them on a nearly equal basis; except women will always have child bearing duties-- that has been ordained by nature herself."

" I can see that would be an improvement over present conditions. But what do you see happening regarding war and violence?"

" Alas, that has a rather gloomy outlook. It will take millennia to overcome those twin evils. But when they are overcome, it will be because of men like you."

" You are very generous, but please explain."

" Well, mankind has mental skills that appear to be greatly superior to those of the animals. Sooner or later, people will not only expand logic, as you, Socrates and others have, but they will see the wisdom of applying it! There will be golden ages in mankind's future that will dwarf ours; but there will be times that try men's souls, as you have just encountered."

" I'm beginning to feel better. Thank you, dear friend. Now tell me what else you see in the future. Tell me about the machines and other things you mentioned earlier."

" Why they are simply marvelous: men will harness the forces of nature to do most of the physical work; horses and chariots will be replaced by self-powered vehicles that run along smooth highways at great speeds; airborne craft will travel through the atmosphere at even greater speeds; great cities will arise with buildings a thousand feet high; pictures and messages will be transmitted instantly great distances through the air; the arts will flourish and be accessible to the poor; the rockets the Chinese use as playthings will be developed into craft that will take men to the moon and beyond; science will make huge strides, and engineering will convert the knowledge it uncovers into a virtual plethora of products and services; agriculture will produce more and better food, so no one need be hungry; knowledge will be conveyed to the masses through public schools and mass produced writings..."

" Ah, you paint a verbal picture of paradise itself. Will there be no problems at all? "

" Perhaps someday problems will be minimized, but not within the future I foresee. You see, my vision is cloudy beyond the year 1994 A.D."

" That is far in the future—almost two millennia!"

" It is over 2300 years in the future! You see, men will change the calendar system to date history from a great event that will occur about 330 years from now."

" Does that mean we are not part of their history?"

" No, dear friend, we will be an important part of their history. They will date our time as B.C. and then count backward. For example, you were born in 384 B.C. by the future calendar."

" Yes, I understand, even though at first I thought it illogical. Unless we go back to the beginning of time, which is impossible, there will always be history before and after anyone's calendar year one. But what is the great event you prophesy?"

" You are familiar with the Hebrew people and their insistence that there is only one God, aren't you?"

" Yes. And truth to tell, it seems more logical than our belief in so many gods. But I dare not voice that opinion except to good and trusted friends like you. I do not wish to take the hemlock, as did Socrates. But please explain the meaning of 'A.D.' and 'B.C.'."

" As part of their belief, the Hebrews prophesied the coming of a

Messiah who would save all mankind. There will arise such a man, about 330 years from now, who will fulfill the prophecy so well that many will say that HE is the Messiah. Eventually, the authorities will change the calendar to honor his life. ' A.D. ' means anno domini, from the Latin 'in the year of the lord'."

" And what does 'B.C.' stand for?"

" Before Christ--you see this unusual man will be known as Jesus Christ."

" He must be a remarkable person to influence the world that much. What will he do to get such acclaim?"

" He will preach love and forgiveness, and the brotherhood of mankind under the fatherhood of God. He will promote the repentance of past evil deeds and the practice of justice and good deeds. He will perform miracles to help those in need and confirm his divinity. He will even promise eternal life to those who truly follow his teachings. His small following will grow into a worldwide following that numbers in the billions."

" Remarkable! And will he become rich and powerful, and spoiled by too much adulation as do so many with far less cause?"

" No, he will not! In fact, he will come to an early death at age thirty-three by the hands of his own people, and their conquerors, the Romans."

" Ah, so he will do evil and deserve to be executed? Or will he be unjustly sentenced, as was Socrates?"

" As always, Aristotle, you have a clear and open mind. He WILL be unjustly executed, or so future history will confirm. His fatal claim will be that he is 'God Incarnate'. That will so upset the Hebrews that they will demand the Roman Governor crucify him like a common criminal."

" What a shame, to be snuffed out so early in life. Could not he muster his followers and save himself?"

" Yes, he could save himself in many ways, but his mission will be to save mankind, not himself; so he will decide to sacrifice his own life as an example for all people. That one act will so set him apart from most men that his message will reach all over the world; but the qualities in men that caused your ills will delay its being accepted and followed universally for millennia."

"I wish it were possible to meet him and spend many hours in discourse. Do you think he really could be God Incarnate?"

"With God, all things are possible. Certainly his life and message will be so powerful that he will have divine qualities. One thing seems sure: if mankind eventually follows his message and quits quibbling about small details, life on earth will be much pleasanter and more wonderful. But best of all, is his promise that those who become his disciples will be eligible for eternal life in God's spiritual world."

"Do you suppose that could include those of us who came before his time on earth?"

"That is a difficult theological question which is bound to cause many arguments. My feeling is that it would be just, and God is certainly the fountain of justice. I believe there is a strong possibility that someday you will meet him!"

" Ah, friend Maconius, you have cured my frustration and depression, and given me hope for the future. I thank you most sincerely"

" I hope I have been of service, for it is important that your life and thoughts be added to humanity's treasure trove."

" Again you are too kind. And I confess that your descriptions have the ring of true prophecy! They are too logical and detailed to be pure speculation, as I first thought."

" They are more than prophecy, my friend, they are future history! "

" But how can that be? And how do you know so much about the future and things to come?"

"Ah, that's easy. You see, I spent most of my life in the twentieth century. I have traveled back in time to visit with you!"

"How is that possible, dear friend?"

"The same way you see possibilities in the future; by using my imagination!"

DIALOGUES THAT MADE A DIFFERENCE

1. THE CONTRACTORS:

"Hey Tony, heard the good news?"

"No, Giuseppe, I've been too busy on our road project"

"We won the contract to build the new edifice-- it'll keep us and most of our men busy for several years!"

"Hey, that's great-- did they accept our bid, or did they chisel it down like they usually do?"

"Well Tony, they did chisel it down a bit, but I think we can still make plenty of money, especially if we get Vincento as the customer's overseer-- for a small bribe he'll let us cheat on some of the specifications."

"I know just what you mean, Giuseppe, and I know how we can save a bundle without anyone being the wiser— even if we don't get Vincento!"

"Well I have a few short cuts myself, but tell me yours, partner."

"The foundation-- it's the one place Vincento or any overseer hates to check closely because it's so dirty and messy. All the overseers are pretty fastidious guys, you know, and I can make a foundation look sound from a distance better than anyone. And to make sure they don't come too close, I'll make the approaches to the foundation real messy."

"Yeah, yeah, I know that Tony, but this is going to be a pretty tall edifice. We don' t want it to come crashing down on us."

"Don't worry my friend, it will last for years and if it ever comes down we'll be long gone. If it lasts one hundred years, as I predict, what difference will it make if it falls?"

"It won't make any difference to us, but our names will be on the dedication stone-- I hate to think that our grandkids will be ashamed of us."

"Well, Giuseppe, you have a point there, but my calculations indicate that it won't really crash down-- it'll just tilt a bit to the right and the engineers of the future can probably fix it before it falls."

"Good, then that settles it. As a matter of fact, I think a slightly leaning tower might be the very thing to put Pisa on the map!"

2. A MOVING STORY:

"Wife, I think we should leave and move to a smaller and safer city!"

"You must be jesting, husband-- you know that my parents and siblings are all located here; besides, the kids like their school and the markets and shops are the best in the country. No, I see no reason to move!"

"Well dear one; maybe we should get your whole family to move. Don't forget that we live in the capital and I fear that it will be the principal target for large scale bombing by the enemy. Those earlier air raids were small, and were mere tokens of what will come soon unless our forces can achieve more victories. If and when the enemy does bomb us, we might lose everything-- even the kids."

"But the city is so large-- why would they want to bomb a residential area like we live in?"

"Well I hate to frighten you, but bombs do go astray, and they are getting more and more powerful. They could kill thousands of civilians."

"Husband, you have frightened me! But if the bombs kill all our relatives and friends, and destroy our city, what difference will it make if we stay alive. Maybe we'd be better off dead!"

"Hush, wife-- let's have no more talk like that-- we've got to think of the children, and someday their children."

"I guess you're right, but promise me you'll talk it over with my father. He's very wise and has more years of experience than you. "

"I promise, and if he says it's unwise we'll stay here."

"Thank you—-and if he says move, then I'll do so willingly."

(Two days later, the dialogue continues:)

"Wife, I talked with your father and he agrees with me; he even suggested a place where we have relatives that will help us relocate. In fact, he thought it such a good idea that he, your mother and most of your siblings will join us. He's sure that we'll all be much safer there."

"Then it's settled— I feel better about it already because the war has gone on much longer than our leaders promised. Sometimes I wonder if they've deceived us."

"I've suspected deception for many months, but it's better not to let others hear such thoughts. It might be as dangerous as the enemy bombs!"

"Then I'll drop the subject and not discuss it further—even with my parents or you. By the way, when are we going to move--and where?"

"Your father thinks we should move sometime this July—that way we can be settled in time for the 1945 August festival. As to the new city, I think you'll like it a lot—it's called Hiroshima!"

3-. LOVE, HONOR, AND OBEY!

"Hey, Sam, I hear your daughter Priscilla is engaged to Tommy-- when's the wedding?"

"This coming June, Joe; you and Vi will be getting an invitation!"

"Gee, thanks. We think a lot of Priscilla— she's such a beautiful and talented girl. Tommy seems nice, and I know his folks have a lot of dough, but do you think he'll make a good husband?"

"Well, I guess we fathers wonder the same thing— most young men seem kinda wild and rebellious these days-- and not nearly good enough for our precious daughters— but my guess is that they'll form a union that will last 'till death does them part'-- just like the vows proclaim!"

"What a beautiful thought, Sam— I sure hope you're right-- but I detect some character flaws in young Tommy. His mother has spoiled him rotten, and his dad is away so much on business that he hasn't disciplined him."

"Now Joe, I think you're being too harsh on the boy. You and I were sort of reckless in our youth— it goes with the territory-- but we shaped up and are now good family men and pillars of the church, aren't we? And look at your Katherine and Jack-- I remember how worried you were about him, but they both seem happy to me!"

"Well, I guess you have some good points there-- Katherine and Jack are getting along fine and Marge and I dearly love our young grandson; and you and I did sow our share of wild oats, didn't we, Sam? So what difference do those dam* wild oats make now, especially if our wives don't find out?"

"Yeah! That's what I mean when I say it comes with the territory. Practically all red-blooded young boys get into some sort of mischief before they settle down, don't they?"

"Well Sam, I guess so, but a few never seem to mature. They want to have fun all the time; and the ones with lots of money not only have the wherewithal, but think they're entitled to break the rules of society."

"Yeah, yeah, but you must admit they're the exception rather than the rule; I predict that Tommy will settle down properly with my Priscilla, and double the Manville fortune!"

EAR WITNESS

"Hi, Diana-- it's me, Carol. Have I got some great news for you. David proposed last night and we've set the date for June 15. We want you to be the Matron of Honor if you'll accept. Will you?"

"Of course I will! After all, you were my Maid of Honor and turn about is what makes the world go around. I think the date is clear, but if it's not I'll give you and David top priority."

"That's wonderful, Diana. And of course Max is invited. David would like him as an usher, if he will accept."

"I'm sure he will, but I'll have to check it with him. I'm delighted with your great news, and I'm sure you and David will be very happy. Much as I would like to chat some more, please excuse me and let me call you back soon. We're in the middle of something important, which will be a surprise for you."

"Of course you're excused. Call me back as soon as you can. Bye, I love you."

"I love you, too-- and give my best to David."

Diana closes down her cell phone, or at least she thinks she does. Actually she pressed the wrong button and it is still on. Carol is cradling her phone in her arms while glowing and meditating about all the wonderful things waiting for her in the future. Her reverie is shattered by loud voices on her phone. She puts it back to her ear and listens in utter shock. Here's what she overhears:

"I've had about enough of you--you bitch-- and I want a divorce!" It's Max's voice, and Carol cringes at each surprising word.

"You've had enough." Diana yells. "How do you think I feel? But then you never think of me, do you?"

"Of course I do," Max replies. "But ever since I suspected you had an affair with that Yale man I lost all my respect for you. And when I discovered you had an affair with the apartment handyman, it blew my mind. How could you do such a thing?"

Carol can't believe her ears when she hears these words, and is tempted to yell into the phone. She then thinks she should hang up, but decides to keep listening to get the true, but horrible, facts about her best friend.

"Well, you started it, you S.O.B., when you had that affair with your secretary. At first, I wanted to confront you and try to get an explanation, and maybe try to work things out. But when I found you had mistresses at several of the companies you visit, I decided things had gone too far for reconciliation. So I decided to play your game and see how you liked it."

"You're a typical wife, bitch. When are you women going to understand that our hormones make us not only want some variety, but need it. You should know that we expect you to be faithful. After all, you don't have the raging hormones we do, so it's easy to control your sexual urges."

"And you're a typical husband. You think you're the masters of the world and that women are your servants. Well let me tell you, Buster, we women are equal to men, and in some ways superior. If you don't believe me, look at the mess the world is in now and think who's responsible for it--Men, you bastard--Men!"

"That does it!" Max yells. "You're hopeless and I insist we have a divorce!"

" Fat chance, you male oaf. I won't give you a divorce unless I get everything and a big alimony settlement."

Carol is now rooting for Diana, almost audibly, but suppresses it before it can be heard.

"No way, bitch. You're as guilty as I am in the eyes of the law. The most you'll get is half, maybe less since I can pay a lawyer more than you can."

"Aha, I've got you there. I hired a detective to find out about your affairs, but none of mine are true. They are all rumors I started to trap you."

Carol is pleasantly surprised, and her faith in her friend's character not only returns, but her admiration increases. But then she gets the shock of her life.

"Goddamn you to hell, you sly bitch. I hoped I wouldn't have to do this, but you asked for it." BANG! BANG! BANG!

As the three shots are fired, Carol hears Diana scream in agony and fall to the floor. She instantly shuts down her phone and starts sobbing. After a minute or two, she composes herself. She decides she must call 911 and report this horrible crime, with the hope that Diana can be saved and Max apprehended while the evidence is still hot. Once 911 answers, the conversation is like this;

"This is 911. May I help you?"

"Yes, yes, I want to report the shooting of my best friend."

" A shooting you say. Did you see it, or is this a joke?"

"No, it's not a joke, and I didn't see it. I heard it over my phone just after I finished talking with her. They had an awful argument, her husband went into an uncontrollable rage and I heard three shots fired. Then I heard my friend scream in agony and fall to the floor. She could be dead by now-- oh,

I hope not-- but maybe some quick help could save her. It was her husband who shot her, so he may still be dangerous."

"That does sound serious. We'll get on it right away. Don't hang up, because I need more information."

The 911 man then asks a number of questions which Carol answers, after which Carol asks, "Would it be O.K. if I went over to their apartment?"

"Yes," the 911 man replies. "But stay outside until the ambulance and the police arrive. The husband may be dangerous."

Carol readily agrees, then puts on her coat and starts walking toward her friends' apartment, which is only three blocks away. Her heart is heavy and she is so nervous she shakes like a child about to get its first beating. As she approaches, she hears the siren wailing. As she draws nearer, she sees the police and paramedics enter the building-- with the police leading in case Max is still dangerous. Her wait seems interminable, but eventually the police and paramedics come out. Diana is not on a stretcher, and Max is not in handcuffs, so she is both disheartened and bewildered; she imagines that Diana is dead and maybe Max shot himself. She approaches a police officer, identifies herself, and asks for an explanation.

"They're both O.K., Miss. It was a false alarm."

"What do you mean a false alarm?" Carol is both puzzled and agitated. "I distinctly heard an awful argument, followed by three shots and screams of agony. How could it be a false alarm?"

"Well, Miss, you did the right thing by calling 911, but when we got there they were still rehearsing the community play they're starring in. Why don't you go up to their apartment and get the lowdown first hand."

Again, Carol has mixed emotions. She thanks the officer and is greatly relieved that her friends are both safe and not having marital troubles. However, she feels a bit foolish for jumping to conclusions. When she gets to their apartment door, Max answers.

"Hi, Carol. Diana is calling your phone now. The police explained your call, and seeing us both well and happy, and rehearsing a play, understood the confusion. They even got a chuckle from it, and accepted a beer before they left. Hey, Diana! Carol just got here, so you can hang up now!"

Diana runs to Carol and they both embrace and start laughing until tears roll down their smiling faces. Carol is first to speak.

"Oh Diana and Max, I'm so sorry. But after you shut down your cell phone it was still on, and I over heard all the lines of the play until I heard the shots and your scream. I didn't know it was a play and it was so real that I panicked and called 911. I hope you'll forgive me."

"Of course we will, Carol, if you'll forgive me for pushing the wrong button on my phone. After all, if I had shut it off properly, you wouldn't have heard anything." Diana then patted Carols back gently.

"Gee, I guess you're right. But I still feel like a fool. No, change that-- I feel like a happy fool-- happy that you're both O.K. and still in love! By the way, what was the surprise you were going to tell me?"

"About the play, of course. We just got the parts yesterday and started rehearsing with each other today."

"But Diana, why did Max fire three shots during a rehearsal?"

"Oh, you know how Max is--sort of a perfectionist. He figured it would be more realistic and he'd get used to handling a gun again."

"But how about your neighbors-- weren't you concerned about their hearing the shots and calling 911, like I did?"

"Yes we were, so we warned them in advanced. They're all good sports and went along with it. As a matter of fact, two of them are in the same play, so they really understood."

"By the way, what's the name of the play and when is opening night?"

"Its name is *Eye Witness to A Murder,* and it opens on April first. The second act is a doozy, because it's about the trial of the husband, who happens to be a poor shot with a pistol."

"I can hardly believe what you just said, Diana."

"Why do you say that?" she asked.

"Because I was an <u>Ear</u> witness to a murder, and it's opening on April Fools Day. Get it? I feel like a fool by what I did as an EAR Witness!"

AN ENCOUNTER WITH LEPRECHAUNS

I was walking briskly down a hillside path toward a small New Hampshire village called "New Ireland". It was a bright, blue-sky day, the temperature was around 70 degrees F and I felt at ease with God and nature. Little did I imagine that the coming events would strain my credulity to the breaking point.

As I neared the village, a narrow road lay about twenty feet below me, and I noticed a lovely young woman walking down the adjacent sidewalk. Her hair was dark black and hung well below her shoulders; her cheeks and lips were rosy without noticeable make-up; her light complexion was flawless; and her figure was stunning---slender waist, shapely bosom and smooth, fascinating legs. She was dressed for summer in tasteful clothes that fit so well they looked tailor made, probably by her. Her beautiful face looked worried and extremely agitated, quite out of keeping with her lovely looks.

A red-haired young woman came out of one of the houses, and upon seeing the dark-haired beauty called out: "Hey Kate, its me, Mary Malone; wait and I'll walk with you to the village. Kate glanced back briefly and then started running away from her friend. It was obvious to me that Kate wanted to be alone, but I had the advantage of seeing the distress in her face.

Startled, Mary increased her pace to catch up, but she was no match for Kate. Sensing that something was terribly amiss, Mary yelled to two approaching friends to stop Kate. This they did, midst loud vocal protests from Kate, and an ineffective attempt to go around them. The disturbance also brought two men to see if they could be of assistance. I scurried down the remaining path and joined them, not only because I wanted to get a closer look at Kate, but because of humanitarian concern for her obvious distress.

Kate was protesting loudly," Leave me alone, leave me alone, I'm beyond redemption!"

Mary said, "Then let us try to help you-- that's what friends are for!"

"No. No", Kate insisted, "I'm beyond help!"

The older of the two men said, "Miss, I'm Doctor Greenspan, a psychiatrist from Boston; it has been my experience that the more severe the problem, the more talking with friends will help. Consider all of us your friends and share your problem with us-- perhaps you are not as far beyond help or redemption as you think." His kind countenance, his soothing voice, and his air of authority calmed Kate down, but she still didn't speak.

"Here, come and sit on this bench and relax, and when you are ready, share your problem with us, starting from the beginning," the psychiatrist said.

Kate walked slowly to the bench, took a few deep breaths and said, "I'd like to tell you, but I'm afraid you'll think I'm crazy; and after what happened I just might be."

Doctor Greenspan put his arm gently on her shoulder and said, "I for one will keep an open mind, and I believe the others will respect my professional judgment. If it turns out that you need psychiatric counseling, which I doubt, I can make arrangements to help you recover." We all nodded our heads in agreement.

"Promise you won't tell any one else?" Again, we all nodded in agreement, and some of us crossed our hearts.

"Doctor, you said start from the beginning, and I shall. Well, believe it or not, I just encountered three Leprechauns. At first I thought they were just little men in funny garb, maybe going to a costume party. But their clothes did look like pictures I have seen of them --dark green with accents of light-brown leather, and funny-looking, green conical hats with up-turned brims. Their faces looked 'Leprechaunist' too." We all nodded and the Doctor said, "Go on, go on!"

"They addressed me politely, said they were lost Leprechauns, and would I be so kind as to tell them the name of this village. When I replied. New Ireland, New Hampshire, they wanted to know where New Hampshire was, and when I said the United States, they started arguing among themselves. The short one said, 'I told you we should have turned left at that last moon beam, didn't I?' 'Yeah, yeah,' the plump one replied, 'but you must admit that it was confusing when we got the "Ireland" signal. How could I have known there was a "New" in front of it?' "

"The plump one then asked me where they could sample the local food, so I told them how to get to Kelly's restaurant. 'Will they take this kind of money?', the thin one asked as he showed me a large gold coin. I suggested they go to the New Ireland Bank, or the pawnshop near it, and convert it to American money. They thanked me kindly, and I started to walk away, wondering if they were really Leprechauns. The short one said, 'Wait a minute. Miss, we would like to give you a proper reward for your kindness to us-- after all, we are strangers in a strange land.' "

"Think nothing of it," I said. "This is a friendly village and strangers are always welcomed."

"'We insist!', the thin one replied. 'It is our custom to bestow rewards for such kindness, and since you are so young and beautiful, we have decided to give you our greatest reward--love making!'"

"I was shocked at their indecent proposition, and tried to refuse it diplomatically, explaining that I had an appointment. Their faces grew livid with anger and they explained that mortals must never refuse a Leprechaun, or else an evil spell will be cast upon them and their whole family. When they said that my father would die within a fortnight, my mother would have a debilitating stroke, and my two brothers would end up in abject poverty, I grew worried. My pleas for mercy were to no avail, even when I told them I was still a virgin. The last revelation made them all grin; and to show their power, they made a strong wind arise and blow down a nearby tree."

"I was frightened out of my wits at their obvious power and the thought of all those terrible things happening to my parents and brothers, so I reluctantly complied. They smiled, took me to a nearby-secluded spot and made me disrobe completely. I was very ashamed, but what could I do? One of them waved his arm, and a luxurious comforter mysteriously appeared. They beckoned me to lie down on it, and then proceeded with their evil deed, taking turns and fondling and caressing me when it wasn't their turn."

"Well", I said, "You were forced against your will and you should not feel guilty. In fact, you made a noble sacrifice to save your whole family from the Leprechauns' evil spell, so you should be condoned, not condemned."

"But you don't understand", she replied, "My guilt is not because they forced me, but because of my reaction. It was a bit painful with the first one, sort of pleasant with the second one, and sheer ecstasy with the last one. How can I possibly explain it to Father Murray at my next confession? No, it is a mortal sin and I am beyond redemption!" She dropped her eyes and head in abject shame.

The psychiatrist then spoke, saying: "My dear child, I am not of your faith, but I find it hard to believe that a kindly priest would condemn you so severely."

I then added, "I am a Christian like you, although I am a Presbyterian-- what my Catholic friends call a 'left footer'. Father Murray represents a loving God who has forgiven worse sins-- remember the Savior's words as he suffered on the cross: 'Father, forgive them, for they know not what they do!'"

Kate broke into tears, and rose to hug both of us. We returned the hug, and added more words of comfort. The Doctor then said, "Come, let us escort you to the bosom of your family."

We started toward her home, accompanied by the girls and the other man, whom we learned later, was named Jim.

"Wait", I said. "What are we going to do about those evil Leprechauns? They may do harm to others."

"You are absolutely right," the good doctor responded. "Let's have her friends escort her home, and the three of us will track down the evil little men before they wreak any more havoc on this peaceful village!"

We then said our good-byes to the young women and headed for the area that Kate had described to us. Jim was first to spot the scene of the crime because he detected the crushed grass where the comforter had lain. The Leprechauns were nowhere to be seen, but again Jim spotted signs where they had walked. Soon, with Jim's eagle eye and tracking skills, we found them resting on an old fallen tree. I was puzzled at the color of the bark less tree, because it was a smooth, medium green. I couldn't help but wonder if that was its natural color or if the little men had cast a spell on it. I also wondered if their pleasurable encounter with Kate had made them forget their desire for food. Perhaps they were reveling in their clever accomplishment.

The other two men had elected me spokesman for the group because of my comforting words to Kate, and because "Doc", as we now called him, felt the Leprechauns would resent his professional approach. I said, "Good afternoon, gentlemen! Could we have a few words with you, if this is a convenient time?"

They conferred privately for a few seconds, and the short one said, "Sure, we might find it amusing to hear what you mortals have to say."

"We thank you kindly" I responded. " We come on behalf of the young lass you recently met. We realize you thought you were rewarding her for her kindness to you, but what you did was contrary to our customs. The young lady was very upset..."

The thin one smiled and said, "She didn't seem upset when I finished--she seemed to be enjoying herself beyond belief!"

"Yes, we understand, but that was a purely physical reaction to a brand new experience for her; Actually, once she had recovered, her mental state was awful because she felt she had committed a mortal sin and was beyond redemption,"

"What an ungrateful wench!' he replied.

"Please understand our purpose in seeking you out. We simply want to help you understand our customs and ask you to honor them. We also want to ask if the young woman could become pregnant."

The short one said, "We don't give a damn for your customs, and, yes, she could become great with child, but it is highly unlikely because we are not like you. In fact you are annoying us and I think we shall torture you and then kill you, else you may set the whole village against us!" He then waved his arms, and immediately the three of us were immobilized.

He did not take our power of speech away, so I said, "Please kind sirs, do not harm us. We came to you to seek understanding and hoped you would return to your homeland before there was further misunderstanding."

The Doctor then said, "I agree with my friend. You are destroying the legends we have read about your people. It describes you as mischievous and fun loving, but not cruel and vicious. In fact, legend has it that you may reward us with a pot of gold. If you torture and kill us you will destroy your good name!"

The short one guffawed and said, "Why do you think we are here and not in the real Ireland? Its because we are outcast from our tribe and we are eager to ruin the reputation of the others-- it will serve them right for being so condemning of our so called wrongdoings!"

The Leprechauns then grabbed us around the middle and started their torture. I'm not sure what they did to the others, but my torturer dug one of his sharp fingernails into the base of my skull until I cried out in agony, pleading for him to stop. He just laughed sardonically, and proceeded with his sharp poking.

The pain was awful, and I felt I would soon pass out, or maybe die. In utter desperation, I came up with an idea. I said, "Now it is my turn to punish you, so be prepared."

He stopped poking, saying, "And just how will you, a mere mortal do that?"

"I will make all of you disappear into thin air—after all, you are fictitious characters and a product of my imagination. So all I have to do is wake up from this amazing dream and return to the safety of my bed."

And that's just what I did!

Authors note: Some readers may think the dream ending is a cop out, but in reality it was the true ending of my story. I haven't the foggiest idea why I dreamed it, except deep in my sub- conscious mind there must be a storyteller who can meld various bits of information and images stored therein into a viable tale. I confess that I have expanded a bit on the details of the dream, but the basic plot and characters were all there-- and they were much more vivid and real than any written words!

Incidentally, I was in my early twenties in the dream and still a bachelor, so I hope my wife of 52 years will understand. (Kate was some "dish" and I wouldn't mind seeing her in a less dangerous dream sometime.) Since I am now in my late seventies, it shows the mind's ability to travel back in time with ease. Try that in the real world!

Shakespeare wrote a soliloquy about sleep in his play, "Mac Beth", which I learned as a high school student. I take exception to his metaphor that sleep is "the death of each days life...." In my view, sleep may simulate death in the relatively immobility of the body, but the brain can be busier than ever with highly imaginative dreams. They are a LIFE in themselves, and frequently, are more exciting and interesting than our daily life!

EXPERIMENTAL ELIXIR FOR ETERNAL YOUTH

"Good morning, Mark. You're looking very chipper today."

"Good morning, Steve. I'm feeling very chipper. How are you feeling today?"

"O.K., I guess. I had a bad night, though, and still feel a bit sleepy." He stifles a big yawn and both of us chuckle.

"Well, I hope you're wide awake for the meeting at the clubhouse. The speaker at the Men's Club is supposed to be one of the funniest ones we've had in Leisure Village, and I know how much you appreciate a sense of humor." Steve smiles and slaps Mark's back. They chat as they walk their regular 125 yards, then Steve says:

" Here's our usual bench. Don't you want to rest a bit, Mark?"

" Nah, Steve. I think I might be able to walk all the way-- non-stop!"

"Are you sure? There aren't any more benches before we get there."

"Yep, I'm sure. Besides, I brought along my cell phone in case one of us can't make it. How about you? Would you like to rest on this bench?"

" Not as long as you have your cell phone and any rescuers don't put us in a cell!" They both grimace at Steve's bit of humor, then they chuckle softly.

A week passes, and the two are walking to the clubhouse again. Steve is the first to speak. "Did I see you jogging the other day, or was it a look alike?"

"Yep, it was I, alright. I'm feeling so good that I decided to get back into shape."

" I know you play doubles tennis, Mark, but don't you think jogging might be a bit too much? Doesn't that strenuous an exercise bring back some of the aches and pains you used to complain about?'

" Not anymore. I haven't had any aches and pains for several months. I've even given up my afternoon nap because my energy has increased."

"Wow! That's great, Mark. Can you tell me your secret?"

"Well, it's not exactly a secret, but I'm not supposed to talk about it . But since we are good friends, I'll tell you. I'm taking an experimental elixir as part of some UCLA trials on old folks. Their tests on monkeys indicate that it can make the mind and body young again, especially for males."

"That sounds great, Mark. How did you learn about it and do you think I could be part of the experiment?"

"I learned about it from my son-in-law, James, who's a professor at UCLA. He heard about it and told me two months ago. After some preliminary test on me by the UCLA experimenters, they felt I qualified. Unfortunately for you, they have all the trial subjects they need. Besides, you're too young. They only want men over 85 for these first human trials, and at 87 I sure qualified."

"Are there any women in the experiment?" Steve has a quizzical look on his face.

" Not yet. They want to do more trials with female monkeys first. They think the elixir needs modification for females. But when they are ready, my wife, Beth, is on the waiting list."

" Wow, that sounds great, Mark. I hope it works out because you are such a great couple. Maybe I'll live long enough to see it leave the experimental stage and be available on the market."

"I hope you will, Steve. I understand that the trials will last only three years, so hang in there and you'll make it!"

Another week passes, and the two friends are having cocktails on Steve's patio. Beth is there, too, and so is Steve's lady friend, Margaret. Later on, Steve takes Mark aside and says:

"Hey, you're looking great. Your facial wrinkles have almost disappeared and I spot some brown roots developing in your hair. Your eyes sparkle more than I've ever seen. I guess the elixir is really working."

"You bet it is, Steve. I haven't felt this good in years. I'm now running three miles four times a week with some younger guys from my church, and I'm playing golf again. That elixir is really wonderful!"

" How's Beth taking it? Is she jealous?"

" She's taking it very well, especially since my libido has increased. In fact, she's starting to feel and look younger herself. The UCLA people think it may be because of the larger number of sperm deposits she now receives, and she is now the only woman in the experimental program."

"That's great, Mark. I wish you both the best of luck! I can hardly wait for the elixir to be on the market."

Several more weeks go by, and Mark has become involved in an old hobby-- oil painting. While at an art supply store, he approaches a very pretty young clerk at the checkout counter with his purchases. His hair is now light brown, with just a few touches of gray; there are no wrinkles; and his youthful muscles have almost returned. Although he looks the proverbial 39, actually he's an 87-year-old hunk!

"Did you find everything you need, sir?

" I think so, Miss."

"I'd be glad to show you some of our other supplies, if you like."

It's obvious that she is interested in Mark, so he decides to see where it will lead.

" Well, there were a couple of colors I couldn't find. Perhaps you can spot them for me." He wonders how old she is, and guesses 28. There's no ring on her fingers.

"I'd be glad to help you." She then yells to the other checkout clerk, "Cover for me," and then says, "Follow me, sir."

While following, Mark notices how trim and sexy her figure is, with a walk that's even more so. When they reach the back of the store, she finds the missing colors, but is able to brush up against Mark while looking.

"There you are, sir! I wish you great success in your painting. If you ever need a model, I would be pleased to pose for you at no charge. My apartment has some great backgrounds you could use." She then whispers, "I'll pose in the nude if you like, and I'm available most evenings."

"Thanks for your kind offer. I'll get in touch with you if I decide to do that sort of painting. So far, I've only done landscapes and flowers."

When they returned to the checkout counter, she whispers again, "Remember, I'm available most any evening, and you can reach me here by telephone. Just ask for Hazel. Or we can make contact whenever you need more supplies."

As Mark leaves the store his head is spinning. "Wow", he says to himself. "This elixir is working better than I ever dreamed! But after 63 years of happy marriage to Beth, I think Hazel's offer might be too tempting. Maybe if I brought Beth along I could try that type of painting. It always intrigued me."

Two months have now passed, and discretion prevents the writer from telling what happened between Mark and Hazel. All he can say is that Mark now has several nude paintings, and they're <u>not</u> in the style of Picasso or Dali. Beth is still happy and looking younger, but nowhere as young as Mark, who looks like he is in his early thirties. Strangely, he is better looking than he was when he was thirty, because he doesn't have the extra weight he once had. Beth approaches and says:

"What did the UCLA man say during your visit today, honey?"

" He thought I was doing great. As you know, I haven't felt any bad side effects, and their tests confirm that there are none. He did suggest that I stop taking the elixir, since physically and mentally I am equivalent to age 25. Best of all, I remember all the things that happened during my entire life more clearly than ever. He thinks we should wait a year to see if there are any signs of aging. If there are, I can start taking it again, but in smaller doses."

"Great, honey! I'm so pleased the way things are going. I hope you're not getting tired of being with me, since I look more like your mother than your wife."

"Don't worry, dear. It's a matter of time until we are the same age. Meantime, it's good to have a mature woman around to help me find my way in this new world. I don't think I could manage without you."

"What a sweet thought, honey. Here's a big kiss for you, with something even better tonight."

"I can hardly wait. By the way, dear, the UCLA man wants us to go on an all-expenses-paid, world show-and-tell tour to other university experimenters. He has a DVD that will show the before, in between and after, so they can follow our progress. How does that sound to you?"

"Great! But there may be some places I don't want to go to. Can we eliminate those and still go?"

"Yep! The same thought occurred to me, and he said it would be OK as long as we visited about 80% of them."

" I'm raring to go, honey. When will we start traveling?"

" In about three weeks. That way we will have plenty of time to prepare and visit the kids and grandkids."

" Speaking of the children, honey, aren't you pleased how well they are handling the changes in us?"

" Well, I figured James and Rebecca would be very supportive, since James was instrumental in our connecting with UCLA. Also, they live close enough to see our changes. Tina and Mike had some reservations, as you know, and they haven't seen us for some time. I'm not sure they think it's part of God's will, so I'm a bit concerned once they see how much younger we now look. You look more like the girls' sister than their mother, and I look like a son. That may be hard to take."

" I agree with you, honey. Guess we'll have to wait and see."

The events in the next two weeks are either fortunate, or unfortunate, depending on one's viewpoint. Mark and Beth never get to visit Tina and Mike, thus avoiding what would have been a huge shock to them. On the other hand, the world tour is postponed. You see, even though Mark had stopped taking the elixir he kept growing younger. Once he reached his late teens, Beth's hands were so busy coping with his juvenile problems that she took him to UCLA to see if they could stop the trend. Mark kept growing smaller and smaller, and was like a nine year old boy before they found an antidote.

It worked slower than the elixir, and it took three months to return him to 25. He remained that age for a few weeks, after which he slowly started growing older. UCLA offered to put him back on the elixir, but he refused. Once he got to age 50, which was Beth's new age, he took enough to stay there.

Three years have now passed, and the elixir is almost ready for the market. Steve managed to get on the program earlier and is now stable at 45, which was the age he wanted. Rebecca and James also got on the program and are now in their late thirties. Tina and Mike are still thinking it over. Their growing aches and pains may convince them that God approves mankind's inventiveness. At least Beth and I hope so. The grandkids aren't eligible because they are still too young. At a recent happy hour on Mark and Beth's patio, Steve is with Alicia, a younger woman. The conversation between mark and Steve is something like this:

"Are you glad you finally got to take the elixir, Steve."

"Damn right I am, Mark. My life has not only been extended, but also made more wonderful. I might even go back to work! How about you and Beth?"

"Well, once I got over my 'runaway youth scare' and stabilized at 50, I couldn't be happier. I too am thinking of going back to work after our next world tour. My old company heard about my new youthfulness and offered me a high position and a big salary to work on their new Manned Mars Landing Program. They figured my experience on the Manned Moon Landing Program, as it is now called, would be useful."

"Are you going to take it, and how does Beth feel about it?"

"Well, I'll let Beth answer both questions."

" I'm all for his going back to work-- it'll keep him from making all those stupid nude paintings!"

Fastidious Sloppiness

Most of my friends know how fastidious I am and how much I hate sloppiness in any form. Well, there was one occasion in which it seemed I couldn't do anything right.

I was taking Emily to opening night at the opera, and naturally we were going formal. I had just had my tails cleaned and pressed and they were simply elegant. My patent leather shoes were immaculate and you could almost use them as a mirror. I showered and then shaved twice to make sure all the stubble was gone. Next, I put on my favorite after-shave lotion, dressed and drove to Emily's house.

Her folks were having a party, so I had to park near the end of their big circular driveway. It was pretty dark and since I had expected to be near my usual place I didn't bring a flashlight. I rang the doorbell and Henry, their butler, led me toward the library to wait for Emily. That was when the trouble began.

Emily's mother spotted me from the living room and waved to me, but her smile quickly turned into dismay and embarrassment. I followed her eyes to the source of her dismay and discovered that I had tracked dog doo-doo all over her beautiful light beige carpet.

To make matters worse, the next guests were coming in, and they had to carefully side step my tracks to avoid the mess. Naturally, Emily's mother had to introduce us and that compounded my embarrassment.

Henry had also seen what had happened and summoned a maid to clean it up. I took off my shoes and apologized profusely. Then Henry led me to a down stairs bathroom so I could tidy up. About that time, Emily came downstairs just as the maid started cleaning. Of course she wanted to know what had happened and the dumb maid not only told her, but who did it! I heard all this and Emily's peals of laughter from the bathroom.

I then started cleaning the mess from my shoes. Both were contaminated, one more than the other, so I cleaned the easy one first to get the knack of this disgusting task. As I was cleaning the messier one, I held it very carefully over the John. Somehow, it slipped from my hand-- right into the bowl with a big kerplunk!

I reluctantly fished it out, finished cleaning it and dried it as best I could; I then squished out to meet Emily, as it was time to leave for the opera. She giggled naughtily over my earlier mishap and my current predicament all the way to the opera.

We arrived at the opera house just before the curtain rose. The other opera buffs gave me hostile stares and snickers when they heard the squish, squish of my shoe. That was one of the longest trips down the aisle I ever had. Boy, was I sorry that we had seats in the fifth row.

The opera was Verdi's Aida and an amazing thing happened during the Grand March scene. The elephant that Sir Thomas Beacham insisted on for realism, turned out to be a bit more realistic than even he envisioned. It performed a gross indiscretion right in the middle of the stage for all to see. Sir Thomas was equal to the occasion. He stopped the music and got two stagehands to clean it up with a giant shovel and a big mop. He then turned to the audience and said something like this:

'Ladies and gentlemen, I apologize for the untimely interruption. It seems that an elephant leaves something to be desired as a colleague—-but my God, WHAT A CRITIC!'

The audience roared with laughter. Emily and I exchanged knowing glances as we joined their laughter. In fact, it was the source of the fourth embarrassment I suffered that evening. You see, Emily and I got the silly giggles and kept laughing long after the opera resumed. Talk about Murphy's Law-- that night it worked overtime!

FIRE BRIGADE

It was 1943, and the Thanksgiving Parade would soon begin. My buddy Dave and I had driven to Cold Spring Harbor to park my car and do a little window-shopping before going to our favorite parade-viewing place. It was on the hill between Cold Spring Harbor and Huntington, and was on a grassy knoll just opposite the Huntington Country Club. As usual, we were among the first to arrive.

Autumn leaves covered the ground, so we scrambled them into small piles to act as cushions. Our spot was high enough so we could sit down and still see over anyone that stood in front of us. We were pleased with our foresight, and doubly pleased that we had brought a thermos of coffee, paper cups, and some doughnuts to pass the time until the parade reached us. I was a bit concerned that the recently finished coffee, plus that from breakfast, would overload my tank.

Sometime later, more spectators started arriving on both sides of the street, mostly from the neighborhood and the country club. When we heard the band music in the distance, we knew that the parade would reach us in less than ten minutes.

There were several cigarette smokers in the country-club crowd, plus quite a few mothers with small children on both sides of the street. In those days, no one complained about cigarette smoke outdoors, even when small children were present; but I had a huge distaste for it, and avoided the stinky fumes whenever I could. I was thankful to be on the opposite side of the street on this glorious Thanksgiving Holiday.

I saw one of the country club men carelessly toss his cigarette butt in the leaves, and as the parade came into view at the top of the hill, the dry leaves burst into flames and started spreading rapidly. Smoke rose quickly, and the gentle breeze wafted it toward the mothers and their kids. I was horrified when a mother with a baby-in-arms started coughing from the smoke, and even more horrified when the fire started overtaking some of the young kids. Although some country-club men tried to stomp the fire out, it was spreading too rapidly. They then concentrated on helping the women and kids escape, but the smoke, the slippery terrain, and a bit of panic made it slow going.

I looked at Dave and he looked at me, and we both knew what to do. We ran across the street to the edge of the fire, unzipped and started putting it out with what had once been coffee. We waved to the other men to join us, and about twenty or more did so.

It wasn't long before the fire was subdued enough so we could stomp out any residual flames with our feet, and the parade still hadn't quite reached us. Dave, all the men, and I felt good about our accomplishment, until we heard loud complaints from the women and kids down wind. It seems that urine and fire make a stinky smell, and its power overshadowed their appreciation for our fire-fighting exploits. Once the parade reached us, the smell was still strong enough to cause the participants to look around and hold their noses.

Many of the town's firemen were in the middle of the parade, and some figured out what had happened. The chief even left the parade to get the details of the fire. By that time, some of the women had regained their appreciation of our quick action, and pointed at Dave and me as the heroes. The Chief got our names and other information, and said he would be in touch soon. Not all were thankful for our actions, because we overheard an older woman complain about our "indecent exposure in front of women and small children."

For the rest of the weekend, we wondered what would happen to us. Would we be arrested for indecent exposure in front of women and small children, or would we be honored for putting out the fire, and maybe saving people from burns, or even death? Would the terrible odor be considered a public nuisance or a health problem? And would we be charged for encouraging the men that joined us to break the law?

Unfortunately, we were too young and inexperienced in such matters to avoid worry, so it wasn't a very happy Thanksgiving for us. We even concocted severe punishment scenarios for our actions. I knew that ignorance of the law was no excuse, so my worries were even greater than Dave's. Whoever said, "Knowledge is power" hadn't considered <u>my</u> predicament.

On the following Monday we both got a summons to appear in local court the next Thursday. All of the above charges were listed, plus one we hadn't considered: "Assuming firemen's duties illegally." Dave wondered if we should hire a lawyer, but since money was scarce, I easily convinced him to wait until we found out more.

We had to take time off from work, and our boss was very sympathetic. He had heard about the incident, so he said, "You boys (He was 55 and still considered us boys because I was 23 and Dave 22) shouldn't be prosecuted, you should be commended; maybe get a medal or something equivalent." His words reduced our worries, but didn't eliminate them.

When we arrived at the court building, we had to wait our turn. A reporter from the *Long Islander,* our local weekly paper, was present and wanted to interview us. I told him to wait until we had finished with the judge, and Dave agreed.

When we went to the Judge's bench, he read the charges again and asked who would speak for us. Dave had agreed that I should because I was a year older. The Judge then asked, "Did you men do the things you were charged with, and why did you do them?"

I was pleased that he had called us men, and my answer was something like this: "Your honor, once we saw the fire start and spread so quickly, we felt immediate action was required because of the women and their kids. One woman in the fire's path was even carrying a baby in her arms. Many others were in the path of the fire, and a few had already started coughing from the smoke. Some had even fallen down because of panic and the slippery terrain. Their safety was our main concern, and violating other laws was secondary. We subconsciously recognized that exposing ourselves was wrong, but the danger was so imminent that we went into action anyway. The other charges didn't enter into our minds at that time. Oh, and one more thing. Some other men had tried to stomp it out, but it was too powerful. Our actions were a last resort!

He then said, "Are you aware that ignorance of the law is no excuse?"

"Yes I am your honor; but isn't there something in the law that lets emergencies overcome lesser rules? I ask the question because I am ignorant of any remedies, and must rely on your knowledge and sense of justice."

The Judge then asked Dave if he agreed with my statements, and Dave said, "Yes, your honor". The Judge nodded at Dave and smiled as he replied to my question, "Yes, there are remedies in case of emergencies, and because of them I am going to dismiss your case. I was required by law to interrogate you to see if the facts and your attitude made them relevant. Now if you two will go into my chambers, the Fire Chief and the Town Supervisor have a pleasant surprise for you. Next case!"

A clerk escorted us into an adjoining room, where the waiting officials took turns making complimentary statements, with the reporter present and taking notes. The Fire Chief gave each of us a certificate making us "Honorary Firemen", and the Supervisor gave us one making us "Outstanding Citizens Who Put Community Safety Above Self".

The reporter then took several pictures of the four of us with his flash camera, and we answered some of his questions. The front page in the next edition of the paper had a picture of the event, but it showed more of Dave and me than it did the two officials. The accompanying article was discreet in explaining how we put out the fire, but remember that was in 1943. We even got some non-front-page publicity in other papers.

We were frequently kidded, and sometimes praised, by our friends and co-workers. At the time, I sometimes wished the incident had never happened. Eventually, talk of it died out and we became regular guys again.

As I later learned from Dave, there were some unexpected benefits for him and some of the other "leaf firefighters." It happened that one of the country-club members took photos while we were in action, and posted them on the club's bulletin board for all to see. A few of the sexier ladies were impressed with the quality of some of the exposed fire-fighting tools, and contacted Dave and a few other men.

However, I had to be content with the certificates I had been awarded. I like to think it was because I was facing away from the camera!

ACTOR'S PLIGHT

Brian Johnson was a damn good actor, but he needed a break. During the winter he had some minor roles in a Broadway play, and was now starring in an original play at a Long Island summer theater. The play had received good publicity from the local newspapers and even the N.Y. Times had mentioned it favorably. The media had given strong approval of the relatively unknown playwright and Brian's sterling performance. Both were overjoyed when they heard that a Broadway producer and Hollywood scout were coming to their summer theater, and figured this might be their golden opportunity.

The playwright was eager to see the outcome and a bit on edge, but Brian, who had to deliver the goods, was nervous the whole day before that evening's performance. He was a bit grouchy and ate very little of the supper his wife had prepared. Worse yet, he had a flat tire on the way to the theater, and it took him so long to put on the spare that he barely made it before starting time. During the turmoil, he kept telling himself, "Keep cool, man. Tonight could be the turning point in your career!"

As most actors know, the right amount of pre-performance nervousness can stimulate the mind and get it to do great things. That was the case for Brian, because his performance was flawless. That is, until he got to the last scene and became overconfident. In that scene, the leading lady was angry with the leading man, and his strong, emotional rebuttal ended the play with a bang.

Apparently, the leading lady was even more nervous than Brian, so she misspoke her lines badly. So badly that he forget his long speech. After a pause, he had an inspiration:

"Frankly, my dear, I don't give a damn!" He then walked off the stage and the curtain fell.

The Broadway producer was shocked, but the scout was impressed. Hollywood next stop!

DRY SPELL

Bill and Harry were good songwriters, and had several songs that were big hits during the roaring twenties. They were making a good living with their songs, but when the great depression of the thirties hit the nation, they got depressed too. Result: COMPOSERS' BLOCK!

When they went into their favorite restaurant, they sat at their usual table and started discussing their plight. Harry was the first to speak. "We've got to get rid of this damn composers' block. Have you got any ideas?"

"I think we should come up with a few catchy titles, jot them down along with a few ideas, and maybe the words and music would come to us."

"Great idea, Bill! But this city depresses me. Maybe if I was back home on the range I'd think of something."

"Yeah, I'm sorta depressed and homesick too. Why don't you take the train to Texas, Harry, and I'll take the Chattanooga choo-choo back to Tennessee. Maybe if you saw that girl you left behind she could cheer you up. What was it you called her?"

"Oh, I used to call her my Yellow rose of Texas, because she always wore a yellow rose in her red hair. But you know I can't take a train, Bill. They nauseate me when I hear the rails clicking, and clicking in the same dull rhythm. It sounds like <u>music going round and round</u> !"

"Guess I forget how they affect you Harry. But we've got to do something to remove this composers' block. It makes my brain feel like it's full of <u>deep purple</u>."

"I know what you mean. But cheer up, Bill; <u>happy days'll be here again!</u>"

"Not with my <u>dry bones</u>!"

"What you need, pal, is some water--<u>clear water</u>."

"Nah, but I wouldn't mind some tea. How about you?

"Sounds good, Bill. Waitress, please bring us <u>tea for two.</u>

As the waitress leaves, both nudge each other, and Bill says, "Boy, she's looks like <u>a million dollar baby</u>! Maybe we should pray that heaven sends us a big pile of money."

"I agree about the waitress, pal, but I doubt if we'll get rich. All we're getting now is <u>pennies from heaven!</u>"

Note to younger people, which is almost everybody: The underlined words were the titles of hit songs when I was a youth. Too bad Harry and Bill didn't realize they had some good titles when they were searching for them, but life is like that. Many never see the obvious.

E. T. EVENT
(Translated conversation from a remote site)

Earlier in the century, the explorers had left their over-crowded homeland for something that was totally different. Although it was quite a hostile place, they had come prepared and worked hard to make it livable. After many years, it was now quite civilized and comfortable, thanks not only to their diligent efforts, but because they were highly intelligent and inventive.

Most of them were very happy, and because the surroundings still appeared hostile, they figured other explorers would leave them alone. That was not only their devout hope, but it had become ingrained, so they kept guards on duty just in case some newcomers arrived.

The guards at portal 53 were a young married couple, and their recorded conversation was as follows, with the husband speaking first:

"Honey, did you see that flash in the sky?"

"Yes, dear. What do you think it is?"

"Maybe one of those space ships we've heard about on the electronic media.

" You mean it might contain some of those dangerous extra-terrestrial beings? If so, I'm frightened, so put your arms around me, dear, while I inform headquarters."

" I think we should investigate it first. It might be just a shooting star that landed.

"Guess you're right. What should we do?"

"Hop into the patrol vehicle and let's see where it landed."

They drive about a mile over the rough terrain before they spot a strange-looking object. Parking behind a large boulder, they walk closer, cautiously and arm in arm, so they can get a better look. The husband is carrying a weapon and the wife the communication equipment, which she puts on "alert" so headquarters can monitor their conversation "

"There it is! Good lord, it is a space ship, but it sure is an ugly one, honey. In fact it doesn't look anything like those renderings we've seen in our library. Look at that fat body and those skinny legs."

" You're right, dear. It is ugly, and a bit frightening looking. What now?"

" Let's wait a bit, honey, and see if there are any extra-terrestrials aboard."

" Good idea, and if any come out I think we should get instructions from headquarters."

They wait a short interval "Look dear, one is climbing down that ladder now!"

"Yes, I see it. Gosh, it sure is a puffy creature-- and look at that funny head."

"Why do you think it looks so strange, dear?"

"Probably because it needs to protect itself from our hostile environment. Remember how long it took our engineers to develop our protection, which is now barely noticeable?

"Yes I do. Listen, it's talking!" They turn on their automatic translators and hear : "One small step for man, one giant leap for mankind!"

FAVORITE SONG

When Martin and Debbie Anderson finally had their first child, they considered it a real blessing. It had taken them four years of trying, which of course was pleasant, but three miscarriages were very unpleasant. In fact, it was extremely discouraging, but their desire for a child was so great that they persevered.

When a baby girl arrived, they named her Karen. Not only did they like that name, but also it represented their attitude--to be "Caring" for all people, especially their own dear child. Unfortunately, they had to do more caring than most parents, because Karen had a serious heart problem. She had several close calls as she grew up, but the most serious one came after she was hospitalized shortly after her 16th birthday.

Unless Karen's parents found a heart donor soon, she was doomed to die. They were fifth in line on the waiting list and they prayed frequently for a break. It finally came, but it was a mixed blessing.

Her Dad was in an auto accident a mile from Karen's hospital and died upon arrival. The card in his wallet gave his organs to Karen and his wife. Some wondered if the accident was deliberate, but there was no proof.

When her doctor heard about the new heart he operated immediately and saved Karen's life. Of course she and her mother were happy about the successful operation, but saddened by Martin's tragic accident. Once Karen recovered she had a new favorite song:

" My Heart Belongs to Daddy!"

MOON WALK

It was their third day on the lunar surface, and Pete was eager to explore more of that desolate landscape. As he and his buddy, Jim, left the safety of the Lunar Module, Jim said, "Wow, the sure is bright today."

"Remember, there's no air to filter the sun's rays." Pete responded. "Hey, let's see what's behind that hill."

"Don't you think it's too far away?" Jim sounded concerned.

"Nah, we've got plenty of oxygen and our space suit cooling systems will protect us from the bright sun."

They walked and bounded in the low gravity for about six hundred feet, enjoying the light feeling it gave them. It was only one-sixth of earth's gravity, and in spite of their cumbersome space suits, they enjoyed the feeling as they bounded around like school kids.

Pete then picked up a shiny rock about the size of a baseball and looked at it carefully. He then said, "Look Jim. My hunch was right. This rock's full of diamonds!"

Jim then bent down to pick up one too, and it wasn't long before he confirmed Pete's finding. "Hey, you're right. Mine's full of diamonds too, and I think I spot some gold chunks."

They both wondered aloud whether or not they could keep them, but concluded that N. A. S. A. would want to examine and analyze them in their usual careful way. Jim put both of them in his specimen bag before he said, "That's a great find, Pete, but I think we should go back, pronto. It's getting awful hot!"

Pete also felt the heat rising, so he took one look at the sun through his sun shield and yelled, "My God, Jim, it's a solar flare. Run for your life!"

Pete was sweating and gasping as his wife woke him. "You shouldn't nap at the beach, you've gotten sunburned. What sort of crazy dream did you have this time?"

HORACE HORNBLOWER

Honk! Honk! Honk! The guy in the red convertible behind me was impatient, but I wasn't about to go any faster on such a steep, curvy, two-lane road. If there had been any shoulders, I would have pulled over to let him pass; alas, they were scarce on this road and I saw none ahead.

I raised my arm in an 'I'm doing the best I can' gesture, but it did no good. He kept honking and waved his arm in a 'speed up or pull over sign.' To make matters worse, the late afternoon sun made visibility tough. When it wasn't directly in my eyes, it filtered through the trees and made a strobe-light effect. I was not only starting to get dizzy, but a dull headache was surfacing.

'Hang on', I thought. 'It'll set in thirty minutes. My wife, Doris, frequently takes the other driver's side when I'm driving, but this time she sided 100% with me.

"Can't he see that there are no pull-outs and it's dangerous to go faster?"

"I know," I replied. "If I spot a decent one I'll pull over and let him pass." We went for about five minutes before we found one, but with all the honking it seemed like an hour.

When I finally pulled over to let him pass, he was livid with anger, gave a last sustained honk on his horn, and made an obscene gesture. He was yelling something too, but I couldn't make it out. 'Just as well', I thought, because profanity upsets me almost as much as it does Doris.

After he safely passed, he sped up and we could hear his tires squealing around the curves. Doris, who wouldn't hurt a June bug, then made a surprising remark. "I know it's uncharitable, but when I see an oaf like that I almost wish he would have an accident. Nothing serious, of course, just enough to make him slow and calm down, and maybe learn some manners."

"Me too," I agreed. "He certainly needs to be taught a lesson." We then discussed several scenarios for harmless trouble: a flat tire; a fender bender accident; a reckless driving ticket; maybe something worse, with a few bumps and bruises to him.

Doris clinched the discussion with, "Maybe a hard blow on his cranium would knock a little sense into him!"

Actually, Doris and I frequently developed imaginary scenarios for dangerous situations, including how to overcome them. One that we had dreamed up several years ago was put into practice later on. I also conjured up a name for him--Mr. Hornblower. (With apologies for the hero of the novel, Horatio Hornblower.)

About fifteen minutes later our wishful thinking bore fruit. He had hit the post of a guard rail and his neat convertible seemed to be severely damaged. One wheel had snapped off, and the right side seemed to be completely creamed. Not a total, but at least a half total. Hornblower was no-where to be seen, and since there was no shoulder I only slowed down. A few minutes later, we spotted him. He had walked to the next shoulder and waved his arms frantically when he saw us.

"Shall we?" I asked Doris.

"I hate to," she replied, "but I guess we have no choice. He may be badly hurt."

"O.K.," I said. "But be prepared to use plan H. S. if he gives us any trouble. I don't trust guys like him." She nodded in agreement and checked her pocket book.

I then pulled over and Doris opened her door and got out. "Here, take my seat-- you'll need the leg room," she explained as she climbed into the rear seat.

"Thanks," he mumbled softly.

"Your car looks quite damaged" I said. "How about you? Do you need any medical attention?"

"I'm just a bit shook-up; no broken bones as far as I can tell but my chest and head ache a bit. Damn sun got in my eyes, otherwise I'd have made that stupid curve." He sounded and looked as arrogant as ever, so my heart sank. Apparently he hadn't learned the lesson that Doris and I had wished.

"I'll take you to North Conway and to the hospital, if you like; otherwise, I suggest you take a taxi and find a doctor. Either way, you should be checked for internal injuries. Once you are O. K., you can get some one to tow your car." He nodded in silent agreement.

I then said, "I'm Henry, and this is my wife, Doris." He then told me his name was "Horace." 'Funny name for such an nasty-tempered devil,' I thought. About five minutes later he got very fidgety.

"Can't you drive any faster? I don't like to go this slow."

"Can't drive any faster and stay safe," I replied.

"Look, you old goat," he snarled. "I think I'd better drive!" he then pulled out a switch-blade knife to prove he was serious."

"You shouldn't do that after we helped you; I hoped you'd be nice to us." His reply was shocking to both of us.

"Don't be asinine, grandpa. Can't you see I'm a mean devil?" He then stuck the open knife to my face and waved it menacingly.

"O. K., O. K. I get your point-- just don't frighten my wife-- she has a weak heart." I exchanged glances with her and her eyes said "Plan H. S." I pulled over on the next shoulder, undid my seat belt, opened my door, and started to get out. He did the same, and once he was out, Doris executed our plan.

"Excuse me sir," she said sweetly.

"What do you want, lady?" His voice was impatient and he waved his knife at her.

" I want to give you something." She then squirted her hair spray directly into his eyes. He staggered backward blindly, rubbed his eyes and cursed. I quickly got back in my seat and gave it the gun. Fortunately, no other cars were coming, so I pulled out quickly, before he recovered. I drove about a hundred yards and slowed down so Doris could climb into the front seat and close the dangling door

Once we were safely buckled up, she said, "What nerve--he's a real bastard if I ever saw one. I hope no one picks him up and he has to walk all the way to North Conway. It would serve him right!

"I couldn't agree with you more, my dear. Guess some people never learn. I'd hoped the accident would have taught him some sense." I silently marveled that she had used a naughty word to describe him.

"That kind never seem to learn," she said. She then chuckled and said, "Guess we showed old Horace Hornblower that Senior Citizens know a thing or two!"

"You executed plan Hair Spray beautifully." I said. "Your poise and timing were perfect."

"You did real well with your fake exit-- and your quick re-entry and pull away were splendid."

In about twenty minutes we got off the treacherous road and onto Route 16 near Intervale. "Who would have thought our trip to Evan's Notch to see the fall colors would have been so exciting," I said.

"Or dangerous," Doris added. "Guess we were lucky--and pretty clever too."

We held hands in mutual admiration all the way back to Dover-- except when I paid the toll in Rochester!

EPILOGUE:
The next evening, Doris showed me an article from the Portsmouth Herald: MASSACHUSETTS MAN WRECKS CAR

Horace Nastase, from Springfield, was shaken up and sustained minor injuries following a collision with a guard rail on the country road between South Chatham and Intervale. Apparently, Mr. Nastase lost control during the steep descent. According to Mack's Garage, in North Conway, the 1998 Chrysler Le Baron suffered about $8000 in damages. County officials said he would be billed for the guardrail damages The Herald also discovered that his insurance had just lapsed. Mr. Nastase also suffered exposure to a twenty-degree wind chill factor and exhaustion during his long walk down the steep road during the waning twilight. He complained that none of the few cars on the road had the decency to pick him up. He's expected to be discharged from Memorial Hospital later this week.

"How do you like that," I said. "His last name is almost the same as his disposition--nasty! Do you suppose he finally learned a lesson?"

"I doubt it," she replied. "But I'll say one good thing about him."

"What on earth is it?" My curiosity was at its peak.

"Shakespeare said, *Know thyself ....* He sure demonstrated that virtue when he called himself a *Mean Devil!*" We both laughed heartily, and my admiration for her rose a few notches higher!

Note: This fictitious story was inspired by a trip from our home in Dover, NH, to Evan's Notch to see the fall foliage. New England, especially the mountain area, has some of the most spectacular foliage in the world. Yes, the sunlight was severe and I was honked at a few times. However, no one like Horace Nastase appeared, for which my wife, Elizabeth, and I are grateful. L. M. E.

HOW I WAS "SAVED"

"Young man, have you been saved?" That was the question posed to me as I left the Sunday service at a small, evangelical church in 1941. One of the members had spotted me as a stranger and talked with me, so I was the last one in the greeting line. I wondered if the minister had asked such a blunt question of others, because I was surprised by it and a wee bit offended. The minister was an old man, probably in his late 70's or early 80's, so I tried to be polite.

"Sir, I was baptized as an infant and confirmed at age 12, so I suppose I have been saved." I hoped that would satisfy him.

"No, no," he insisted. "That's not what I mean. Have you been born again in the spirit? Unless you have been born again, you haven't been saved!"

He was starting to annoy me because he dismissed baptism and confirmation so quickly, and I decided to be less polite-- not impolite, just less polite. "I suppose by your standards I haven't been saved. What else do I have to do? In fact, why should I do any more than I already have?"

He grew quite agitated at my words and went into a long diatribe. "You must turn over your entire life to Jesus Christ and abandon all sin-- not only in deed, but also in word and thought. Then when you die, as we all must, you will enjoy God's company in heaven forever and ever. Does that answer both your questions?"

"Well partly," I replied. "But what you suggest sounds like a pretty tall order. I'm not sure it's humanly possible."

"It is a 'tall order', as you said, but it's exactly what is required if you want to be saved and receive salvation's many blessings."

"But I'm only 21 years old-- can't I wait until I'm a lot older, so I can have more fun while I'm young?

He grew calmer, almost reverent, as he said, "Serving the Lord is the most 'fun' you can have in this life. It will bring unspeakable joy to all your days. As to waiting, that is the Devil tempting you because we don't know when we are going to die. Suppose you are killed in an accident tomorrow? What then?"

I paused to think that one over. "In that case, I suppose I may not make it to heaven, unless the Lord is merciful, as my former pastor used to preach."

"It's worse than that," he insisted. "You'll roast in Hell for eternity!"

"You mean God would be that cruel and punish me forever for a few measly sins during my short lifetime? That doesn't seem fair."

He was unyielding in his reply. "That's exactly what I mean, but don't take my word for it." He then proceeded to open his Bible and quote several passages on the eternal punishment of Hell, and how to avoid it via rebirth.

I wasn't entirely ignorant of scripture, so I said, "How about the part that says even if we are dead, we can be saved if we believe? To me, that means God will give me another chance at the end of my life, even if I die in an accident."

"I'm glad to see that you have had some good teachers in your life, but didn't they explain that it meant "dead in sin", and not physically dead? Unless you have been born again, you are dead in sin. Are you willing to risk your eternal life on that false interpretation?" He had a look on his face that said, "Let's see you wriggle out of that one!"

Undaunted, I decided to change the subject. "What is sin anyway? What you consider sin may not be sin in my eyes, or even in God's eyes. For example, if I find a young girl so attractive that I want to kiss her, is that a sin?"

"If you contemplate marriage it may not be a sin; but if it's a lustful thought, it is. It will be punished unless you repent."

Pushing on, I said, "But isn't desire for love and affection from the opposite gender a normal, God-given instinct that is necessary to keep the human race alive?"

"Yes", he reluctantly admitted, "but it still has to be free of lustful thoughts."

"Suppose the young lady starts disrobing and seduces me. Am I sinning if my flesh is weak and I succumb to her charms? And is she sinning, or just fulfilling a normal, healthy desire that could land her a husband?"

"Young man, why do you ask such complicated questions? I think you are not only disrespectful, but are testing me."

"Why do you take such a simplistic and unyielding position? Although I respect your age and calling, I'm not sure you can speak for God with the authority you pretend. In fact, you may be committing a terrible sin yourself-- the false pride that your interpretation of scripture is the only one?"

His face grew ashen and he looked visibly hurt. I began to regret my harsh words and tried to make amends. "Sir, I'm sorry if I got carried away and my words offended you. I think I've gone too far in this discussion.

Please forgive me."

He nodded and gestured in the affirmative, but he seemed to be choking, or having some sort of physical problem. Two of the ushers who were closing up the church came rushing to his aid.

"I heard some of your conversation" one of them said to me. "What have you done to our beloved pastor? You should be ashamed of yourself. I hope you never come back to this church again."

The other one was even harsher. "Get away from here right now! And don't ever come back, you heathen!"

They then led him inside and laid him down on a bench to calm and comfort him. I hung around as long as I dared to see if he recovered, but as I walked away I still heard coughing sounds. By the time I walked the few blocks to my rooming house, I heard the siren of an ambulance headed for the church. I felt terrible, and resolved to keep my big mouth shut in the future, especially when discussing controversial subjects with old religious zealots. I prayed silently for his quick recovery.

I went directly to my room and read my Bible most of the afternoon, seeking solace for my misdeeds, and wisdom for the future. I even skipped lunch, making do with a few pieces of fruit I kept in my room.

Later in the week I learned that the old pastor had a bad choking spell, but recovered quickly and was preaching again the following Sunday. 'Thank God he didn't die', I thought, 'Otherwise guilt could weigh heavily on my mind.'

So how did that experience "save me"? Well, it saved me from a bad guilt complex, because my prayers were answered and he recovered quickly.

It saved me from any further, intemperate arguments with the old pastor. In fact, I never went back to his church, and the one time I saw him in public I walked the other way.

It saved me from becoming prey to extreme religious zealots in the future. I looked for pastors with a sense of balance who were willing to discuss matters of faith calmly and with reason. After a few years of "heathenism", I joined a church whose pastor accepted me-- warts and all. In time, I became a lay leader, holding many positions in support of the church's lofty mission.

Later on, I found solace in the words of a neighbor's son who had left the business world to become a minister. During an inspiring conversation on my patio, he told me of some research his denomination, was doing regarding the best way to convert unbelievers into believers. The research showed that over-zealous pastors frequently drove more people away than they converted. The conclusion went something like this: It is a pastor's job to preach the word as the spirit and his intellect reveal, then stand aside and let the Holy Spirit do its work.

I said a loud "Amen" to that conclusion.

But, you may ask, "Was my immortal soul ever saved?"

To which I reply, as I approach my eightieth birthday: "I'm still a work in progress, although I know the years ahead are far fewer than when I was twenty-one. I'm trying to keep all avenues open for the Holy Spirit to continue doing Its wondrous work. Most of all, I'm willing to wait for God's final judgment of my life.

Hopefully, He will say, "My son, you have now been saved;"

Author's note: This story is mostly fiction, but it was inspired by a brief encounter with an old pastor who wanted to save me on the spot, and became agitated when I politely resisted. I did become a lay leader, and the experience on my patio is true.

KISSES ON MAIN STREET

While strolling down Main Street on his eager feet, a young man, called "Pete", saw a very pretty girl who put his head in a twirl. The setting sun was almost done, and its ethereal glow of gold made him unusually bold; so he said, "Pardon me, lovely Miss; could you spare a kiss? It would give me bliss!"

Her face was red, as she sternly said, "No, I won't give you a kiss. It may be bliss for you but it won't be bliss for THIS Miss, so consider yourself dismissed!"

Pete sighed as he replied, "Come on. Miss; would you really miss just one little kiss, and deny a fellow poet bliss before he's dismissed?"

She smiled a wee bit at this poetic nit-wit, then said, "Not that I care a dime for your rhyme, but how small a kiss would it take to give you bliss?"

With great alacrity he spotted her uncertainty, so he passionately took her into his arms. He could feel her charms as he gave her a quick, soulful kiss before he could be dismissed. She started to slap his face in disgrace, but he restrained her, saying, "I'm just answering your question. Miss. A kiss like that one would be about the smallest kiss to give me bliss; but a kiss like THIS would bring SUPERB bliss!"

Again, he took her in his arms and felt her charms, and gave her a longer, even more soulful kiss. She struggled a bit, but the kiss was such a hit that she returned it. Still holding her, he whispered, "There, Miss; didn't that kiss give you a tiny bit of bliss?" His head was no longer in a twirl; it was in a swirl over this stunning girl!

Before she could answer, her father came out of his Art gallery yelling, "What's going on there? Young man, how dare you act like this with my sweet Miss-- take THIS!" He was about to strike Pete, who didn't retreat, but quickly said, "Wait a minute. Before you hit me one little bit, take a look at that sunset of gold. It made me unusually bold and I felt, before I grow old and cold, that I should seek a bit of bliss by getting a kiss from your lovely miss.

As an art connoisseur, don't consider me a cur; instead, please understand that I 'm a sensitive young man who is touched by great art deep down in his heart. In the presence of such beauty, I felt it my sworn duty to do my little part to honor such great art. I couldn't kiss the sunset, but your daughter I'll never forget.

So before you strike my cheek, take another little peek at both. Then see if you don't agree just a tiny bit with me. '

Her father wasn't immune to rhyme, so just in the nick of time he restrained his blow, saying, "I'm going to let you go. You are an unusual and poetic young guy who doesn't deserve to die!

Fortunately, he remembered his own youth, and, to tell the truth, his eyes had a glow that said, 'I know, I know.' He took the arm of his Miss, and, with a gesture, forgave all our bliss. Then father and daughter began to fade into the sunset, and its lengthening shade.

Before long the sunset was gone, so Pete basked in the wonderful afterglow, which you and I know will grow stronger with the years and keep away many tears.

Remember this as the poetic story of a young man's moments of glory, with a charming Miss and some kisses of bliss, during a sunset of gold which made him bold, and a father's understanding way beyond society's demanding.

It was a stupendous feat, which I suspect can't be beat, because it was done on Main Street!

THE MANSION

While walking along a tree-lined boulevard filled with stately mansions, I was particularly attracted to one. It wasn't the largest one I saw, but it was the one most architecturally suited to my taste, and the landscaping was out of this world. The emerald-green lawn was carefully mowed and seemed to be completely weed free; the foundation plants were luxuriant and full of various colored blossoms that complemented each other; and the circular driveway and walks were lined with gorgeous flowers and shrubs. It was a visual feast to anyone with an eye for beauty.

The mansion itself was of gray field stone with a slate roof of a darker gray. The windows were large, casement type, and placed in just the right positions. Its crowning glory was the large cupola in the center of the roof, which I imagined gave a splendid view of the craggy mountains and sparkling lake in back of the mansion.

I desperately wanted to go inside, but felt it would be a terrible intrusion on the owner's privacy to even ask. I had already noticed that there were no fences or walls protecting the mansions, but I took this as a sign that the neighborhood was crime free, and not necessarily that it was friendly. The homes of the wealthy aren't noted for their friendliness, especially to outsiders like me.

After I had gazed a long time at my favorite mansion, I continued my walk along the almost deserted boulevard. I spotted a car coming toward me and started marveling at its sleek lines and ultra-quiet engine. I could tell immediately that it was a luxury car, so I focused my eyes to see who the lucky driver was. It was a dark-haired, attractive woman. As she drew closer, I recognized her-- it was my own mother!

She spotted me at about the same time, slowed down, and then pulled over to the curb, rolling down the electric window en route. We exchange greetings, and she invited me to hop in and drive home with her. After a big hug and a kiss, I took my seat. I looked for a seat belt, but to my surprise there was none. I soon forgot the oversight because I had not seen her for some time and was eager to catch up with the latest news. I was burning with curiosity about her elegant car. What had happened to her old Chevy? Where did she get the money for this car, which must have been in the eighty thousand dollar category-- maybe higher? And where did she get those stylish clothes, which exceeded her usual tasteful dressing in both color and charm? I repressed my burning curiosity and decided to talk about more mundane things first.

We chatted amiably for a minute or so, then to my surprise she turned into the driveway of the mansion I had admired some minutes ago. Surprised, I asked, "Why are you pulling in here?"

"Because it's now my home. Come on in and I'll show you around after we have tea on the terrace. I have a surprise there for you." Was this a coincidence, or was she expecting me?

We pulled up near the front door and a servant opened her door *and* would have opened mine, except I beat him to it. As we approached the front door, another servant opened it, greeted my mother respectfully, and said, "The others are waiting on the terrace. I presume this is the son you mentioned earlier?"

Mother nodded affirmatively and introduced us. As we entered the large hallway I thought, 'Aha, so I was expected. The mystery deepens!'

The hallway floor was made of rich marble and the walls were decorated with fine paintings and tapestries, and a few busts of people I didn't recognize. The ceiling was of wood, heavily carved with various designs. "Wow", I thought, 'Mother must have a job here as companion to some rich lady who is away. She can't possibly own this place, unless she won a big lottery and hasn't told me yet.'

Next we went into the spacious living room, which outdid the hallway in elegance. It had colorful oriental carpeting on the wooden floor; hand-carved, antique furniture strategically placed; more tapestry and paintings on the wall; a central fireplace with logs ready to light in case it grew chilly; and a concert grand piano in the corner. I observed all of this as we walked toward the stone terrace, which was at the far end of the room and in the back.

When we walked onto the terrace there was my surprise-- my two sisters. They were already seated and enjoying tea and delicate finger sandwiches. Apparently they hadn't been there long, so after Mother and I greeted them we all enjoyed the tea and sandwiches, plus some light conversation.

Mother then said, "I expect all of you to have dinner and spend the night here; so, if you will excuse me, I will make arrangements with the servants." We all nodded in agreement.

I could tell that this was the opportunity we had all been waiting for. Once Mother was out of earshot, we started speculating as to how on earth she seemed to be in charge of such a glorious home. My older sister, Ruth, thought she had hit it big in the stock market. We all knew that she had done well in previous years, so maybe she bought shares in Microsoft, or another dot-com company early on that multiplied its value tremendously.

My younger sister, Louise, scoffed at Ruth's suggestions, saying, "She was mostly in mutual funds. Besides, even if she bought a winning stock her initial capital wouldn't have been enough to acquire all this. I'll bet she married a multi-millionaire! (My father had died many years ago).

"One of you may be right," I tactfully said, "but my guess is that she either won a huge lottery or is a companion to a rich old lady who is away for a while."

Before we could reach a consensus, a difficult task among my siblings, Mother returned. After tea, she took us on a tour of the house, showing us along the way three elegant bedrooms where we could stay as long as we liked. Her bedroom was magnificent, but we noticed that there was a smaller one near it. That gave some credence to my "companion" idea, as knowing nods and subtle glances from my sisters implied.

Dinner was a real gourmet treat, and we all noticed the great respect the servants had for Mother. If she was a rich lady's companion, she must be a very valuable one, because the servants treated her as if she were the owner. My "companion" theory was now on shaky grounds, but the "lottery" one was still viable. It too had a flaw, because none of us could ever remember her gambling, a practice she had frequently admonished us to avoid when we were children and young adults.

After dinner, we retired to the living room, where a cozy fire was going to subdue the night-air chill and enhance the ambiance. We talked about many topics, except none of us was brave enough to ask Mother the question burning in our mind-- 'How did she come by this wonderful mansion?' I was pleased with Mother's comprehension of every topic we discussed, and I could see that both sisters seemed amazed. Obviously, Mother had been doing a lot of reading, or perhaps had taken some courses, or both. At my request, my sisters and our Mother played the piano before we left the living room.

It was after midnight when we went to bed, and I noticed that the servants had done their job again. The bedclothes were turned down, there was a nice pair of silk pajamas for me, and the adjoining bathroom had proper dental equipment. They even had several books and magazines on my night table, but there was no television in sight. I read one of the magazines for about fifteen minutes, and then fell into a deep sleep.

When I awoke the next morning, I was back in my own bed in my New Hampshire condominium. Suddenly, it dawned on me. It wasn't the stock market; a multi-millionaire husband; a rich old lady; or the lottery that were responsible for Mother's mansion. It was something more important and much longer lasting. A passage of scripture flashed through my mind: "In my Father's house are many mansions."* It was then that I surmised that I had caught a brief glimpse of Heaven and the rewards my Mother had earned on earth.

While this story is fiction and an embellishment of my dream, the vision was as real as: sunshine on a snowy peak; silvery moon beams on sparkling water; the perfume of fragrant flowers wafting in a gentle breeze; the angelic smile on a baby's face; or any of the thousands of wispy things that reach our senses and create great pleasure, but which can never be fully explained!

*John 14.2, King James Version

Note: The absence of my Father bothered me at first, but I figured he was away temporarily during my visit. Likewise for my two younger brothers, one of which is deceased. Or maybe they will be included in my next dream of Heaven!

THE MOST AMAZING WOMAN IN THE WORLD!

As managing editor of a major newspaper I was invited to the first press conference for "A Most Remarkable Woman." I toyed with sending one of my top reporters, but there was something about the announcement that intrigued me.

First, it was from my old friend and sometime rival. Sir Geoffrey Barnstead. That old fox was noted for his ability to uncover things that were both unusual and authentic.

Second, the destination was tempting. My only trip to Ethiopia had been during the last major uprising, and I never really got to see Addis Abba, the capitol.

Finally, Sir Geoffrey had made it pretty clear that he wanted me in person with his hand-scribbled note: "This may be the story of the century, possibly the millennium! G.B."

The flight to Addis Abba was somewhat routine, except the sunrise over the Sahara desert was spectacular. I checked into my room at 9:30 a.m., went to bed and left a call for 1:00 p.m. After a shower and a shave, I lunched in the coffee shop and had plenty of time to get to the press conference before the starting time of 3:00 p.m. I greeted some of the managing editors from papers and TV stations around the world that I knew, and took a seat in the second row.

Promptly at 3:00 p.m. Sir Geoffrey appeared on the stage, accompanied by a strikingly beautiful African woman and two distinguished looking men, whom I recognized. After thanking us for coming, he introduced the two men, both of whom were Nobel Prize winners. Dr. Ernest Graves had won his prize for discoveries in genetics, and Dr. Forrest Greene had won his prize for computer inventions. I could see that the old fox was getting first-rate backup for his big story. I turned on my recorder so I wouldn't miss any of his clever tricks.

Sir Geoffrey then introduced the young woman thusly:

"Ladies and gentlemen of the media, I would like you to meet an amazing young woman who came to my attention about a year ago. One of my reporters heard that a woman led a remote southern tribe, which as you know is unheard of in this part of the world. When he told me that she had overcome the long tradition of male leadership among the tribes by sheer intellect, I was intrigued. When I visited her and her tribe, I immediately saw her great beauty and wondered if that wasn't the dominating factor in her success. But no, great as her beauty is, her intellect far outshines it."

"My staff and I found that she had mastered six languages and most of the facts in the Encyclopedia Britannica while attending a rather primitive village school. Her usefulness as an interpreter and her knowledge of just about everything else led her to the top post, but not without some struggle. Suffice it to say that the tribe eventually knew a good thing when they saw it and common sense triumphed!"

"With great effort, lots of diplomacy, and substantial financial aid, we persuaded the tribe to let her come to England so that she could develop her skills to their utmost. She was eager for more knowledge, so she willingly came once she saw that her people would be provided for."

"Our next task was to educate her as much as possible without giving away our secret prematurely. We housed her at my private estate and hired the most learned professors we could find. At first we thought it would cost a fortune, but when the professors discerned her great intellect and her ability to learn from books and computers, they agreed to work almost free provided they could publish the results after two years. I am happy to report that she mastered twenty-six languages and twelve major fields in less than a year. Each of the professors has confirmed that she could easily obtain fifteen doctorate degrees from either Cambridge or Oxford, and we plan to pursue that goal shortly."

"Her physical side was not neglected, and we set up an exercise program with an expert trainer. It was he who discovered that she was a world-class runner and all-round athlete capable of winning championships in any ladies' sport. Furthermore her eyesight was as keen as a cat's at night or an eagle's during daylight, and her sense of smell and hearing equaled a bloodhound's. Her sense of touch and taste were also outstanding, as were her sense of balance and presence."

"Now I know these statements seem incredible, so we sought a rational explanation for them. The two Nobel Prize winners on stage and their assistants have performed extensive research on her, and have concluded two things:

"1. Her genetic make up combines the best characteristics of the Jewish race, which history says settled in this area several millennia ago, and the Ethiopian race. In addition, there is some genetic material that is completely unknown to science. Its origin is a mystery, and even evolutionary accidents cannot explain it adequately."

"2. Her brain seems to operate on a binary principal, similar to a computer. In fact, her memory capacity rivals the best mainframe computer, as does her computation and recall speed. Even her speech can be speeded up, and she can utter 15,000 words a minute. Of course they are unintelligible to ordinary humans, but when recorded and then played back at very slow speed they become completely intelligible! She also has the ability to perform manual tasks at twenty times the most proficient expert."

"She has graciously agreed to answer questions and demonstrate her remarkable ability. Ladies and Gentlemen, I am privileged to present Miss Marta Sencobia, of Ethiopia."

When Marta arose, there was polite applause, indicating that the skeptical attendees wanted real proof. I heard a few people softly muttering such phrases as "Who does he think he's kidding?" "Does he think we're complete fools?" "What a bunch of baloney!" If her hearing was as good as Sir Geoffrey claimed, she probably heard them all, including the ones in other languages. She smiled graciously and said, "Thank you Sir Geoffrey. I hope I can meet the high standards you have set. Ladies and Gentlemen, please give me thirty questions in your native language on the most difficult topics you can. I will wait until all questions have been asked and then I will repeat each one verbatim in the order asked and in the proper language, following which I will give my answer. These gentlemen (she waved her hand at two men wheeling laser-disc recording equipment on stage), will record my words, which will be at high speed as indicated by the rate meter shown to the right. Don't be surprised if they sound like the high-pitched tones of whales, and if you hear nothing, it is because the pitch exceeds your auditory powers. I will then sit down, and the recording engineers will replay my words at an intelligible speed. Who has the first question?"

There was a scramble for the three microphones in the aisles, and the questions came pouring forth. In addition to English, I recognized French, German, Italian, Spanish, Greek and Japanese, not because I am fluent in them, but because I know a few common phrases in each and could discern the special lilt each one has. There were several obscure languages, which I could only guess at, from the dress of the questioner. Only about one-third of the questions were in English!

The questions in English were very difficult to my way of thinking, and involved details in nuclear physics, quantum theory, Heavyside operational calculus, eighteenth century history, classical music, current sport events, current theater, old movies and TV, etc. I could only imagine the difficulty of the foreign language questions.

Marta listened attentively to each question, repeated it to assure the questioner that she understood it, and when all thirty questions were completed, she waved to the recording engineers, and got an o.k. signal. The equipment then gave out her high pitch response. True to her prediction, about a third of it was beyond my hearing capacity. The rate meter indicated between 15000 and 16000 words per minute, and stopped at 15,433, which the lead engineer explained was the average rate.

During her discourse, which lasted about two minutes, she opened her knitting bag and knit over a linear foot of a sweater. That demonstration alone confirmed part of the claims Sir Geoffrey had made. But the acid test would come when the engineers re-played the disk. After a brief rewinding session, they started the slow-motion replay.

The assembled group was completely captivated by her performance. First, they marveled at the accuracy of her repetition of the questions. The questioners generally nodded their heads in agreement, or did so orally. Others shook their heads sideways to show how baffled they were at her uncanny memory. But her answers were the most startling. They were accurate, detailed, and full of charm and wit. She apologized at one point because she didn't have as detailed an answer as possible, explaining that she was ill during that tutorial session.

When the recording was finished, the group rose to its feet to give her a boisterous standing ovation. She seemed half-pleased, and half-embarrassed. I noticed that Gwendolyn Foster, from a Chicago African-American paper, was very reserved in her applause. When the ovation died down, she rose to her feet and said she didn't believe what she had just seen, claiming it must have been some sort of Hollywood visual effect or a master magician's illusion!

I rose to my feet and said, "Gwen, I am surprised that you, of all people, would question what your eyes and ears have just witnessed. Not only is she the same gender as you, but basically the same race, so why should you be the Doubting Thomas?"

She looked embarrassed and mumbled a brief apology, but said she still had major questions. Sir Geoffrey then rose and said, "Thank you for your doubts-- it is the perfect lead in to a question and answer session. Please address your questions to any of us on the stage, first giving your name and your affiliation."

The questions were long and varied. Some of the most interesting and pertinent ones were:

Q. (To Dr. Greene) "Most of us realize that you have been a pioneer in artificial intelligence, in which you are attempting to make computers reason like humans. Would you say that Miss Senobia has beaten you to the draw, but in reverse order?"

A. "Yes she has, and I am delighted. Do you remember the movie 2001, in which HAL, the reasoning computer outwit the human crew and did them in? (The questioner nodded yes). Well, as a human, I hope we stay a few steps ahead of our computers and always maintain the upper hand. I realize that humans are flawed creatures, but if we ever get the data base and processing skills of computers, as Miss Senobia seems to have, I believe human decisions will advance the human race into a glorious future-- one that exceeds our fondest dreams!"

Q. (Follow up) "Since words can be multi-syllabic, how does the rate device compensate?"

A. "The rate device measures each syllable, and then divides by the number of syllables in an average word. Check it out in a newspaper column and you will find it is about 1.73."

Q. (To Dr. Graves) "Do you think the unknown genetic material could be of extra-terrestrial origin-- possibly from an alien male mating with Miss Senobia's mother?"

A. "Remember, I am a scientist and I deal mostly with facts. However, even we scientists must postulate theories and try to confirm them with facts. So my answer is this: It is in the realm of possibility, and perhaps probability. In short, it is a good theory, but until we get more facts it will remain just a theory."

Q. (Follow-up) "Your research indicated she has the best traits of the Jews and Ethiopians-- What are they?"

A. "Basically the Jews are noted for their emphasis on learning, high intelligence, ability to survive adverse conditions, and their spiritual insights, as shown by the huge influence their early writers and prophets had on the world. The Ethiopians are noted for their love of the land and environment, their athletic ability, and their joy of living."

Q. (To Sir Geoffrey) "What are your motives in revealing this amazing woman to the world, and what will be the final outcome?"

A. "Well, Marta has expressed appreciation for our interest and aid in her case, and has signed a joint partnership contract with us. She has realized from childhood that she was special, but limited because of her surroundings, and we both believe that an organization like mine can be of substantial help.

She would like to become a consultant to world leaders and help them guide the nations of the world to a future in which poverty, hunger, disease, violence, ignorance and other ills of the world are eradicated, thereby releasing humans from their awesome burdens. She believes the key is to eliminate war and preparation for war, gradually turning their huge expenses into productive programs to cure the world's ills and eliminate the root causes of war.

We will be her sponsors and, in addition to our journalistic advantage, we will share in earnings over 100,000 pounds per year. But our main motive is to see that her talents are used to solve major world problems and uncover new opportunities! As to the outcome, it will depend much on how we in the media, handle things. If we can rise to the level of journalistic statesmen and promote good causes, the world could benefit greatly. If, on the other hand, we treat this unique opportunity as just another news story, sensationalize it and look for a lot of negative aspects, we can do immeasurable harm!"

Q. "Are you suggesting censorship?"

A. "Of course not! What I am suggesting is that we recognize that we have just started a new millennium and that we have a chance to help the world reach its full potential. That is why I have invited you key people from all types of news organizations. Your voluntary help will be invaluable. Remember how Marta's tribe overcame age-old tradition and used common sense to better their lives by using her skills? Is our common sense less than theirs? I think not!"

Q. (To Dr. Graves) "From what I have heard, she is a unique person, and her skills will die with her unless she propagates. Will she propagate? And if so, with whom?"

A. "That is a very insightful question, and one that we faced ten months ago. She is only twenty and not ready for marriage, so with her permission, we have used her ova for in-vitro fertilization, using the sperm of highly stable and intelligent male donors. The fertilized ova are now growing in the wombs of superior female volunteers. Of course we will not know the results for many years, so keep your hopes high!"

Q. (To Sir Geoffrey) "If she is so wonderful, and I believe she is, why don't we get her elected to run the U.N., or perhaps appointed Secretary of State?"

A. "I agree, but such things take time. By consulting for major-nation heads of state, she can start doing good immediately, and in due time work up to a position of world leadership."

I stayed in Addis Abba for an extra day, as did most of the others. We agreed with Sir Geoffrey's suggestion to let the Associated Press file the report to our papers, and have radio and TV. releases from a single, English language source, with appropriate languages dubbed in. The extra day was spent talking with Sir Geoffrey and Miss Senobia briefly, and at length with my colleagues from the media. I even snuck in a brief tour of the city. Most of us vowed to let our "common sense" equal or exceed the tribal people.

When I returned back to my office, I assembled the entire editorial and writing staff and explained the situation, much as I have here. Some were skeptical of the associated press release, so I wrote an editorial that was the best of my long career.

The response was overwhelming, with favorable replies out-numbering negative ones 50 to 1. Best of all, the President invited me and several of the other attendees to the White House for a detailed briefing, and followed it up with an invitation to Sir Geoffrey and Miss Senobia to meet with him and his cabinet. It looked like things were moving rapidly forward.

However, we started getting reports about other highly-gifted youths in other countries. On a hunch, I called Dr. Steven Gruber, who was noted for his investigation of extraterrestrial life and intelligence. He said his latest contacts told him that Marta was a forerunner to test the wisdom and tolerance of earthlings. That was why they chose a third world woman. The others were back-up reinforcements designed to make sure their mission didn't fail. The space visitors had decided that earthlings were headed for self-destruction unless they intervened. Dr. Gruber said it demonstrated their wisdom and magnanimity when they chose this method of intelligent persuasion!

I went to bed that night feeling confident that the three year old New Millennium was off to a wonderful start!

MY MOST INTRIGUING INTERVIEW

When my editor assigns me a new interview, I am usually intrigued. Most of the subjects are rich and famous people that I would never get to meet, so talking with them is a treat. I also enjoy seeing their fabulous homes and their art and other collectibles.

My job is to uncover things which will show that they are human, and have much in common with ordinary people, like me. Usually, they are not only human, but warm and friendly, and they make me feel welcomed.

However, some are full of ego and very haughty, so I can't wait to end the interview. Even so, I write about their admirable attributes because my editor doesn't want to offend the powerful.

My latest interview was not only intriguing, but a big surprise. In fact, I wondered how I could do it. You see, I was to interview someone in the un-famous, un-rich masses. What some call the lowest form of human life. Someone with such a common name that men laughed and women blushed when it was mentioned.

I also wondered if it would be difficult to converse, so I studied more than usual to prepare myself. My editor had told me to keep the last name secret until the end, so readers would be pleasantly surprised. (No fair peeking.)

Here is my interview, which was transcribed from my tape recorder:

Me: Mr. S., what do your friends call you?

Mr. S.: Plain old Joe; you can call me that too.

Me: Thanks, Joe. Tell me, do you have any brothers and sisters?

Joe: Lots of brothers, but no sisters.

Me: How many brothers do you have?

Joe: Gee, I never counted them. All I can tell you is that it's pretty crowded in our place.

Me: Do you live with your parents?

Joe: We only live with my dad. If I have a mom, I never see or hear her.

Me: Do you have any female friends?

Joe: Not yet, but I hope to have one soon.

Me: Do you hope to get married some day?

Joe: Well, I like to think of it as sort of a union. Marriage isn't a custom in our family, except maybe higher up.

Me: I realize you're still pretty young, but do you have a job?

Joe: Nah! My father supports us, but he plans to kick us out soon.

Me: What'll you do then?

Joe: Work hard to find a female so we can form a wonderful union.

Me: What do you think are the odds for success?

Joe: Gosh, I suppose they're real low; you see, there's lots of competition. Even so, I'm gonna try my very best.

Me: That's an admirable trait, Joe. Do your brothers share it?

Joe: Well, most of them do. Unfortunately, some of them are weak and sickly, so they won't have the energy that we healthy ones have.

Me: What'll you do if you don't make it?

Joe: Father won't take me back, so I guess I'll become an outcast. In that case, I probably won't live very long.

Me: That's a pretty bleak future. How do you handle something that frightening?

Joe: I just have to face the reality of things. If I don't make it, I hope one of my brothers will.

Me: Suppose we look at the brighter side and assume that you make it?

Joe: That would be great. My mate and I would work real hard to make something wonderful of our union. I expect that we will grow more and more wonderful each day, and some day our union will produce a miracle!

Me: A miracle? What do you mean?

Joe: Well, our union will start from nearly nothing, and grow in size, complexity. and wonder until it is a living, breathing, thinking little baby.

Me: Oh, I see. You're planning to have children?

Joe: No, you dope. We will be that baby!

Me: Of course! Now I guess I can reveal you full name. You're Joe Sperm, and the mate you hope to get is Annie Ovum.

Joe: You got that right, mister. I hope your editor approves and your reader's like it. After all, it's how they started, and look at them now!

Me: Thanks, Joe, for this interview. Now I fully understand why you call it a "miracle!

Note: Now that you know Joe's last name, re-read this piece of fantasy and see how well the dialogue fits. L.M.E.

NEAR DEATH?

"Two flat tires? You've gotta be kidding!"

Thus speaks Tom, my deputy leader, as we are returning to our cars after a long visit to assess a suitable site for our new Research facility.

"No, I'm not kidding," I respond. "Come and look for yourself."

The new site is in a remote area, with grassy meadows and some very dense woods. It is just what we were looking for since our research people like to be away from the noise and hub-bub of our main manufacturing plants, and there is a new housing development being built a few miles away where they can buy or lease homes.

When he gets to my car, he says, "Well I'll be damned. Both of them are flat and they're on the same side of the car. I'll be glad to take you to the nearest place where you can get a tow truck, or someone to fix your tires. Do you think somebody is pulling a trick, or maybe thieves are planning to steal your car after we leave? "

"Gee, I don't know. Could be either one, but if someone IS planning to steal my car, maybe I should stay here while you go for help."

"Good idea," Tom replies. "I'll go back to my car and leave as soon as our other riders get back. We should be back here in less than an hour."

"Great," I say as I pat him on the back.

A few minutes later our riders return, so he starts his car, waves as he passes me and drives into the late afternoon sun.

I am parked on a small, unpaved road that goes about 100 feet into the dense forest, so I pick up a heavy stick and find a suitable place where I can watch my car. If someone comes back to steal it, I hope I can take him by surprise and use the stick to subdue him, or at least protect myself.

After waiting about a half -hour, I feel a sharp blow on my head and soon pass out. When I wake up, I find that I have been dragged deep into the woods. I figure the car thieves re-inflated my tires and drove my car away, hoping the blow on my head will give them plenty of time for their getaway.

I then realize that I should try to find my way back to where I left my car in case Tom is waiting there for me. I feel the bump on my head, and it's quite large. Worse yet, my head is pounding and my balance is a bit shaky. Even so, I keep walking in the direction I think will lead to my parking place.

The sun is now setting, and the forest is getting darker and darker by the minute. A wave of panic goes through me as I wonder if I can find my way back, or if Tom and the others will organize a search party. My panic increases when it dawns on me that even if Tom comes back to my parking place and finds the car gone, he might decide that I fixed it myself and drove off.

Fortunately, my common sense prevails, and I subdue my panic with these thoughts: 'Hey, you've been in worse jams before. Keep your cool and use your brain, even if it's aching a bit.' I pick up a long stick to help me navigate through the woods and fend off any branches that strike me during my journey. Hope soars when I see a break in the forest, but it plummets when I find myself on a steep cliff overlooking the deserted housing development. There's no way I can climb down the cliff, even if I were in a better condition, so I reverse my steps toward what I hope will be my old parking place. I'm thankful that I saw the cliff while there was still a bit of daylight, thus saving me from an accidental fall. I'm also thankful that I saw the housing development, since it told me I was 180 degrees off course.

Pretty soon it's pitch dark. I'm hungry, tired, aching all over, and growing colder and colder from the night air. All I have on is a lightweight jacket and an open collar shirt. It was just right for the daytime explorations of the property, but it's pitiful for the growing cold. I button my shirt, zip my jacket up as far as I can, turn up its collar, and find a comfortable place to lie down for the night. It's at the bottom of a big oak tree, so I pile some fallen leaves to support my aching bones and maybe spread over myself to fend off the cold. I keep my long stick beside me for protection in case any marauding animals come my way.

I don't know how long it will take me to fall asleep, and I grow so lonely that I wish some animal, maybe a friendly dog or cat, will come along to keep me company. Alas, none come by. After some fitful sleep, I wake up shivering intensely from the cold night air. I stare at the stars I see through the trees. They look cold and distant, and remind me of what a tiny part I am of the vast universe. It is then that I realize that death is approaching, and is not far away. I doubt if I can last through the night, so I start making peace with God, myself and my predicament.

'So this is how you're going to die? O.K., old boy, you might as well face it since it'll come sooner or later. Meantime, why don't you review all the good and bad things in your life before it's too late.'

This I start to do. My thought process is something like this:

'Today is Sunday, so it's a good day to die. But wait a minute. Sunday isn't a workday, so why was I looking for a new research facility on Sunday?'

'Furthermore, I don't remember proposing a new facility in the management-approved Research Re-organization Plan I prepared. So why am I looking for one at all?'

'And why did you refer to yourself as "old boy" earlier? Ah, I remember-- I am now 86 years old and retired twenty years ago!'

'I am about to reach an inevitable conclusion, but my shivering keeps up and I am really cold, so how can it be just a bad dream?'

'Well, there's one way to find out. Open your eyes, spread your arms, and yawn.'

Once I do so, I find my self warm and toasty under my down comforter, my dear wife sleeping peacefully beside me, and the night light partially illuminating our bed room in Leisure Village, our new retirement community.

I give a big sigh of relief and fall back asleep, while marveling at the awesome power and frightening reality of a dream!

NEW MODELS

Most of us are familiar with the custom of developing new models every few years. Thanks to modern technology, and a bit of imagination, I was able to over-hear and record a dialogue between the Chief Designer and the Production Manager regarding an interesting new product, which will be identified later. For this story, I will use the initials of the two principals, G.A. and M.N. respectively, but by the time it ends I suspect you will guess their real names.

The revelation shouldn't be too difficult, because both are world famous, and I hope they will be a rewarding surprise. Incidentally, the conversation happened some time ago, and again you will probably guess the approximate time period once you know the principals and the product. Here is the dialogue:

M.N. : " I hear you are working on two new models. Care to tell me about them?"

G.A. : "Sure. The first new model is going to be a utility one. It will be able to carry heavy loads for long distances and over rough terrain. It will be rugged, but quite attractive. The second one will be designed with the family in mind. It will be smaller and less powerful, but will have some outstanding qualities."

M.N.: "Like what?"

G.A. : "Oh, a finer finish, more streamlining, better response, and more graceful styling."

M.N.: "It sounds like every family should have one!"

G.A. : "Absolutely. In fact every family will NEED one, and there is bound to be a big market once it is in production. Families will also need the utility model, but not in the same close-knit way."

M.N.: "How about the engines for these new models?"

G.A. : "They will be similar to the earlier models, which you and your work force helped get into mass production, except both will have much longer lasting engines than most of the other models."

M.N.: "Sounds interesting. What sort of fuel will they use?"

G.A. : "They will run on standard fuel, except it will be cleaner and more refined. It is one of the reasons the engines will last so long.

M.N.: "What sort of performance will they have?"

G.A. : "During the break-in period their performance will be inferior to many of my previous models in acceleration, speed, and endurance. But they will have a built-in feature which, eventually, will let them greatly surpass all previous models!"

M.N.: "Can you tell me more about the built-in feature?"

G.A. : "Certainly. Both will have an on-board computer that will be the best I have ever designed. Even my latest production computers will seem rather primitive compared to those for the new models, which will be able to process much more information, do it quite rapidly, and produce some truly astonishing results!"

M.N.: "Will the computers be the same for both models?"

G.A.: "Basically, yes, but with some subtle differences to enhance their specific usefulness."

M.N.: "Sounds fascinating. How about production quantities?"

G.A.: "The production line will be quite limited at first, but I expect it will increase rapidly with time and your valuable help. In fact, eventually, the new models will become the dominant models in the world market and stand a good chance to retain their market domination longer than previous models."

M.N.: "I detect a bit of uncertainty in your last statement. That's not like you —please explain."

G.A.: "You are correct. My uncertainty lies mostly in the on-board computers. I have designed them to do things never before tried, and if they are misused it could be catastrophic. But it is a risk I want to take, because I have become completely enamored of both new models!

M.N.: Does that mean that I will have to stop producing some of the older models?"

G.A.: "Of course. You know that we must be pragmatic and keep production going only for the most useful models—remember how we had to stop production on those large, inefficient models recently?"

M.N.: "Yep! But I was kind of disappointed because they were so fascinating. I hope you will exhibit them in a museum some day."

G.A. : "All in good time. In fact, I foresee the day when they will be the most admired models in many museums."

M.N.: "I'm glad to hear that. Guess I'll have to be patient a bit longer. How about maintenance and repair?

G.A.: "That's another improved feature. I have designed them for minimum maintenance and repair, especially if the on-board computers are used properly. If not, we may have to set up some maintenance facilities and a few spare parts depots."

M.N.: "By the way, what do you plan to call these new models?"

G.A.: "Oh, something simple, but catchy. I'll call the protypes ADAM and EVE, and the product line MANKIND!!

Author's note: I trust that you now know the identity of the Chief Designer and the Production Manager, and the approximate time period of this story, which was thousands of millennia ago. You may want to re-read it and see if you agree with my characterization of the two models. In case you are still in the dark, I have given explanations for the purposely obscure descriptions below and in small type. Before you peek, see how much you can figure out on your own!

G.A. is God Almighty, M.N. is Mother Nature; Engines are the cardiovascular system; fuel is food; on-board computer is the brain; eventual higher performance will be autos, aircraft, sensors, and other technological innovations; production line is population, which has grown to alarming numbers; uncertainty is due to mankind's free will; large, inefficient models are dinosaurs; maintenance facilities are health services establishments; spare parts depots are organ banks.

AN OLD SHOE

It was such a beautiful October day that I decided to take a walk in a nearby park. Mothers were wheeling their babies or holding their children's hands; older kids were tossing brightly colored Frisbees to and fro; even the birds were chirping happily. Everything looked peaceful and safe, but as the old adage says, "Appearances can be deceptive."

I was wearing a pair of old loafers because they were both comfortable and easy to slip off and on. At age 84, I figured I might have to sit on a bench and remove them if my feet started aching. I had recently done so when the ugly incident happened.

I had walked about fifty feet from the bench when my left shoe came off. Before I could bend down to pick it up, a teen-aged boy came from behind and kicked it 15 feet in front of me. Then, with a mighty kick he sent it soaring in the air. It went over 100 feet away and he laughed rudely, saying: "Go fetch, Grandpa!"

He then quickly ran away, still laughing loudly and skipping merrily. Obviously, he was pleased with his mean trick. I wondered what sort of values he had been taught and how anyone could do such a thing to a harmless old man.

My old shoe landed on a crosswalk, and I saw a young man pick it up.

He held it over his head to see if anyone claimed it. I waved my arms, he spotted me, and we walked toward each other. Actually, I was limping more than walking because one foot was shoeless. On the way, I thought: 'Now there's a decent young man, so maybe that mean teenager will be better when he grows up.'

As we met, I reached for the shoe and started to thank him, but he put it behind his back, saying: "What's it worth to you, old man?"

Although I was surprised and disappointed, I kept my wits. "Well, young man, it belongs to me as you can see by its mate on my right foot. I will give you a big thank you and a pat on the back for your kindness."

"I mean money, you jerk," he replied. " My kindness costs dough--say ten bucks?"

"Then I suggest you keep it, because I don't have ten dollars on me. Besides, it's old and ready for the trashcan." I smiled amicably as I spoke.

"Yeah, yeah," he barked. " So give me five bucks and you won't have to limp all the way to wherever you're going."

" No deal," I said. "I'd rather be uncomfortable than have you learn the wrong lesson in life. The world's already too full of people who victimize others for their own selfish purposes, and you don't want to go down that path, do you? So please keep the shoe with my blessing."

There were other people nearby, so I felt he wouldn't attack me; however, the frustration and rage on his face indicated he wished we were alone. I then left and went back toward the bench, and he returned to the crosswalk. I sat on the bench until he was out of sight, then I followed his path until I came to the next trash basket. Sure enough, there was my old shoe. I quickly retrieved it and put it on. No more limping for me that day.

Several days later, I went to a nearby construction site to see what progress the workers had made that week. It was Friday afternoon and the workers had left early to get a head start on the Columbus Day holiday. When I reached the back of the site, I saw a pick-up truck hidden between two buildings. It was partially filled with lumber, so I surmised that a thief was still on the premises. I decided to go back to the entrance and notify an authority.

Before I got there, I heard a weak voice say, "Help, help! Is anyone up there?"

I finally found the source of the voice; it was coming from a deep hole near which were some two-by-fours scattered on the ground. Obviously, they were dropped when the culprit fell in the hole. While there were signs and barricades around the hole, he must have been looking back to see if anyone saw him with the lumber before he fell in.

A strange feeling came over me when I saw a left shoe near the hole. As I peered into it, I was shocked. Staring up at me was the young man that I had encountered in the park!

He recognized me too, and said, "Can you help me , sir? Maybe toss me a rope?"

"Let me see if I can find one, young man. I'll be back soon."

Fortunately, I found two ropes: one long and strong, and the other long but frazzled. I returned to the hole and said, "I found a rope."

"Well toss it down so I can climb out." His voice was impatient.

My mischievous streak took over, so I took him literally. I tossed him the frazzled rope--all of it. I also wanted to test him, so I kept the strong rope in reserve.

"No, no, you dumb old bastard. You should'a kept one end and tied it somewhere so I can climb out. Now I'll have to throw one end back up, if I can." He tried to do so, but there wasn't enough room in the hole to succeed. He was completely frustrated.

"Don't worry," I said, "I have another idea. There's a hose near a cement mixer which I can pull over here and fill the hole with water. You can then float out with no effort and no harm."

He pondered a minute before he said, "I can't swim, and even if I don't drown I'll freeze to death after I get out. So please look for another rope. "

Gently, I said, "By the way, how much are you going to pay me? You see, I have another rope up here."

"What'a you mean, pay you? Can't you see I'm in a desperate situation?"

"Well, you wanted me to pay you 10 dollars for my old shoe the other day, so I figured saving your life would be worth a lot more-- maybe thousands of dollars."

There was a long silence, and I knew I had put him in a quandary. Finally, he said, "I hope you're kidding me--are you?"

"I'm just doing what you tried to do to me, only the stakes are higher. I even let you keep my old shoe and walked away. Tell you what- here's your shoe, which you can keep without paying me a penny, and I'll walk away again." I tossed it to him and he muttered unintelligibly.

"Wait!," he shouted. "It's getting cold down here and the workers won't be back until Tuesday because of the holiday. You wouldn't let me die over an old shoe, would you?"

"Not if you have enough money to make it worth my while. And to make sure you don't double cross me when you're out, I've written down your license plate number so the law can get you for stealing all that lumber."

There was another long silence, and he finally said, "Well, sir, I guess you've got me by the balls, so I'll get you as much money as I can. I've got over five thousand saved and I'll give it all to you if you'll rescue me and tear up the license plate number. And believe me, sir, I'm sorry for my bad behavior the other day, and I've learned an important lesson."

"I hope you have," I replied. "But you might change your mind and kill me if I get you out. I'm going home and write a letter to the police. It'll tell them about the lumber and the hole. If you harm me, my wife will mail it Tuesday. So long for now- I'll be back in an hour." I then walked away while he was pleading for mercy in a sincere way.

When I got to a telephone, I called 911 and asked for help. They responded soon and I led them to the hole. They had their own equipment and quickly and gently hauled him out. He thanked them and me and tried to leave, but the 911 medics said he had broken several ribs and they would have to take him to a hospital for treatment and further examination. They also needed to meet with both of us for interrogation when he was up to it. They drove him away in an ambulance and offered me a ride home, but I told them I preferred to walk as it was near by. The firemen got my address and telephone number, and asked a few questions which I answered carefully. They then thanked me, and drove away.

Once they had left, I went back to the pick-up truck. The key was in the ignition for a quick get-away, so I did some deep thinking. Should I unload the lumber and drive his truck to my home? Or should I let the law take its course? If I helped him avoid the law, would I be charged for aiding a thief and get in trouble myself? Or would there be no crime if he hadn't actually taken the lumber away? And who was to know if I acted quickly on this deserted site?

I decided he had suffered enough and would learn a better lesson if I was merciful, so I quelled my conscience about breaking the law. I then unloaded the lumber and drove the truck home for safe-keeping.

The next day, I visited him in the hospital. His chest was all bandaged up and one leg was in a sling and elevated. The reaction on his face was mixed. I could tell he was angry about my getting 911 involved because of the lumber problem. On the other hand he seemed grateful that he was out of that frightening hole and didn't have to spend a miserable weekend there. I learned later that his leg had been severely bruised and was elevated to help it heal.

When he finally spoke, he said, "Thank you, sir, for helping me. I'm willing to pay you for saving my life, but I'll have to reduce the amount. I'll need to keep a good bit to defend myself against the lumber charges. I hope you understand."

"I understand perfectly. I think you'll be pleased to know that I unloaded the lumber and drove your truck home. You see, the way I figure, you didn't steal the lumber because it's still there."

He looked surprised, but said, "That was clever of you. I suppose I'll have to pay you all the money now to keep you from telling the police during the interrogation."

"That would be blackmail and I couldn't do that. Instead, I'm going to set an example which I hope will guide you to a new path in your life. I'll tear up the license number and return your truck once you are discharged. As to money, forget that. I only mentioned it while you were in the hole to make you think about the course you were taking in your life. You see, I have found that our actions have consequences.

Bad deeds frequently come back to us enlarged, as your fall into the hole demonstrated. On the other hand, good deeds work the same way. Their rewards, though perhaps delayed, can be surprisingly great. All I ask of you is that you be smart enough to let your good deeds greatly outnumber your bad ones. I think you'll find it will lead to much happiness and success."

He gripped my hand, bent his head, and started sobbing. I gave him a warm hug and left. The next day, I returned with some flowers and a gift box. I told him not to open it until I had left. We talked for over 30 minutes, and as I started to leave he promised to be my friend for life. At 84, that wasn't a long-term commitment, but it was very important to both of us.

After I left, I could only imagine his reaction when he opened the gift box. All it contained was my old left shoe!

Note: This is a true story because it happened in a dream. I was the old man and the other characters must have been part of my reality, embedded in my memory cells and released to play their roles. Park scenes, construction sites, even 911 equipment, have also been part of my reality, then embedded and released for the background settings. Did I embellish my dream? Of course. On the other hand, some parts, like the dialogues with the young man, were more vivid and dynamic than I could recall.. Reality is transient, then embedded in memory cells, then released when we recall them or rearrange them in dreams.

Someone once said, "Life is but a dream." To which I respond, YES!

O P E N !

O P E N HEARTS

The big day had come at last. David was going to be honored by his co-workers at a retirement dinner in honor of his 45 years of service to the company. There would even be several high ranking officers present, indicating the great esteem most people had for his hard work, clever innovations, and sterling character. Both he and his wife, Elaine, were not only looking forward to the event, but the wonderful plans they had made for their retirement years.

She, of course, knew better than anyone else what a great guy he was, but even so, she was tremendously proud of all the accolades various speakers gave David, some of which were impromptu, and obviously from the heart. They were equal, perhaps even better, than the ones she had received two years earlier when she retired from her twenty years of service on the staff at the local Methodist church. And both were delighted that several of their four children had come to both events with their spouses.

It was a memorable evening, but like all good events it came to an end. Both David and Elaine were full of happiness as they drove home, knowing that this special evening would stay in their memories for many years, probably for the rest of their lives. And the awards he received would be prominently displayed beside hers as a daily reminder.

They slept late the next morning, and finally awoke to a heavy rain storm. Elaine spoke first. "Look dear, it's raining real hard on the first day of your retirement. Do you suppose it's a sign?"

"Sure! It's a sign that the grass will grow and I'll have more time for mowing it. It's a sign that the vegetables in my garden will be more luscious than ever, and the flowers in your garden will be even more fragrant and beautiful. Best of all, it's a sign that we can finish planning all the trips we will take, starting less than a week from today for the first one!" David smiled broadly as he gave her a good-morning kiss.

"Oh, you're such an optimist," she replied. "I wondered if it was a sign that we might have some unforeseen problems now that we are both retired. A rain storm on the first day could be a bad omen, you know."

"Yes, it <u>could be</u>, but I doubt if it is, so why worry about it? Let's go down stairs, have breakfast, and then finish our travel plans. I'll even take you out to dinner and a movie tonight. How does that sound?"

"Great," she said, as she planted a kiss on his willing lips.

The next day was bright and sunny, and they started adjusting to their new-found freedom from his structured work routine. Each day seemed better and better, and the next Friday they started packing for their trip to Europe, which left on Sunday. They were both full of eager anticipation, because two earlier oversea plans had been spoiled by business emergencies and sickness.

As they were preparing to go to bed that night, the telephone rang.

"Who could that be at this hour?" Elaine then picked up the phone and handed it to David.

David's face grew sad as he listened to the message. During a brief interruption, he whispered, "It's Harriet--Harry's been in a car accident." He then resumed listening while Elaine went to another telephone. She picked up the receiver just as Harriet said, "It's real serious, Dad. The doctor said even if he lives he'll not be able to walk for the rest of his life."

Elaine then spoke, saying, "Oh, we're so sorry, dear. What can we do to help? We can drive down to your place tomorrow, and we'll call your siblings if you want us to."

"That's very nice of you, Mom, but aren't you flying to Europe Sunday?"

"Well we <u>were</u>, but we can cancel it. You and Harry take precedent over a silly trip to Europe. Don't you agree David?"

"You bet," he replied. "Listen Harriet, we'll come tomorrow as your mother said. We should arrive early afternoon, and we'll call our other children so you don't have to worry about that. Anyone else we should call?

"Oh, you and Mom are such great parents. I'll try to be home when you arrive, but if I'm still at the hospital I'll leave a key under the side door mat. Both Jeff and Susan should be home from high school by four o'clock." She forgot about calls to other people and started weeping again. Elaine and David took turns consoling her until she composed herself and said goodbye.

The next week was sad and busy. Harry died, and David and Elaine took care of the funeral and burial arrangements, while Harriet took care of her kids, her siblings, and the many friends who sorrowed with her. Once the burial was completed, there was a day of adjustment. Then came the discussion of what to do for the future.

"I'd like to stay here," Harriet said, "but our finances were kind of shaky even before the accident. And the parents of the young woman in the other car are threatening to sue for their daughter's injuries, which were quite severe. I'm afraid our insurance won't cover it, so I might have to sell the house, find a job and rent a place for me and the kids."

David and Elaine looked at each other, read each others mind, and then David said, "Tell you what-- why don't you and the kids come and live with us until you can get back on your feet. We have lots of room, and the school district is first rate, so the kids will still get a good education."

Elaine then spoke up. "I agree with your father. It's the best thing to do." She then went into detail as to which bedroom each one would stay in, where Harriet could store her furniture, etc.

Harriet hugged both of them, and said, "Let me go and tell the kids the situation and your kind offer. They might resist at first, but I'm sure they'll see the wisdom of moving. Jeff will probably think it's a new adventure, and Susan will be thrilled at the new and bigger room she'll have."

David and Elaine stayed with Harriet and the kids until all arrangements were completed. Once the move was made, it took six years for Harriet to get back on her feet. By then both her kids were well along in college, and David and Elaine paid most of the bills. They even snuck in a trip to the Caribbean the third year, and had enough spare money to finally take that canceled European trip after Harriet moved out .

Only a few people knew about the generosity of David and Elaine, but their open hearts let them join the huge number of loving parents who have come to the aid of grown children, grandchildren, even great-grandchildren, that were in need. MAY THEIR TRIBES INCREASE!

O P E N MINDS (A Dialogue Between Two Nameless Men)

"The president sure is getting us into a big mess. He shouldn't have led us into this war in the first place; we keep losing troops; he keeps changing generals; and the budget is soaring out of sight. He sure is stubborn, and in my opinion, he's also stupid!"

"Well, at least he's taking the war to the enemy. Most of the turmoil is in their territory."

"Yeah, that's true, but I don't see an end in sight. Do you think he should have gotten us into it in the first place?"

"Well, Congress agreed to declare war once the enemy attacked us, so at least he followed the constitution. And he convinced a lot of people that it was a just cause. But I agree that we shouldn't have gone to war in the first place. We should have waited longer and used more diplomacy."

"Now you're thinking right. War is too dangerous to enter unless it's a real necessity. Too many lives are lost; too many families disrupted; and too many are wounded for life. Then there's the terrible destruction and huge costs; think of all the good we could have done if we spent all that money on worthwhile projects that helped people and promoted peace."

"Those are all good points, and I agree; but I wonder if we should take a longer-range perspective?"

"What do you mean by a longer-range perspective?"

"Well, our minds are now overwhelmed by the heat of current events, so our thoughts are short range. I wonder what future historians will think? Will they agree with us, or will they agree that the President was right, even with all the blunders? After all, war is a messy business and errors come easily. And our leaders sometimes see further into the future than we do, so maybe future historians will agree with them."

"Well, I suppose they might see things differently than we do today. But I still think this President will go down in history as a damn fool for getting us into this mess, and keeping us in it so long!"

"Suppose we open our minds a lot more. Can you visualize that the outcome will be so well thought of by future generations, that the President will be regarded as one of our greatest leaders? Suppose they think so highly of him that they erect a national monument to him that will be visited by millions of people. Would that surprise you, assuming you live long enough to see it?"

" Are you kidding? I have as good an open mind as most people, but I'll be damned if I can visualize the President going down in history as a great leader. As to a national monument, I think he made monumental errors, so I doubt anyone will have the guts to erect one in the capital; maybe they'll put one in a remote mountain site, but even that's hard to visualize for a lousy leader like President Lincoln!

Note: The Civil War killed 624,000 American military; 2/3 were Union and 1/3 Confederate. The South not only suffered great hardship and destruction, but ill feelings for decades. Yes, the slaves were freed and the Union preserved, but was it worth the awful price? Could more diplomacy and time have solved the vexing problems of that era? Open your own mind before you answer these questions, and use this and other historical perspectives when evaluating present and future wars.

O P E N DOORS

Sam and Sally had just been on their first grocery-shopping trip after their honeymoon. As they approached their apartment door, Sally said, "Open the door dear, this insulated bag is getting very heavy."

"Are you kidding, honey? Look at all the bags I'm carrying. Why don't you put that heavy insulated bag down, and use your keys to unlock the door?"

"OK, OK." She put the bag down, breathed a sigh of relief, and then started searching her shoulder bag for her keys. "I can't find them-- I think I left them on the kitchen counter."

"Well reach into my left pant pocket and get mine. And please hurry, honey--my bags are getting damn heavy too."

As Sally reached for the keys, her fumbling made Sam say, "Take care of what you're touching. You're getting me all excited again."

"Calm down, Romeo," she said as she inserted the key and then opened the door.

They then entered the kitchen, put their bags on the counter and started opening more doors. Sally the refrigerator doors for frozen food and fresh vegetables, and Sam pantry doors for everything else, except fresh fruit, which he put in appropriate bowls. Sally was the first to speak.

"I think I'll take a shower, dear. I got all hot and bothered climbing all those stairs and carrying that heavy bag."

"Me too, Honey. Mind if I join you-- like we did on our honeymoon?"

"OK dear, but let me adjust the water. I like it hotter than you do."

They then went to the bedroom, where Sam opened the door and carried Sally over the threshold, just like he had done when they first entered their new apartment. After they disrobed, Sam opened the shower door while Sally got the water the right temperature. They were like two playful children in the shower, and even as they were toweling off. They were both still "hot and bothered", but it was a different type.

Sam then said, "We have three more doors to open, Honey. I'll open the first one, you open the second one, and we'll both open the third one."

He then proceeded to open the first one by pulling the covers away from the bottom sheet. Sally opened the second one by lying down and opening her arms. The third one was opened after Sam put his key into her lock and they both opened the door to Earthly Paradise!

Normally, the story would end here, but in a way it was just a beginning. One of nature's miracles started when one of Sam's 300 million sperm cells reached Sally's tiny ovum and opened that door. It began one of the greatest creativity periods humans can experience--the creation of another human being!

Later, a fourth, more wonderful door, was opened-- PARENTHOOD!
Note 1: I hope any men who read this story will remember that women are the principal creators of human life, and deserve full support during these wonderful but sometimes painful days.
Note 2: I was inspired to write these stories by the Camarillo Methodist Church's motto, "Open Hearts, Open Minds, Open Doors, and our Writing Club leader saying. "There's no special topic this week-- it's OPEN.

A POWERFUL MIND

Milton loved mathematics, mountains, and his new marriage. Since he had just solved gravity-nullification equations, he found a way to use his mind to actually nullify gravity. It was a real case of "mind over matter." He first tested it in his laboratory when no one was around, using a rope to tie himself to a large table to make sure he could get back down. Thus secured, he closed his eyes and willed himself weightless. He felt himself rising slowly to the ceiling, so he held his hands over his head to cushion the soft blow. He tugged on the rope, let himself down a foot, then rose back up.

Now came the big test. Could he get himself back down again by using his mind, and if he did, would he do it too quickly and injure himself in the fall? Again, he pulled on the rope and lowered himself to three feet from the floor. Then he closed his eyes and willed gravity to return slowly. When his feet softly touched the floor, he felt elated. He repeated the process several times to make sure it was safe, and then decided to test it outdoors. Using a rope that was 200 feet long as a safety measure, he slowly ascended until it was tight. He had not only levitated himself, but the rope, which weighed quite a bit.

"Aha," he said. "I can not only lift myself but quite a bit more, probably another person." That means I must do some more lab work to see just how far my new discovery can go. His head started spinning with thoughts on how best to accomplish the tests, and what to do when they were completed. But the test must wait, because he and his new wife, Madeline, were headed for Yosemite Park the next day.

After checking in at the hotel, they took a walk to the 5000' cliffs of El Capitaine, where they saw climbers laboriously working their way to the top. "Don't be frightened, dear," he said to Madeline, but I'm going to show you something that I have safely tested. Leaning against the cliff, he mentally nullified gravity locally. Then standing perpendicular to the cliff, he started walking up it effortlessly.

Madeline and some new climbers were amazed, but turned down his offer to let him carry them up a few hundred feet.. A vacationing official from the Department of Defense accepted. Once they safely descended, the onlookers applauded, cheered, and patted them both on the back, especially Milton. Madeline gave him a huge hug and multiple kisses, which was surprising to Milton because she was shy about public displays.

Although there were lots of questions, Milton refused to explain his new power, saying, "All I can tell you now is that its not a magical illusion."

He, Madeline, and the official then went back to the hotel, where they talked late into the night. Two days later Milton signed a huge contract!

A RUDE AWAKENING

Two days had passed since Alan got lost in the mountain wilderness. He cursed himself for deciding to go it alone when his close buddy turned down his offer because of an impending business trip. His food and water supplies were exhausted, and hunger pains were starting to get worrisome. Finally he found a small stream, and immediately knelt down to quench his thirst. He figured it would not only provide sustenance, but lead to civilization. For the rest of that day, it provided water, some blackberries, and a couple of small raw fish, so Alan felt better, but still plenty worried.

Rain came at dusk, so he plodded on hoping to find shelter. It was pitch black when he groped his way through an open field. Finding a large drainpipe, he crawled in-- wet, cold and a bit hungry. Exhausted, he fell asleep, but his dreams were both bad and good. In the first one, he fell into a roaring stream and was quickly swept into an underground cavern. The cavern slowly grew smaller, the current faster, and soon there would be no air. Escape seemed impossible, but he did so by waking up shivering like a strip-tease queen. He hugged himself and went into the fetal position, and soon was warm enough to go back to sleep.

His next dream was about food--lots of food. He was at a large banquet and the guest were picking up plates, filling them with all sorts of gourmet dishes, and chatting amiably. Alan got in line, and was even talking with a lovely lady while waiting to pick up a plate. Alas, when they got there, the last plate had been taken. Someone said, we'll have more plates in five minutes, so why don't you take a round on the dance floor.

Alan looked at the lady, she nodded OK, and they started dancing to a lively tune. He could feel the warmth and softness of her shapely body, and when she shared a piece of luscious cake she had picked from the table, everything seemed OK. In fact, it seemed heavenly, and almost cancelled out the frightening dream.

It was morning when he woke up. He was still entranced with the lovely lady, but puzzled by a whirring noise. Before he could move, hot air blasted him dry. Too dry.

He was in a private airplane's jet tailpipe!

SURF'S UP!

Tom liked to surf when others weren't around to bother him. He was an excellent surfer, and disliked having to cope with less skilled ones. He especially disliked it when they ran into his board and he had to save them. Fortunately, he could pick his time because his bungalow was 12 blocks from the beach and his job was one he could do mostly at home.

Early one morning, after a huge storm, he hurried down to the deserted beach to catch the big waves. While driving there, Tom had heard a news flash about a dangerous surf, but he switched stations before the announcer gave details. All that danger stuff is for surf amateurs, he figured, as he picked a station with some good classical music. As he was parking his car, the radio was finishing Chopin's Funeral March. Talking softly to himself, he said, "It is a bit gloomy, but it sure has some powerful melodies. Maybe I'll have them play it on the organ at my own funeral. But that's years away."

Once he entered the water, he was in his element. "Wow, what fun," he yelled exuberantly, as he finished his third ride. As he paddled back for his fourth ride, he was elated with the size of the waves and his great skill. "Man", he said, "I'll bet I could ride those giants in Hawaii, maybe some even bigger."

He was now quite far from the beach, and was eyeing a really big wave headed for him. In fact, it was the biggest one he had ever seen, but he was very confident about his surfing ability. Too confident. When the 100' tidal wave the radio announcer had warned about reached him, fate was tricky. It deposited his lifeless body on his front porch!

Some days later they played Chopin's Funeral march, but he couldn't hear a note. He was too busy making arrangements with St Peter to go surfing in Paradise!

THE PRIZE

John was 78 and loved taking care of the test animals at the lab. He lived alone and made his own lunches, using various healthy herbs and spices. Usually he ate alone at the lab, because the skilled researchers went out for lunch. But that was OK with John, because he loved being with his animal friends, especially the chimps.

One day a research scientist, Dr Edward Kemp, said to John: "Please isolate the chimp called "Mack". He's dying of cancer and none of our experimental drugs are working. You can put him in the cage in that small room just outside the lab. OK?

"Of course, Dr. Kemp. I'll take care of it immediately."

Once lunch time came around, John went to Mack's new cage and started talking with him. "Sorry you're sick, old boy. Here, have some of my lima bean soup. It's got some really good herbs, and maybe it'll ease some of your pain."

He then poured some of the soup in a paper cup and handed it to Mack, who gratefully took it and gulped it down. When his hairy hand reached out of the cage and stroked John's hand, both of their eyes were full of tears. John returned the strokes, and then left to resume his duties. He repeated the lima bean soup feeding for the next three days, because Mack really liked it and he seemed to be getting better. In fact, he was getting so much better that John called it to Dr. Kemp's attention.

Dr Kemp was amazed, and said, "John, have you any explanation for his apparent recovery? Have you fed him any thing special?"

"Only my lima bean soup."

"Well bring some tomorrow, and I'll run some test on it. OK?" John nodded his head in agreement. "And keep giving the soup to Mack. We'll pay you twenty bucks extra for each cup."

John tried to refuse the money, but Dr. Kemp insisted, saying, "We might be on to something really big, and you'll deserve a lot of credit if we do."

Dr. Kemp's scientific tests resulted in a miracle cancer treatment and five years later the Nobel Prize for Dr Kemp and, at the good doctor's insistence, his co-worker John.

John was reluctant to accept until Dr. Kemp told him that Mr. Nobel had discovered dynamite accidentally while seeking a cancer treatment, and the money he made from dynamite paid for all the Nobel prizes.

Serendipity deserves great rewards: Nobel a fortune, John honor and more money than he dreamed possible!

AN UNLIKELY GREAT LOVER

When the sexual revolution hit America, most young guys rejoiced. Gals would hop into bed more quickly and participate more actively than ever. Many of them even started being the aggressor and became very demanding, dropping poor performing guys frequently. For some of the young and better-looking guys, their rejoicing turned into sorrow, or at least frustration.

Their frustration peaked when they learned about Sam Perkins. Now Sam wasn't a prototypical great lover, but he had more beautiful women chasing him than anyone else. He was short, wire sculpture skinny, with bright red hair and freckles. Hardly a Lothario, so what was his secret?

In spite of much cajoling, Sam was reluctant to tell anyone his secret. Finally he told his friends, "It's because of my red hair. The gals think it makes me a red-hot lover."

Some of the guys dyed their hair red, but it didn't do any good. "Come on Sam, tell us the real secret," they begged.

"It might be my freckles. They cover up some of my blemishes and the gals think they're cute."

One of the guys found a way to put some really god fake freckles on his face and torso, but even when he tried them on new gals they didn't do much good . So back to Sam for more cajoling.

"Well," he said, "It's probably because I'm short. Most gals are shorter than you guys, and they kind'a resent it. Now I know you can't make yourself shorter, but maybe if you slouched more, or dated taller girls, it would help."

Well, that did help a wee bit, but it still didn't explain Sam's phenomenal success with the gals. When he said, "It might be because I'm so skinny", there was a run on the diet food and gyms. After several months of misery, the guys again approached Sam. But he refused to tell anyone any more. The guys pooled their dough and hired a private eye. Here's what he found:

In addition to his wit, understanding, politeness and skill, he applies the motto of former Brooklyn Dodger coach, Leo Durocher, to love making"

"Nice guys finish last!"

A PIECE OF PAPER

Hi! I'm a piece of paper. I've been languishing in a drawer for a long time, but now I feel wonderful. You see, someone is actually writing on me! When I was young, my folks told me that the paper family was very important to the human race. They said same humans curse us, many bless us, but almost all depend on us. So I was anxious to join the mainstream, or should I call it the paper stream? But, alas, it didn't happen. In fact, I waited so long that I thought I'd never be written on and end up in the garbage dump or burned up, like so many of my kin.

What sort of wait have I had? Well, when I left the factory I had a pretty yellow color, blue horizontal lines and two red vertical lines, which someone told me made a margin. I felt sure that all those colors would attract an appreciative human and I would soon fulfill my destiny. No such luck—I waited, and waited and waited!

There was one consolation—I didn't have to wait alone. Some people bound me into a nice pad with about 49 of my siblings. Then they put five pads together and damn near suffocated all of us with a clear, plastic shrink-wrap. Fortunately, we don't suffocate easily and I guess the plastic wrap did save us from dirt and bruises when people handled us. But nobody, I mean nobody, took us home; so we just sat on a store shelf-- lonely, unused and dejected. (Sigh)

After a long wait someone put us in a bin that said "Clearance Sale." I'm still not sure what that is, but anyway, this gray-haired man picked us up and took us home. One of my siblings said, "Don't expect too much, because 'Clearance Sale' means a cheapskate has bought us!"

When we got to his home he tried to open the plastic with his hands and it didn't budge a bit. Then he took his teeth and tried to bite it open, but that didn't work either. He then mumbled a few curses, stamped angrily into the kitchen and got a sharp knife. That did the trick and the fresh air we got sure felt good. We all yelled, "Free at last, free at last, thank God almighty, we're free at last!" Some one in the past must have made a big impression on us.

The gray-haired guy then took the top pad and threw the rest of us in a drawer. Unfortunately, I was in the bottom pad so I had to wait still longer. I could tell when he used the other pads, because the weight on me got less and less. Even so, it seemed like an eternity before he took my pad out of the drawer.

Then I got to thinking. If this guy is some sort of a writer, he sure takes his own sweet time. Maybe he doesn't have many good ideas, or is lazy, or too busy with other things. Maybe I've got a real clunker with no talent, no energy and no imagination. Someone once said, "People are no damn good," and boy that was exactly how I felt about him during the long wait.

Finally, on September 23, 1991, he took us out of the drawer. He wrote a poem called "Others" on the first page. Next he wrote another poem called "Seasons." Then he started a poem called "Life," but never finished it—instead he took the next page and made a sketch of a floor plan. I was confused. Was he a poet or an architect, a doodler or a bum? Talk about erratic, this guy takes the cake!

I knew about these writings, because I could feel the impression of his pen clear down to my level. Incidentally, one of the poems was pretty good, but I won't tell which.

Finally, on October 6, 1991, after a wait of almost two weeks, I was next! Would he finish his poem called "Life", would he make another floor plan, would he doodle and throw me away, or what? This guy is really unpredictable, so I began sweating bullets.

Then I had a great idea. My folks had told me about psycho kinesis--the ability of a human mind to make an inanimate object move, wiggle, bend, etc. I wondered if I-- a simple piece of paper-- could reverse the process and implant some ideas in his head. Perhaps make him see things from paper's viewpoint.

I discussed it with the siblings below me and we agreed it was worth a try. When the time came, we would emit our thoughts for him to write down. We figured if we concentrated it might work, and by golly it did. The guy didn't have much talent, but he did have a receptive brain.

What you are reading is the result of our emittance. We realize it won't go down in history as a great paper family achievement, like the Ten Commandments, the Sermon on the Mount, Magna Carta, the Declaration of Independence.... However, it may give humans something they sorely need: more smiles and a better understanding of the importance of a piece of paper!

What sort of an audience will it have? That's hard to foresee. We're sure he'll read it to his wife, maybe to his grown children and grandchildren. Most likely, he'll type it up and show it to his writing group. If it passes muster with them, they'll publish it in their quarterly review, and several dozen may see it.

There's even a long shot that some perceptive editor of a major magazine will publish it. After all, editors can't survive without paper - and it's about time we got our day in court!

A POLITICAL FANTASY

The old man with the flowing white hair and gold-tipped cane entered the visitor's gallery of the U.S. House of Representatives. He walked slowly and with great dignity. The nearby visitors sensed that he was not the usual tourist, but was charismatic and had an important mission. As he took his seat, the usual inter-party bickering was reaching new heights of exaggeration, deceit, and name-calling. He listened patiently for a while, shook his head sadly, and then pointed the horizontal handle of his cane directly at the Speaker. The golden handle had a strange, ethereal glow.

The results were amazing. The Speaker rose and politely asked the bellowing representatives to refrain from so many invectives. He then said: "Let us suspend all debate and observe a day of confession and atonement. Without objection, I will start."

A murmur of soft voices rippled through the House, but there were no objections, so it fell silent. The Speaker spoke thusly:

"My dear colleagues. It suddenly occurred to me that the problems facing our nation are much too serious to let party politics destroy our future. Are our positions as congressmen so dear to us that we must continue to mishandle the nation's business? Each of us has enough talent to re-enter the private sector and earn a good living, so we should make our decisions based on what is best for our beloved country, and not what will trick the people into re-electing us."

"Yes, we enjoy the powers and privileges of our office, but you must admit that they have their downsides. Campaigning every two years is bothersome, and the constant verbal abuse and lack of privacy should prick the thickest skin among us. So let us concentrate on doing good for the country, even if it means we are not re-elected!"

"I confess that I have played the political game for many years, and I have decided to atone for my past misdeeds. My conscience demands it! From now on, I pledge to treat all members fairly and with respect, and to cooperate with any member who sincerely promotes the best policies and laws our nation so richly deserves."

"I know that many think I lack compassion for the less fortunate, so I will listen more carefully to those who voice true concern. I also realize that special interests have an inordinate influence on our decisions because of their campaign contributions, so I vow to reform the election process. We must make it fairer, free from outside distortions, and so clean that each victor will be beholden only to his constituents and the common good."

"I promise to be more objective during conflicts between the business community and environmentalists. I will seek data from impartial experts on ALL problems so that we can make sound decisions based on fact, not rhetoric."

"I believe that we should not only lead our people, but also set such a sterling example that they will renew their lost trust and respect. Let us acknowledge our past errors and abuses, and pledge that we will be fully accountable for our actions, and politely honest and frank in our speech. And let us lead personal lives that reinforce our national values so that we may stamp out evil, or at least make its practioners re-think their wicked ways. Above all, let us adopt policies and laws that will promote education, high ethical and moral values, and prevention in health and criminal matters."

"In our dealings with other nations, let us support democracy, free and fair markets, and the welfare of our fellow humans, wherever they may live. Let us put a heavy emphasis on eliminating war and its root causes. In the wrong hands, the world's rapidly advancing technology could end mankind's very existence on this beautiful planet. These things I pledge to do, so help me God!"

The house sat in silent, thought-provoking awe. The golden handle then pointed to the Minority Leader, who rose and said:

"Mr. Speaker, I am deeply moved by your words and pledges. I sense that you are completely sincere and that your word will be your bond. I too, have played the political game, fooling myself that it was necessary, and perhaps even desirable. I confess that I have shed many crocodile tears on behalf of the poor and working class, when my real motive was to buy their votes. I surreptitiously helped business leaders get their way in return for large donations. And I admit that I enjoyed many floor fights, mostly because they let me display my debating skills. I acknowledge that our government has undertaken many programs which did more harm than good, and should have been left undone, or to the states and the people, as the tenth amendment proclaims. Henceforth, I will support only those programs which truly help people, and I will do all in my power to make them honest and highly cost- effective. The legacy we leave our children and grandchildren must not be a crushing debt or bankruptcy!"

"I fully agree with your enlightened positions on the environment, education, prevention, our relationship with other countries, and your other vows. I pledge to work cooperatively with you and your party, and to encourage my fellow party members to do likewise. Let us LEAD our nation and MAKE our words come true, even if we risk our positions."

"Mr. Speaker, I believe sincerely that if we follow the precepts you have so ably described that there will be a new birth of freedom and progress in our country, and a grateful electorate will reward those responsible. And our example could spread our blessings throughout the world. The possibilities boggle the mind, but I believe strongly that we can make them all come true, with God's help and in the fullness of time!"

The rest of the day was spent recognizing other members, each of whom clamored politely for recognition. The old man catalyzed the startling proceedings for an hour and bowed his head momentarily; he then took his gold-tipped cane over to the Senate. The results were equally amazing, but the Senate took two days to complete them.

When the President was informed, he ordered C-Span tapes so he could review the newsworthy proceedings. They were so unique, he suspected a conspiracy to undermine his Presidency and ordered an investigation. At his next news conference, the old man with the gold-tipped cane was there. After the gold-tipped handle glowed and pointed at the President, the reporters were shocked at the many confessions he made, but knowing his fertile mind and his propensity for long talks, they easily accepted the wealth of new ideas and approaches he proposed. The President even out-did the Speaker in his sincerity, boldness and enthusiasm!

The old man smiled, pointed the glowing handle at the assembled reporters, and went outside. He glanced around to make sure he was alone, slowly lifted his cane and swiftly rose toward heaven. Mission accomplished—the Golden Era had begun!

Author's Note: Quite a few years have passed since I wrote this fantasy, and although I gave it to several Presidential candidates during the 2000 NH primary, no one ever wrote me. A few answered some letters I wrote on important issues, but the issues are still unresolved. Unfortunately, most of our elected officials seem more interested in getting re-elected than in solving some very dangerous problems facing the nation and the world, so I guess we voters will have to show up at the polls with our own golden-tipped cane! L. M. E.

THE REALM OF PURE IMAGINATION

Come! Fly with me to the Realm of Pure Imagination. It is a realm with a plethora of wonderful people and places; ideas, innovations and inventions; challenges and conquests; events and excitement. It is a realm where good is much stronger than evil, where joy greatly outshines sadness; and where every problem has a wonderful solution that unveils huge opportunities. In short, it is much like the world; not as it was yesterday or even as it is today, but the way we want it to be tomorrow!

To get there you have to discard your usual baggage, so leave behind your fears and inhibitions; your worries and cares; your long list of unfinished tasks. Forget those unpaid bills, the unopened mail and those worrisome stock market fluctuations. Don't even pack any clothes or do-dads, stop the mail, or get a neighbor to water the plants and feed your pet. If you have young kids, don't worry; they'll be O.K̦. during your absence from the rigorous realm of reality.

"Impossible," you may say; but I say, "All of the above are huge impediments to your visit to the Realm of Pure Imagination, so abandon them immediately and I will prove that nothing is impossible!"

I realize that these instructions are difficult to comprehend because most people take some of their usual baggage along during Flights of Fantasy. But note that my invitation is to the <u>Realm of Pure Imagination</u>, and burdensome baggage has no place there. All you have to do is relax, assume a comfortable position, read on, and let your mind do the rest.

Let's start your journey to this marvelous realm this way: You are now in a large room full of well-dressed people enjoying cocktails and light refreshments. You spot the Vice-president of the U.S.A. and his wife up near the microphones on the dais. If you don't like the current V.P. and his wife, substitute ones you admire. With them are high government officials and heads of state of several major countries, so you know it is a very important event.

The television cameras are scanning the distinguished guests and you spot a number of movie and T.V. stars, top athletes, business executives and other notables whose faces appear frequently on the world stage. A small orchestra is playing light classical music which adds to the importance of the event.

You wonder why you are there, but it is so pleasant and exciting that you put the mystery on the back burner. Suddenly, the orchestra starts playing "Hail to the Chief", and the President and First Lady enter the room amidst applause. Again, if you don't like the current ones, substitute ones you admire. The President is escorting a stunningly beautiful woman whose shapely figure causes the movie and T. V. stars to gasp in awe. She is wearing a gorgeous evening gown, which rumor says she designed and made herself. The fashion designer guests surreptitiously take out sketchpads to capture the ideas displayed.

The First Lady is with a handsome, distinguished-looking man who is tall, muscular and well groomed. The honored couple seem to be in their early forties, but recent publicity indicates they are much older. Some of the skeptics present whisper that it must be a damn good make-up job. Surprisingly, all eyes are not on the President and First Lady, but on the couple, as confirmed by oohs and ahhs, and favorable comment.

Then a strange, inexplicable thing happens. If you are female, you suddenly morph into the elegant lady at the President's side. If you are male, you transfigure into the handsome man with the First Lady. The mystery deepens, but you are now hopelessly trapped in the circumstances and are eager to see what will happen next.

The President places you and your mate together, and goes to the microphone. T. V. Lights grow brighter and almost hurt your eyes, but you rise to the occasion and remain cool, calm and collected. You wait for the President to speak, and after the usual acknowledgement of top-ranked guests, he says:

"We are here tonight to honor this fabulous couple" (He gestures toward you and your mate and says both of your names) "As you know, last week they became joint winners of the Nobel Prize for their outstanding research in longevity, and for the development of their longevity capsule, which is called *Methuselah*, and a healthy life-style regimen to insure the capsule has maximum benefits."

"Extensive clinical tests have indicated that regular use of Methuselah capsules and the life-style regimen will not only greatly increase users' life span, but keep them young in body, mind and spirit as well. There are no known adverse side effects and they have been approved by the FDA. Best of all, they have made arrangements with nutrient companies to ensure that the capsules will be priced such that they are within the financial reach of most Americans and many from other nations. Furthermore, they will NOT be sold or made available to any person with a criminal record or severe inheritable traits. "

He then beckons to both of you to come toward him, and says, "On behalf of a proud and grateful nation, and with the full consent of Congress, I am pleased and honored to present you with the first and only 'Most Beneficial to Mankind Award' ever given." He then hands both of you a golden plaque with the awards message inscribed, and a check to each of you for five million dollars. He then continues: "I hope you will place these plaques in your home and laboratory as a constant reminder of the nation's deep gratitude, and use the checks to further your magnificent research."

He then starts applauding, and the guests follow with even more vigorous applause and a number of yells. Both of you are almost speechless, but manage a polite thank you, a short statement, and friendly waves to the guests.

The President then says, "Our honored guests have graciously agreed to answer questions, and I will start the ball rolling with the first one: "Is it true that the royalties you will receive from the sale of the capsules will let you greatly expand your research, and even build a state-of-the-art new laboratory?"

By prior agreement with your mate, you answer his question thusly: "Yes, it's true. The manufacturers have given us enough advance money to do so, and even now plans are being drawn up. We expect to break ground in a month or two. It will be located on a ten-acre plot our hometown has given to us, tax-free!"

The President says, "That's wonderful! We wish you great success in your future research. Now for questions from our distinguished guests."

A notable M.D. asks: "I understand that clinical tests have shown that your capsule greatly improves the immune system, and that test subjects are effectively inoculated against most diseases, both infectious and degenerative. Won't that put a lot of physicians out of work? "

Your mate answers thusly: "Well, there will still be accidents, a lag in curing old diseases, and potential new diseases to treat, as well as help with monitoring and testing our new life-style regimen. In short, there will still be much for physicians to do. Any slack time could be spent in better care for patients and new research in treatment methods. There will probably be a period of adjustment, but we are confident that the profession will rise to the occasion and eventually become even stronger. After all, we've overcome similar problems when other significant advances occurred. It's part of the American spirit, or perhaps I should say the human spirit!"

A leading expert in population growth asks: "Although there has been insufficient time to fully quantify the longevity period, early indications suggests that our life spans could double, or even triple. Have you considered the possibility that earth's resources will be insufficient to sustain the population increase from the additional longevity? "

You answer, "Yes we have, and we admit it may be a problem. However, America and other nations are taking vigorous steps to reduce the birth rate and increase economical natural resource recovery. Our life-style regimen uses high-energy foods that are easily grown throughout the world, and each capsule supplies a significant amount of daily energy requirements itself and quells over zealous appetites. Furthermore, our research trials have shown that individual I.Q. is substantially increased, so we should have an abundance of creative people who can overcome any unforeseen problems that develop. Finally, it will take many years to make our development available to the whole world so there should be time to make necessary adjustments."

A prominent movie actress asks: " How long have you been taking the capsules and following your regimen? Also, if it's not too personal, how old are you now? Judging by your looks, you don't look a day over 40!

Your mate answers thusly: After about five years of trials on monkeys, we started trying it on ourselves in 1960. We made a number of improvements before we tried it on volunteers in 1971, and started clinical trials in 1984. Incidentally, the monkeys quadrupled their normal life span. If humans do as well, we could look forward to living to age 360, because current life span in the USA is about 90. Since it is now 2020, that means we have used it for 60 years. We were both born in 1910, so we are now 110 years old, and we thank you for your compliment.

There are a few more minor questions, following which the President ends the meeting and the foreign dignitaries and high officials congratulate you and your mate personally, as do many from the crowd. As you leave with the President and First Lady, there is a thunderous applause. The presidential limousine then takes you to spend the night in the White House, where you talk with them far into the night.

Your journey into The Realm of Pure Imagination is now ended!*

* Until the next installment, or you create your own journey.

REFORM SCHOOL

There were twenty-three guys in my reform school class, which was led by a man named "Mr. Paul" . He was not a large man, but he had: an air of authority; a deep, vibrant voice; a trim figure; gray flowing hair; and a very pleasant, almost handsome, face. Although we were youthful looking, we felt we were big enough to be called men; but Mr. Paul usually called us "boys", some times even "children". When one of us protested, he said, "Why do you think you are here? It's because of your previous childish behavior."

Joe, who was tall and slender, with curly brown hair and mean-looking eyes that always scared me, then said, "Yeah, but when are we gonna be promoted to a better place? This one stinks!"

"My dear child, how many times must I tell you that you are lucky to be here. There are much worse reform schools, and this one is really a moderate one. And don't forget that there are prisons where you can never get out. I will transfer anyone who wants to leave here to one of the worse places, but you have to earn a promotion to get to a better place."

"No, No," Joe replied. "Don't do that; but how long will it take until we are promoted to a better school? And will we ever become free so we can join regular people?"

"That depends on how you behave here and how much you learn. I predict that your promotion will come when you least expect it, so be patient and work hard." Mr. Paul seemed dead serious as he spoke.

George was the next one to speak. He was big, somewhat plump, and had straight blonde hair and rosy cheeks; but his most unforgettable feature was his disarming, dimpled smile. In spite of his size, his general appearance was one of a-- well, a sissy.

"Excuse me, Mr. Paul, but this place is all lessons, study and work. Would it be possible to organize some sports?"

"That's not a bad idea, George," he replied. "I'm willing to try it if the rest of the class agrees; but I must warn you-- any quarreling or fighting and I'll stop it cold!"

The rest of us shouted, "We agree, let's play some sports!"

Sam, who was red-haired, freckled and very strong and trim, then said, "Maybe I shouldn't play. You know I have a quick temper and I wouldn't want to spoil it for the others." Sam was my best buddy.

Mr. Paul looked pleased. "That's a good thought, Sam. It shows you are getting more mature because you are concerned about others and not just yourself. Tell you what-- I'll take your quick temper into account and punish only you. In fact, I'll do it for each boy, but if it happens too often I'll have to stop everyone."

Sam smiled, and the rest of us nodded our heads "yes".

Mr. Paul then said, "What sort of sports would you like?

"How abut football," George replied enthusiastically.

"That sounds too violent," Mr. Paul responded. "Boys with tempers cooler than Sam's might lose them when they are hit too hard. I suggest you pick a sport without body contact."

George looked disappointed as he said, "Well, that eliminates most other sports, doesn't it? Baseball, basketball, hockey, soccer, boxing, wrestling-- what's left?"

Little Tyler then spoke up. He was only five feet four, scrawny but wiry, and had big blue eyes that didn't seem to go with his dark curly hair and impish face. "Well, there's tennis and golf."

"Yeah, but they need special equipment and facilities-- where are we gonna get 'em?" George looked disheartened as he spoke, and Tyler just shrugged his narrow little shoulders.

Mr. Paul waited a few seconds while the rest of us started thinking. Finally, Jason, who was the quiet, shy type in spite of his large frame, dark complexion and big grin, spoke up. "How about horseshoe pitching? All we need are some iron stakes and some left over horseshoes. There's plenty of space behind the mess hall to accommodate a lot'a stakes."

"That's a good idea, Jason," Mr. Paul replied. "But there's a big problem-horse shoes could be used as weapons, and so could the iron stakes; but I have a good substitute."

He paused a second, and several of us yelled, "What is it?

"Quoits."

"Quoits? What are quoits?" Little Tyler looked puzzled.
Jason then enlightened him by saying, "Quoits are like horse shoes, except you use wooden stakes and rings made of rope. There's no metal involved, so it's much safer."

Tyler nodded his head affirmatively, but George then muttered, "It sounds like a girl's game to me. Couldn't we play horse shoes if we promise to be good?" He looked appealingly toward Mr. Paul.

"Suppose we start with quoits, and if you boys don't quarrel or fight for thirty days, we'll switch to horse shoes. O.K., George?

"Fine with me, Mr. Paul," and most of us nodded in agreement. I couldn't help but notice that Joe and his cronies looked glum during the whole discussion, and Joe looked daggers at George.

The next day, after our lessons and chores were finished, we assembled behind the mess hall where Mr. Paul had set up six sets of quoits. He then divided us into twelve teams and assigned two teams to each set. He then explained how things would work.

"Ringers count three and leaners two; if there are no ringers or leaners, the closest quoit counts one. The first team at each set that reaches twenty-one, wins. Each team will write down the points they earn when scored and the opposing team will initial each entry. I will check the total score and declare the winner. I do this to avoid arguments. During the second and subsequent rounds, winners will play winners, and losers will play losers until it's time for supper." He then paused to see if we all understood and agreed, and since there was silence, he said, "O.K. boys, let's get started."

My team was always a loser and so was Joe's, so we played them during the fourth round. Joe was in a foul mood when we beat them twenty-one to fifteen. He was in a terrible mood when he saw that George's team was the top winner. Joe seemed to hate George, who tried to get along with Joe but disliked and distrusted him.

After playing for about two hours we went to supper in the mess hall. It was a plain, rather dismal place and sometimes I skipped a meal to avoid its depressing atmosphere. I wish I had done it that night, because it was rice and beans again. Ugh! Joe was the first to complain. "How do they expect us to reform when they keep feeding us this awful food?"

George sounded disgusted when he told Joe, "Don't you get it yet? When are you gonna realize that this place is supposed to be unpleasant, so we'll have an incentive to mend our ways and be promoted to a better school; maybe some day we may even be free and can join the people that are happy. Why don't you stop your infernal complaining and shape up?"

Joe got red in the face and said, "Damn you to hell, George! I can't stand your 'holier than thou' attitude, and some day I'm gonna beat the daylights outta you. My guys and I are ready to rebel, maybe escape from this damn school. How about it fellas, are you with me or with old sissy George?"

His cronies and several others sided with him, but the rest of us were silent. Then Sam said, "I think George is right, although I don't like the food and other things here either. But Mr. Paul is too nice to rebel against. As to escaping, how will you climb the steep mountains surrounding us? And how do you know what's on the other side? I think we should be patient and wait for graduation day, like Mr. Paul said." I nodded my head visibly in agreement.

Joe scowled fiercely at him and then me, and his frightening eyes almost made me regret my nods. Then he said, "Yeah, Sam, that may sound good to cowards like you, but how much longer do we have to wait until graduation? We've already been here a long, long time and no one's graduated yet. And how about the fact that we all look as young as the day we arrived? Don't you think that's creepy? I tell ya, I'm fed up with this damn place and I'm gonna leave it at the first opportunity. You sissies and cowards can stay put if you wanna, but me and the other real boys are gonna skip. Right gang?"

Joe looked at his cronies and his new converts and they all gave him the "thumbs-up sign". I sensed that real trouble was about to erupt like a slumbering volcano. I glanced at George, and he had a cool look on his face as if he was concocting his own plan. I was glad I stayed on his and Mr. Paul's side.

After supper, Joe had a private meeting with his followers and I suspected he was concocting an evil plan. When Joe was asleep, George quietly approached Joe's new recruits and some of his nicer cronies, and persuaded them to leave a dangerous leader like Joe and stay with Mr. Paul. I slept fitfully all night in my upper bunk as I was afraid Joe might punish me for agreeing with my buddy, Sam.

Things were very tense all next day during our usual routine, and Mr. Paul seemed to sense that something was wrong; but he took no action. It disappointed us, but no one tattled on Joe. Later, as we approached the quoits field, Joe sprang into action. He and his remaining followers ran ahead, pulled out the stakes, gathered up the quoits, and threatened anyone who tried to stop them. He cursed the "traitors" who had heeded George's advice to leave him. Mr. Paul did his best to dissuade Joe and his remaining gang; however, Joe was unconvinced and his cronies seemed afraid to desert him.

Joe yelled, "O.K. guys, grab the grub we hid last night and head for the mountains. I'll follow you after I settle a score."

His gang yelled "Yahoo", grabbed the food and ran toward the nearest slope. Joe then ran to George, and, before anyone could do a thing, plunged a stake into his chest. He brandished his other stake toward the rest of us and then ran like blazes toward his gang and the mountains. He had told his gang to use the stakes to help on steep slopes, but had said nothing about using one on George.

We let them go because we had more important business at hand--trying to save poor George. He was bleeding profusely and had a pained look on his face that made us think he was a goner. We wanted' desperately to help him, but Mr. Paul intervened.

"Let me handle this, men," he yelled. He then pulled the stake from George's chest, took a handkerchief from his pocket, and applied it to the wound to slow down the bleeding. He then looked up, whispered a few words, and then an amazing thing happened. The excruciating pain on George's face was replaced by a huge smile.

"Thanks," he gulped. "How on earth did you do that?"

"Yeah, O.K.," Mr. Paul mumbled, "But it had nothing to do with earth-- Heaven would have been a more appropriate word."

While we all pondered the excitement, Jason said, "Mr. Paul, you called us "men", and not "boys". What does that mean?"

"You are very alert, Jason," he replied with a big grin. "It means that this is graduation day, and those who followed George will be promoted to the top level school. By his leadership and strong character, George is going to join the people who are free and happy, and I predict the rest of you will join him soon."

Little Tyler then piped up. "That's real cool, Mr. Paul, but what's gonna happen to Joe and his gang? It looks like they escaped like they planned to do?"

Mr. Paul patted his head and said, "Oh, they'll struggle up the mountain and get cold, hungry and tired, but they'll make it to the top; in another day or so they'll reach the next valley."

"What then?" Tyler persisted.

"They'll come to another reform school which is much tougher than this one. You see, their rebellion moved them backward, not forward like your good decisions did for you men!"

That night, as we were in our dreary bunkhouse packing for the next day's journey, we started remembering the things that had been blocked from our minds during our stay. First, we remembered and repented the evil thoughts and deeds that had landed us here. Second, each of us remembered our age when we had died and were sent here. Only little Tyler died in his late teens, during a gang shoot out. The rest of us had been physically mature adults at death, and a few of us were really old. I guess that's why we objected to being called "boys". Then a puzzling thing happened-- we slowly morphed into our death age and lost our reform school youthful looks.

We discussed these amazing developments and then George gave us an even more amazing one, which he had learned from Mr. Paul:

"Hey, guys, Mr. Paul is an "angel-- third class" and this place is one of many reform schools in this region. But get this: the region is not of the world; on earth it's called "PURGATORY!""

Epilogue: George went to Heaven, level one, the next day, but it took most of us ten years to join him. Joe's followers repented, and soon rejoined Mr. Paul. Unconfirmed reports indicate that Joe was a serial killer on earth and stayed rebellious until he was sent to "jail", which we understood to be even more serious punishment than Reform School. Mr. Paul introduced quoits to the other classes, and it was so successful that soon he included volleyball and tennis. He was even sent to other reform schools with his programs. He loved his job so much that he stayed for two centuries, ending up an Angel, 1st class!

SAM'S SUPER SLIDE

Sam Perkins' stellar performance in winning the championship baseball game against Hickory* had made him one of he most admired teenagers in the small town of Newton, N. C. His latest accomplishment, if it can be called that, evoked praise, concern, and condemnation: praise, because he had the brains and skill to do something no one else had done; concern, because everyone figured it would be deadly, or at least highly injurious; condemnation, because it set a bad example of recklessness among the youth.

It all happened when he drove me and several other friends to nearby Taylorsville Dam. Sam was interested in becoming a Civil engineer and wanted to inspect the wonders of the source of so much electricity and the largest structure near us. After looking at the power generating plant, we went to the top of the dam to inspect the floodgates and the big crane that could move across the dam to lift various gates.

The rails that the crane moved on were placed on large re-enforced concrete beams that were about 16 inches wide and several feet deep. One of the beams went over the water side, while the other went over the dam side, which was about 75 feet high.

Fred, who was a good athlete, said, "I bet I could walk on those rails all the way to the next gate." The next gate was about 30 feet away.

Joe, who was the most timid of our group, said, "I'll bet you can't--it's too dangerous-- suppose you lost your balance and fell?"

"So what if I did? All that'd happen is I would fall into the water and have to swim back to the shore."

Now the gate nearest us was slightly lifted, so the Catawba River's normal flow was spewing under it. Joe then said, "Yeah, but suppose you get trapped by the current--it's flowing pretty fast?"

"I'd swim away from it until it was safe-- you know what a fast swimmer I am." With those words, Fred started walking on the rail. He not only made it to the other side, but all the way back.

Everyone except Joe decided to try it, and everyone made it. Harry slipped off the rail once, but landed on the concrete beam so he didn't fall into the water. Fred then said, "Well, I guess it's easy to do when there's water below to protect us. But I'll bet no one can do it over the dam part-- not only is it too dangerous, but the height will make you dizzy."

Now I am not afraid of heights--in fact I enjoy them, so I said, "I'll bet I can do it!"

No one tried to stop me, so I walked on the rail over the dam part all the way to the other side, but I came back over the water part. I didn't want to tempt fate too much. No one else followed suit, not even Sam.

After we left the dam, we went to the Conover Swimming Pool. Not only was it on the way home, but it also had two pools. One for good swimmers, and one for beginners. It also had a cable and trolley so we could have the thrill of flying through the air all the way from the high bank, near the small pool, to the far end of the large pool. It also had a large slide that took you into the shallow part of the large pool. All of us, including Joe, used the cable and slide several times. All, except Joe, also used the high diving board several times. Everyone agreed that it had been a fun day!

The next morning, when I saw Sam, he said, "You know, Macon, I've been thinking about that damn dam again. I think I could jump off the beam over the gate that has the flowing water and ride all the way to the bottom without hurting myself. I'd wear thick clothes and use the flowing water to protect myself from the concrete. I'd protect my fall because the dam curves toward horizontal before it enters the river. It's just like the Conover Pool's slide, except much longer. You might even call it a "Super Slide!"

"Do you really think you could do it without killing yourself?"

"Sure! I'm willing to try it if you and a couple of the other fellows will be at the bottom of the dam to pull me out if I get in trouble."

After a bit of persuasion from Sam and me, everyone except Joe came along. We had an inner tube and a long rope just in case Sam couldn't make it to the shore, and we were all prepared to jump in and swim out if the inner tube failed.

The next morning, we all drove to the dam. Sam went to the first gate, while the rest of us stayed at the bottom, lined up at different intervals. Harry brought a camera to take pictures. Once Sam got to the middle of the gate, he waved vigorously, then jumped into the flowing water. It was a very exciting moment, and I said a little prayer that he would make it safely.

We followed his plunge; saw the smooth curve at the bottom cushion him gently, and then the water carry him down near where we were waiting. Fred threw the inner tube out while I held on to the rope to pull him in. Sam raised his arms in triumph and then swam to the inner tube. We all cheered, and several others helped me pull him ashore, where there was great rejoicing.

Harry's pictures were developed and the story was printed in the local paper. As I said at the beginning, most people praised Sam, some were concerned that he might have harmed himself, and a few condemned him for doing something so foolhardy.

The final result was twofold. Sam became even more popular, and the dam people prohibited visitors from walking to the top from then on!

*Read an *Unlikely Hero.* Note: This fictitious story is based on a true adventure at the same dam. I was the only one to walk on the rails over the dam part. No one jumped off. L. M. E

S.I.R.

" Are you serious-- the President of the United States is calling ME?-- Why?"

"Well, Mr. Epps, he read an article of yours -- 'Senior Citizen Ideas: Unappreciated, Under Utilized and Lost Forever?' He wants to discuss your ideas for changing the situation; you know how dedicated he is to change, don't you?"

" Yes, I do, and I'm all for it as long as it will improve things, is done slowly, and on a modest scale, so we can be sure it works."

"Yes, yes,-- please stand by for the President;"

I wait a minute or so, half-excited, and half-wondering if it is some sort of joke. Then I hear an unmistakable voice that removes all doubt.

" How are you today, Mr. Epps?"

" Fine, Mr. President, and you?"

" Busy as usual, but not too busy to tell you that one of my aides brought your article to my attention. She convinced me that I should discuss it with you. You made a damn fine case that senior ideas could still make great contributions to the country, if only we worked out a decent program. I was particularly intrigued with your thought that the right program would create so much new wealth that it would help solve the great budgetary strain caused by entitlements and unnecessary pork projects. As you know, the people are getting really mad about the unmanageable deficits and the growing national debt."

" I couldn't agree with you more, Mr. President."

" I also liked the short, catchy acronym you gave your proposed program, 'S.I.R.' I understand it means 'Senior Idea Recovery'-- is that right?"

" Absolutely, sir!" (We both laugh at my use of the acronym in my reply).

" Well anyway, Macon-- I hear that's what your friends call you and I want you to think of me as a friend--I would like you and your wife to come to the White House on the 27th for lunch so we can discuss some of your ideas further. I will have people from Commerce, HUD, D.O.E, and H.H.S available afterwards, so you can give them more details than we can cover at lunch. What I would really appreciate is a quick overview at lunch, following which an aide will take you to meet with the department representatives. Do you think you will have enough time to prepare properly?"

" Mr. President, I will find enough time, even if I have to call on my friends for help!"

" Great, great-- then I will expect to see you on the twenty seventh. And thanks very much! Hang on and my aide will discuss arrangements for your visit."

" Thank you, Mr. President."

His aide came on the telephone, identifies herself and gives me details. She cautions that the President may have to cancel lunch at the last minute if a crisis arises, but assures me that the meeting with Department representatives will be firm and high level.

My brain is whirling around like a major tornado, and I quickly jot down some of the ideas I will discuss:

1. Refine my 'Idea Suggestion' form and compose an ad for Senior Citizen and other Publications.

2. Bring my Prospectus for a Natural Energy Dwelling (N.E.D.) and make up a chart summarizing principal features and the great benefits that could accrue when it is successful.

3. Ditto for the prospectus for my Driver Education, Prevention, and Penalizing System. (D.E.P.P.S.). Point out the great savings in lives, injuries and property damage, and the revenue potential for states and cities, and the relief it can provide to their strained budgets.

4. Discuss my ideas for making Hot-Dry-Rock Geothermal Energy a commercial possibility.

5. Bring copies of my new article, 'Cut Spending Now, Stupid', and make a special point of my idea to tax all harmful products, not just tobacco, until they pay all the social costs they create. Point out the benefits to whatever Health Care plan passes—increased revenue; lower medical expenses, a fairer tax system, and a healthier, more productive people.

6. Bring along back copies of my writing groups publication, *Senior Perspectives*, as an example of what seniors can do to preserve the heritage of the past and make the perspectives of their long and productive lives available to many others.

At this point, I pause to reflect. Suppose this story was true, instead of an exercise of the imagination? Should I write a real article, similar to the one I imagined the President read? Should I try to get it published or send it to the President directly? Should I contact my Congressman directly with specific ideas, as I did in N.Y. State when he helped my small corporation start a Hot-Dry Rock Geothermal Energy Program in the nineteen-eighties?

Making a decision as important as this is not easy at my advanced age, so I have started writing up specific ideas to show to someone in authority, probably my Congressman. One thing I know is this: My own mind is full of ideas that I believe could be very useful to both industry and the government. With some 50 million senior citizens in the USA, there must be a large number with good ideas that will be lost forever unless we find a way to ferret them out, select the best ones, and make them come alive.

SHOPPIN' WITH CHOPIN

It was around two-thirty in the morning when I was awakened by a fierce storm. I picked up my bedside flashlight in case the power was interrupted and arose to observe the event. The trees near my house creaked and groaned from the power of the wind, and the electric display lit up the landscape like a gigantic, high-intensity strobe light.

As the storm moved closer it became personal. A bolt of lightning hit a nearby pine tree and the loud boom made me jump a foot off the floor. I was tempted to return to my bed, but the storm was much too fascinating. Once I recovered from the extreme shock--mental not electrical-- I thought: 'Thor must have a grudge against that tree, because the ultra-powerful lightning bolt he hurled split it in two-- lengthwise! ' I looked in awe as one half crashed to the ground while the other half stayed erect.

My wife was in the hospital for minor surgery, so I watched the violence of the storm alone and from the relative safety of our second story bedroom. My emotions ranged from fear to awe-- one minute I was fearful that my house, and perhaps my self, would be destroyed. The next minute my whole being seemed paralyzed by the power and brilliance of the violent storm.

Once it subsided and the distant rumble of thunder was muted, I noticed an eerie glow in the air, with strange balls of blue light darting to and fro. This was something new to me, although I had heard of St. Elmo's Fire; so I watched, completely fascinated until everything returned to normal.

Sleep was now impossible, so I decided to go to my desk and use my new computer, which was outfitted with the latest features that modern technology has to offer. My surge suppressors had done their job and all systems were "go"! Reviewing my documents seemed too tame after the fearsome storm, so I decided to go to the Internet and cruise cyberspace. I punched in "nineteenth-century composers," hoping I could listen to good music while exploring their lives.

Piano music usually calms my nerves and lifts my spirit, so I selected Frederick Chopin from the list presented on the color monitor. The music was just what I needed, and when Chopin's face appeared on the screen he spoke forcefully to me: "Put on your virtual-reality goggles and come join me in Paris. I knew and admired you in your previous life."

Now this definitely was not one of the features described in the computer literature, but being adventurous by nature, I did as he commanded. Once I focused the goggles, his face became animated, his whole body appeared and we were on a nineteenth-century, Paris street corner. It was mid-afternoon and he was dressed in a brown coat, a frilly shirt with the sleeves showing near his hands, and a light brown cravat which matched his trousers. His brown shoes had gold buckles on them. His entire outfit reminded me of some I had seen in the movies. 'Quite a natty dresser, ' I mused. I quickly glanced at my own attire, and it fit the times. I even noticed that my body had grown stronger and more energetic, and was puzzled.

His short, frail body seemed to grow stronger as he spoke. He shook my hand saying, " My dear Richard, it is good to see you again. Our last encounter was much too brief, and we have a bit of unfinished business to accomplish."

Although he spoke in French, I had no trouble following every phrase and nuance. Then these words came from my mouth, also in perfect French in spite of my poor talent for it: "Yes, Frederick, I remember our last meeting and the shopping expedition we terminated. The powerful lightning bolt that struck as we approached the piano salon frightened the horses so much that it took the driver three blocks to stop them. And did you notice the black coach, black horses and coachman garbed in black? It was almost funereal."

"I know," he responded. "It frightened me too-- like I have never been frightened before-- and the eerie glow in the air with those strange clumps of blue light darting around added to my fear. I could see that even a stern fellow like you was upset."

"Well, who wouldn't be! To tell the truth, I had a premonition that some terrible event was about to happen, and it did. Within ten months the world lost you and your wonderful talent."

He smiled warmly and said, "Thank you, Richard, for those kind words. Death so early in my career was hard to bear, but I had grown so weak that I accepted it. I do regret we were unable to finish shopping for the new piano I was seeking. Perhaps you would be kind enough to help me select one now?"

"Of course," I replied without hesitation. We then hailed a coach and entered it. Unlike the coach of the storm, this one was dark green and the gas lamps were gold, not brass. The coachman was dressed in a light green outfit, which went well with the coach and the summer season. The horses were dazzling white and splendid-looking animals. We conversed about music and politics enroute, and the clip-clop of the horses' hooves had me humming a melody to accompany their delightful rhythm. Frederick applauded softly as I finished it.

Within eight minutes the coachman halted his horses outside the premier piano salon in Paris. As we entered, the proprietor, Monsieur Dubois, was delighted to see us. He was a short, portly gentleman with a reddish face and a baldhead that glistened in the salon's gaslights. His thick eyebrows and bushy graybeard gave him a distinctive look, which overcame his physical shortcomings. He not only displayed great admiration for Frederick, but for some unknown reason, immense respect for me. I had a strong feeling that this was not some video game I was playing, but a mysterious return to a previous life. I was simultaneously confused and exhilarated!

The salon had deep red carpeting; carved, wood-paneled walls and ceilings; and busts of deceased great composers strategically located. I recognized Bach, Hayden, Mozart and Beethoven. Although the salon had a display window up front, it needed the gas lamps I mentioned earlier so one could read the sheet music on display. As we passed some of the busts, M. Dubois said. "Someday there will be busts of you two in my salon." Instead of feeling flattered, I felt suspicious of his motives.

There were about twenty pianos in sight, and Frederick spotted one that he decided to try first. "Excellent choice", M. Dubois almost purred. Frederick played a few scales, a waltz, and then a lively mazurka. "What do you think, Richard? Is the tone true and is the dynamic range satisfactory?"

"Yes, but why don't you try that one over there?"

"Certainly," he said. "But would you play something so I can hear it as a listener instead of a performer?" I was startled at his request because of my negligible ability, but some mysterious force compelled me to agree.

My earlier feeling that I had returned to a previous life was confirmed when I played the piano, as did the calendar that said 1848. The few simple pieces I had learned in the twentieth century gave way to some elegant and powerful music. As an admirer of musical virtuosity I often move my hands at a concert, as if I were playing the piano, but now I was living my fantasy. I even like to conduct when listening to a C.D. in the privacy of my home, and wondered if I now had that talent in my computer generated life. Frederick stood enthralled as I played, and asked if they were my latest compositions. I was so dumbfounded at my unforeseen ability that I nodded yes.

We took turns trying all five of the concert grand pianos. Frederick would play and I would listen, evaluating the performance of the piano while enjoying my friend's inimitable style and skill. He did the same when I played, and before long the salon was filled with people, drawn in and mesmerized by the magic of our melodies.

The people had wandered in gradually and pretended to be looking at pianos, or some of the sheet music. Most of them seemed to be students, with a few exceptions. One was exceptional in a delightful way: she was a dark-haired, very shapely beauty! She was wearing an elegant light blue dress trimmed in white, with a very attractive white hat on her lovely head. She was carrying a white parasol decorated with blue flowers. Her beauty distracted both Frederick and me from our task, so it took longer than we planned. The other exception was not delightful; he was a large, shabbily dressed man whose bad breath and loud breathing made me shoo him away. I was beginning to be annoyed with all of them, but finally decided to let them stay, lest the beauty also leave. 'Oh well', I thought, 'a free concert will further enhance Frederick's reputation and perhaps we can meet the beauty.' Alas, it was not to be because she disappeared before we finished.

As to my own place in this era, I still wasn't exactly sure who I was. Of course the music I played gave a big hint, especially if I had composed it and wasn't just playing "Richard's" work. M. Dubois removed my lingering doubt when he called me by my last name, preceded by "Herr". Although "Richard" was famous for his womanizing, my interest in the beauty confirmed nothing; it is a universal trait among most men, even those my age, to admire gorgeous women.

Frederick selected the piano I suggested, and we left amidst the applause of the volunteer audience, which included M. Dubois and his assistants. As we rode away in a gray coach with white horses, Fredrick said something that amazed me: "Richard, the celestial power has told me that you were re-incarnated as a rather ordinary man. They said you were so domineering and egotistical--not without cause-- I hasten to add--that they felt you needed a lesson in humility. How has it worked out for you?"

"Well, it has certainly accomplished the purpose," I replied. "I now like and respect many composers at whom I once scoffed. Surprisingly, I can even detect flaws in my own compositions-- some of my operas are much too long and have too many repetitive and boring passages. And when that monster, Hitler, admired and used my music, I was outraged! I retained some of my stubbornness and ALL of my deep appreciation of great music. However, my musical talent was so meager that I became an aerospace engineer. It is an honorable profession, but trying to cope with the complexities of science and engineering IS humbling. I also learned to respect and obey authority, and had a modest but very fulfilling career. I have been retired for 14 years."

"That's very interesting," he replied. "The celestial power said you helped the astronauts invade their territory by your role in the manned lunar landing program-- that must have been fascinating?"

"It was out of this world, to use some twentieth century lingo. " We both chuckled. "But how about you, Frederick-- were you re-incarnated?"

"Of course! And thanks to the celestial power, I stayed with music. It felt my untimely death warranted a second chance, so I am now the young concert pianist/composer that you met at the Radcliffe's Long Island home."

"Great!" I exclaimed. "That explains the rapport we achieved at the Radcliffes. Incidentally, I noticed that the space program fascinated you almost as much as I was fascinated by your continuing great musical talent. Do you think the celestial power arranged our meeting, or was it just pure chance?"

Frederick looked sharply at me and said: " Do you really think it would leave something that important to chance?"

I shook my head to indicate 'no', and then said, "I suppose it was preparing us for this reunion. It does work in strange and mysterious ways, doesn't it? I suspect that we mortals will never fully comprehend it, although we can appreciate the results." Frederick nodded his head yes.

The coach had now reached our starting point and we both alighted. "Before we say 'Adieu', Frederick, I have one last question: may I tell people your twentieth century name?"

"Only if you let me tell them your nineteenth century one!"

I pondered for a while, and then decided that the world wasn't ready for such information-- no one would believe my former role, although they would see a strong connection in Frederick's new one.

My last words were, "Let's keep it our own special secret!"

Suddenly, the electric power went off and I was back at my desk and in the dark. I picked up my flashlight, shut the computer off, and went back to bed. I was exhausted from all the excitement and soon fell into a deep sleep.

But it was no ordinary sleep. It was filled with fantastic dreams and truly divine orchestral music-- with me as conductor-- and the dark-haired beauty playing first violin!

THE SURPRISED INTRUDER

As I got out of the shower and started to towel off, I heard a strange noise downstairs—like my front door opening. I had left my wife in Syracuse with her sister and returned home a week early. Some urgent business suddenly came up that couldn't wait. I wrapped the towel around myself and opened the bathroom door—yep, there was someone in the house, but who could it be at 7:30 a.m.?

I grabbed the baseball bat that I keep near my bed and crept down the carpeted stairs. If it's a teenage punk trying to rip me off, he's in for a big surprise. I lifted the bat over my head ready to conk him, but he wasn't where I expected-- near my electronic treasures. Then I heard the water running in the kitchen. That was a puzzle -- why would a thief take time to get a drink of water? He must be a cool customer, or at least a thirsty one. Judging by the length of time he ran the water, I concluded he was really thirsty.

I slunk down the back hall, debating whether to jump him at the sink, or wait until he came around the corner. I decided the corner would give me the element of surprise. His footsteps were soft as he left the sink— probably tennis shoes. Yep, it must be a teenage punk. I got ready to spring my big surprise with breathless anticipation. I've got to admit my heart was pounding so hard I was afraid he'd hear it, but apparently he didn't.

Then I began to hesitate - should I conk him in the head, hit his weapon if he had one, or just confront him with the raised bat? Maybe he was a decent kid who just went astray temporarily. I opted for the confrontation.

"Don't move a muscle," I yelled as he turned the comer. Talk about surprised -- we were both shocked!

She screamed and dropped a watering can. I lowered the bat and my towel fell off. She gaped and then slumped over in a dead faint. Quickly, I put my towel back on; ran to the hall closet; got my raincoat; and ran back to revive her.

When her eyes opened they were full of fear, but I told her who I was and she calmed down. Then she told me who she was - a young neighbor girl - probably a teenager- that my wife had hired to water the plants.

"I guess my wife didn't call and tell you I was coming home early," I said.

"And I guess she didn't tell you that I was going to water the plants," I nodded in agreement.

"It's good that neither of us has a weak heart - that encounter was a big shock for both of us." She nodded in agreement.

"You knew," I continued, "My wife complains that my communication skills need improving." "I can hardly wait to tell her what happened when she goofed!"

P.S. I was the surprised intruder in this tale; she was doing what she was hired to do and I intruded into her activity.

P.P.S. If she had entered a few minutes earlier, she would have heard the shower and either called out or come back later. If she had entered a few minutes later, I would have been dressed and she probably wouldn't have fainted. Conclusion: Murphy's Law really works!

Tornado Teasing

Most people fear tornadoes. They are one of nature's most violent forms of concentrated energy and frequently leave a fearsome swath of destruction. But like many other awesome things in life, they can be exhilarating fun when properly handled. If you think that is an outrageous statement, let me tell you about some of my youthful experiences in Kansas during the summer of 1941.

As you probably know, Kansas is famous for tornadoes and flat, grassy land. That combination, plus a little ingenuity and a lot of daring, led my three best friends and me to some wonderful, fun-filled adventures.

Earlier, we had pooled our money and bought an old Ford V-8 Phaeton; you know, the type that had a convertible top over the front and rear seats. The ingenuity part consisted of converting it into a tornado teaser. First, we secured the convertible top in the "down" position, rigged some seat belts and added some foot-straps and hand holds. Later on, we got really clever and attached plywood panels (3'x6') to each running board. (Remember them?) We used strong door hinges and rigged a cable-cranking system so that we could extend the panels from a normally vertical position to an almost horizontal one.

Teasing tornadoes was my idea, but my three buddies helped work out the operational details. We were a good team and there weren't many arguments over who thought of what; probably less than 3 dozen!

Tornadoes were frequent visitors to the plains on summer afternoons and we got pretty good at forecasting tornado weather. After our chores were done, we would drive our car to the deserted barn, rig it for tornado teasing and then play cards, tell jokes, or talk about our other experiences until we spotted one. We could see them coming a couple of miles away and we figured we could get close with reasonable safety because:

o Although a tornado's peripheral winds are around 450 mph, they move slowly over the ground, somewhere between 25 and 45 mph. (We read that in an Encyclopedia)

o Our Ford V-8 could go almost 80 mph and was very maneuverable.

o Gus was a very skillful driver.

The first few times we teased a tornado we didn't have the panels on because we hadn't yet conceived them, but we were sharp enough to wear football helmets and use some aviator goggles left over from WWI. The tie downs, handholds and safety belts were already installed, so naturally we used them.

We spotted a twister the third day after we started looking. As soon as we saw it we headed straight for it! Our hearts were beating very fast and, per our earlier plans, Gus headed for the right side. We figured we should just graze it so we didn't get sucked into the vortex. Gus was going about 50 mph and did an excellent job. Although we barely touched its periphery, our exit speed was over 80 mph and the acceleration was terrific. What a thrill!

We then turned around to try and catch it from behind. Its ground speed was only about 25 mph so we easily overtook it. We were smart enough to enter the new right side so we could pick up speed again. This time Gus got a little closer and we went from 60 mph to at least 100, the maximum on the speedometer.

Acceleration was so great that we "bottomed" the coil springs in the seatbacks. Speed is great but rapid acceleration really gets the adrenaline flowing.

The dust was also thicker, but since there were no bushes or buildings, there was no dangerous debris in the fierce winds. The goggles kept the dust out of our eyes, but our faces and clothes captured more than we wanted. We brushed each other off before returning home, less our folks get curious.

As we started slowing down, Gus noticed that the tornado had changed course and was headed straight for us. That was an unexpected development, but good old Gus made a right angle turn and accelerated. We easily outran the twister and escaped unscathed. We silently wondered what would have happened if the car had stalled. We added an inspection of the car to our check-off list for all future tornado teasing.

The tornado went through a grove of trees and we decided we couldn't catch it for a third try. Besides, we had filled our excitement quota for one afternoon. There was excited chatter all the way back to the barn. Later on, my folks asked me if I had seen the tornado; I said, "yes, from a distance." I didn't volunteer any information about how short the distance became once we got in the car and chased it; fortunately they didn't ask any more questions.

About five days later we spotted another tornado. As usual, Gus was in the driver's *seat;* I was next to Gus; Dave was behind Gus; and Joe was next to Dave. Gus had gotten pretty confident and came even closer to the vortex—too close. Dave damn near got sucked out of the car and into it. Luckily, Joe saw that Dave's seat belt was breaking and grabbed him around the leg-- just as he started to "float" away! For a brief second it looked like the whole car would get sucked in, but our forward speed was so great we broke away. Our instinctive leaning to the left seemed to help too.

We were all a bit shook up, and had to call it a day because of Dave's broken seat belt. Needless to say, we doubled the strength of all four seat belts. We didn't want anyone to float away individually; we figured if catastrophe overtook us, it would be better to die as a group--much less explaining!

The encounter had two benefits: We made the seat belts stronger and got the idea for the side panels. Joe figured that some variable flat-plate area would give us more maneuverability in case of future close calls and subsequent events proved him right.

The next week and a half was spent making the panels, hinging them to the running board and rigging the cable cranking system. We shaped the plywood panels so they would be streamlined and painted them green so they would match the grassy plain and make us as inconspicuous as possible. We also made the rear hinges stick out farther than the front ones so we would get a bigger boost once the circulating winds got behind us while exiting the tornado periphery. We kept the panels and mechanism in a deserted barn so our folks wouldn't know what we were up to.

We got really good at putting the panels and mechanism on and taking them off. Gus and Dave did the right side and Joe and I the left side. We had contests to see which team was fastest-- Joe and I set a record of 5 minutes, 17 seconds for assembly, but Gus and Dave always beat us at disassembly. Their record was 3 minutes, 26 seconds. We inspected their work and they inspected ours to make sure everything worked well. Can't afford sloppy workmanship when you're teasing tornadoes.

We were all farm boys and knew how to build or fix most anything. Gus was 20, Joe and Dave were 19 and I had just turned 18. We double-dated, mostly on Saturday nights, and decided NOT to invite our girl friends to join us in tornado teasing. We also agreed not to tell them, fearing they couldn't keep our secret.

We teased seven more tornadoes during the next five weeks and had more fun than a tree full of monkeys. No one ever saw us because we were pretty far away from the scattered farmhouses. Besides, at the first sight of a tornado everybody else headed for their storm cellar and stayed there until it was long gone.

We felt sorry for the poor, unenlightened folks who were terrified of tornadoes and didn't know how to tease them. Even so, we didn't tell anyone about our new found sport for fear our parents would "kibosh" it.

During those five weeks we experimented with control. We could crank the side panels up or down independently and, of course, we could shift the cars center of gravity by leaning left, right, fore and aft. We were thus able to get closer and closer to the high winds and we achieved great acceleration and high speed.

Dave got a Cord Auto speedometer that would go to 180 mph. Our Ford speedometer only went to 100, and we easily exceeded that most of our runs. In fact, our fastest two runs bottomed out the 180-mph mark so we probably hit 200 mph.

Wow! That surely was a speed record for a Ford V-8—even the new ones, which we couldn't afford. I'll bet we went faster than a Cord, which was the speed car of that era.

During the sixth week, Joe wondered what would happen if we entered a tornado on the left side. We debated the probable consequences for several days and finally decided the only way to know for sure was to try it.

Boy, was that ever a mistake. We spotted a good twister a few days later and let Joe drive because he saved Dave, thought up the panels and was the one who was most interested to find out what a left entry would do. Letting Joe drive was an even greater mistake; instead of just grazing the edge of the tornado as we had planned, Joe miscalculated, or the twister changed course, and we hit it too near the center!

In an instant we lost our forward speed and got sucked into the partial vacuum of the vortex. We left the ground like a homesick angel, and that's where I figured we would end up-- dead and in heaven; or maybe in hell for being so reckless with our lives. The ground was several hundred feet below and we were spiraling upward like a top on a giant screw thread.

Gus yelled, "Lean left and crank the left panel down!" By golly, that worked and we gradually worked ourselves away from the upward suction. We felt good until we realized that we had over-controlled and were falling rapidly toward the ground, headed for a fatal crash for sure.

We leaned and cranked the other way until we got our car into a nearly stable condition and our falling speed slowed down to a snail's pace. We yo-yoed up and down for a bit, and were cursing one second and praying the next.

Somehow, call it luck, native intelligence, or pure fear-filled instinct, we slowed our descent enough to cushion our fall. We finally left the twister unscathed—except our rear leaf springs broke with a mighty crunch. Later on, I discovered a bump on my head. It had hit the instrument panel during the rapid deceleration when we entered.

We checked for any broken bones, (none); watched the tornado fade from view, (relief); and walked back home, (ugh!). Even Joe's curiosity was satisfied regarding the consequences of entering the left side--DON'T DO IT!

The next day we towed the car to our deserted barn with my folk's tractor and kept the car hidden until we could get new rear springs. By the time we found them at the nearest junkyard, the tornado season was over.

On December 7, the Japanese Fleet attacked Pearl Harbor and the United States was sucked into the huge maelstrom called World War II. All four of us were drafted and saw service in different parts of the world. Gus and I joined the Navy and fought in the Pacific theater. Joe and Dave joined the Army and fought in the European Theater. Gus was killed in action in 1942 and Joe was severely wounded in 1943, but recovered completely. Dave and I were lucky and exited the war like we did all those tornadoes—unscathed!

The war was almost as exciting as our tornado teasing, but nowhere near as much fun. I've gotta tell you, 1941 was the most exciting, most fun-filled summer of my entire life!!

It was even better than my recent trip to my ancestral home in Munchausen, Germany, where my great, great, great grandfather was a famous Baron!

But that's another story....

Note: Baron Munchausen is thought to be the greatest tall-tale teller who ever lived. His imaginative stories have been published and even made into a movie, and I have enjoyed and admired both. Like the Baron's stories, this story is pure fiction and neither the author nor the publisher accepts any responsibility for what may happen to anyone who tries to tease a tornado. Our advice is, "Stay as far away from tornadoes as possible—they are dangerous, temperamental beasts that don't like to be teased!

TUNNEL TO ....?

Eight old men were hiking up a trail toward an obscure peak in the White Mountains of New Hampshire. By old, I mean that everyone was well over sixty, and three of us were in our seventies.

The trail started in a small parking area behind a country store, and if you didn't know the storeowner and purchase something you couldn't get a parking space. Most hikers were unaware of the trail, or even the peak, so we felt lucky that Len Richards, our leader, had the right stuff to get us on the trail. Since we were all retired, we were hiking on a weekday and had the trail to ourselves. It went through a heavily wooded area and was barely discernible. We would have lost our way several times except for Len's expertise.

We climbed slowly but surely, in keeping with our age. At noon we had a trail lunch before continuing our climb. Around 2 p.m., we thought we were near the peak because we were well above the timberline and had been enjoying splendid views for about twenty minutes. The stone Cairns guided us until we reached a false peak, at which point we spotted a huge cliff several hundred yards ahead. From a distance, we thought the trail would skirt it, but as we got closer the Cairns led directly toward the cliff and the trail ended abruptly at its base. Since we weren't rock climbers, it looked like we would have to retrace our steps and start over again on another trail.

Naturally, there was considerable grumbling directed at Len. He was a tall, muscular man with brown eyes and thinning dark hair that was gray at the temples. His pleasant, almost handsome face, was blessed with an infectious grin, and his vigorous laugh was irresistible. Since he had never led us astray on previous hikes, I was willing to give him the benefit of the doubt, but Sam Perkins, my trail-mate and best friend, wasn't. In fact, he displayed his fiery, fading-red-head temper by saying, "Damn it Len, you know we can't scale that cliff, so now our whole morning's climb is wasted and we've gotta go back. I'm disgusted with you!"

"Calm down, Sam," I said. "Maybe Len knows another way up without going back. Give him a chance."

"Another way up? How can there be another way up without equipment, and who knows how to use it even if we had it? Just look at how the terrain falls away sharply on both sides of the trail. Any fool can see that we can't skirt that damn cliff, so the only recourse is to retrace our steps. Maybe Len is gonna summon a helicopter or pass out wings!"

Sam gestured wildly during his temper tantrum, pointing at the steep slope on both sides of the trail and moving both hands up in a hopeless gesture at the craggy cliff. He ended with a disgusted look as he jabbed repeatedly at the trail back. His voice was full of sarcasm when he mentioned the helicopter and wings.

Len nodded approvingly at me during my supporting remarks, listened patiently during Sam's tirade, and then said, "Stop your grumbling, Sam, and trust me. I have a surprise for all of you, and its not a helicopter or wings." He then gestured with his arms and yelled, "Follow me, men!" He than lead us to a big boulder a few feet off the trail, slithered behind it and showed us a man-sized opening in the cliff.

"Wow," I exclaimed. "Is it a cave that we can explore?"

"It's better than that," he replied with an impish grin. "It's a long, cave-like tunnel that will take us directly to Hidden Valley, which is one of the most gorgeous places in the world. The scenery is spectacular and there's plenty of food-- fish and waterfowl in Paradise Lake, rabbits, wild turkeys and berries on the land, and game birds in the air. It's a heaven on earth, and getting there will be fun because the tunnel is more fascinating than most caves."

Sam was somewhat placated, but couldn't help saying, "Why didn't you tell us sooner so I wouldn't have lost my temper? I've a mind to go back anyway. "

" Because I wanted to surprise you." Len's big, disarming grin made his statement satisfying to everyone, even Sam. Once he led us into the tunnel, it was all he had said it was, and then some. There were curious shapes, patterns and colors in the rough walls, and the 12-foot waterfall, which fed a small stream that disappeared under some large rocks, was a huge surprise. Len explained that it was 98 percent a natural cave and that an ancient Indian tribe had excavated the other two- percent to make it a tunnel. We must have spent half an hour exploring the first third of the tunnel with our trusty flashlights.

Len then cautioned us, "We'd better move on, men. We need time at the lake to set up camp and have a swim before we start supper. When we return, I'll allow several hours for exploring the tunnel and its many side passages."

Thus assured, we walked more briskly, but the tunnel was so long and twisted that there was no telltale light to mark its exit. Sam and I were more curious than the other guys, and tended to linger behind and wander into the side passages. Fortunately, the Phillips twins, Joe and Charlie, (age 69) were growing weary before we entered the tunnel and slowed the group down.

They were very handsome widowers and much in demand among the ladies, which could account for their lesser stamina. Sam and I were still married and were strong and fit, so we figured we could easily catch up with the others by following their voices and flashlight beams, and jogging if necessary.

Although Sam was four inches shorter and somewhat thinner than I, he was in better shape because of his running. We had been best friends since high school baseball, where he had given me the nickname "Buddy". As we grew older and mature, he shortened it to "Bud".

"Hey, look at this. Bud," Sam exclaimed. "There's a large room down this hidden opening that looks like it has some markings on the walls." Sure enough, when we squeezed through the narrow, convoluted passage, we saw many colorful pictographs of various animals and some primitive looking people, probably a prehistoric Indian tribe. And it wasn't a "large" room; it was a "huge" one.

We estimated that it was 110 feet long, 85 feet wide and 40 feet high. It was somewhat elliptical in shape, as if a giant eggshell had been cut in two lengthwise, except the interior was not smooth like an eggshell. We were so excited with our "big find" that we lost track of time. After oohing and ahhing for about five minutes, I said, "Hey, Sam, we'd better join the others."

"Let me get some photos of these pictographs first, and then we'll leave." After removing his camera from his backpack, he snapped several photos, but it cost us a few more minutes. As we started back, he spotted more pictographs in a side passage and took a few more photos. While in it we heard a muffled sound from the huge room. It seemed like some sort of echo from Sam's clicking and our talking, so we dismissed it from our minds.

We then headed back to what we thought was the entrance, but all we could find were other passages that looked similar. None of them led to the tunnel!

"Sam, I'm worried. That damn entrance must be somewhere in this room, but I'm completely disoriented. What do you think we should do?"

"I'm a bit worried too. Buddy, (he called me "Buddy" whenever either of us got nervous) but let's keep our cool. One of these passages has gotta join the tunnel, so let's start a systematic search. Remember, the passage we came in was only about fifteen feet long before we entered this "ball room." You circle to the left, and I'll circle to the right. Yell, if you find it, and I'll do the same."

Thus reassured, I started circling to the left trying to find the passage that joined the tunnel. We had the presence of mind to leave our backpacks to mark our starting point and lighten our load. After searching carefully, I reached the backpacks. Although I had circled the room, I had not found the connecting passage; worse yet, Sam was nowhere in sight.

I yelled his name for several minutes, but all I heard was a multiple echo that was unnerving. A cold chill went through me, so I took a sweater out of my backpack and put it on. I also took a swig of water from my canteen and sat down on a big rock to contemplate my predicament. Here were my thoughts:

o 'There's something weird going on in here that defies logic. What happened to that connecting passage? Could it have been sealed by falling rock? If so, why didn't we hear the noise? Could it have been something else-- maybe the ghosts of the Indians playing a trick on us--or what?'

o 'What happened to Sam, and why didn't we meet half-way? If he went deep into one of the passages, he would have yelled or left some marker. Could he be playing a trick on me to test my mettle? Nah, he seemed as worried as I was and the situation is too serious, even for Sam, to pull one of his little jokes. Maybe he fell into a pit in one of the passages and is unconscious, or dead. Gosh, I hope not!'

o 'Should I circle the room again in reverse? Maybe I can find Sam or the missing passage.' This I did, going at lest twenty feet into each side passage and looking for pits, but there was no sign of Sam or the passage to the tunnel. There wasn't even a sign of a cave-in, so I remained as bewildered as before and a bit more frightened. I did spot some bats high up and in a corner of the big room and that gave me hope. I'll wait until night and see how they exit. I set my wrist alarm for seven p.m., an hour before sun down.

o Will Len and the other five guys come looking for us? If so, when? How long will it take them to find the partially hidden passage that leads to this room? There were lots of side passages in the tunnel and it may take days to explore all of them. And if there was a cave-in, they-may overlook this room altogether.

o How long will my food and water last? Although Sam had taken his canteen, his food supply was still in his backpack. We had each carried only two days' food supply and we were light eaters, so four or five days was tops for food, and a day or so for water.

o When will my batteries run down? I'd better turn my flashlight off and save them. Also, if I get my spare batteries from my backpack and put them in my pocket, I won't have to fumble around in the dark. I searched Sam's backpack for spare batteries, but he must have taken them with him. I guess my batteries' life will depend on how much I use them. With careful use, maybe they'll last several weeks.

I then took both sleeping bags out and laid them in as soft a spot as I could find. I transferred all the food and supplies to Sam's backpack and used mine as a pillow, but without the sleeping bag it wasn't very soft. I placed Sam's backpack near my head so it would be accessible while in my sleeping bag. Turning off my flashlight, I lay flat on my back, worried sick over my pitiful situation.

I cursed my stupidity and arrogance in not staying with Len and the others. Were they at beautiful Paradise Lake cooking supper, or had they started their search? Perhaps Len thought we had gone back down the trail since Sam had hinted, and even said, we might. If so, he wouldn't worry about us because the buddy system would protect us.

After my eyes got used to the darkness, I noticed a faint beam of light coming from the high ceiling, which was over forty feet above me. 'Aha, ' I mused, 'that's probably where the bats exit' But then my heart sank. If that's their exit it won't do me any good-- they can fly out but I can't. Well, at least it's a source of air, and maybe someone will lower a rope and pull me out. But when I realized how low the odds were for that possibility, my heart sank even further.

I contemplated the irony of the situation: 'Here am I, supposedly the most intelligent and gifted of all the animals, hopelessly trapped. Then there are those lowly bats with their pea-sized brains, but able to come and go at will. Damn!' I closed my eyes and soon fell asleep, but my dreams weren't comforting.

My wrist alarm woke me at seven p.m., and I noted the date--8/1/92. Strangely, the ceiling light was even stronger. I guessed that an overhanging boulder blocked the opening during the early afternoon, and then reflected the rays of the setting sun into the hole. It may sound silly, but conceiving a rational solution to the anomaly comforted me. It wasn't long before I heard the whirring of many wings, and the opening grew darker as the bats made their exit. It was an exciting sight, but it indicated it was the only exit.

I turned my flashlight on long enough to fix my cold supper and swig some water. I didn't fully quell my appetite because I wanted to ration both food and water. Earlier, I had found a place about twenty feet away to deposit my trash and bodily waste. I practiced finding it in the dark a few times to prepare for the time all my batteries discharged. I re-circled the room several times, hoping to find Sam or the passage to the tunnel, but their mysterious disappearance remained intact.

After the sun set, it grew really dark-- so dark that I just had to turn on my flashlight now and then, even though I was snug in my sleeping bag. I established a routine in my mind-- I would sleep as much as possible; eat and drink as little as I could without losing my strength; and use my little "John" only when absolutely necessary. I would also yell now and then so any rescuers could hear me; think as many pleasant thoughts as my mind could conjure up; record my thoughts on my mini-tape recorder; and pray-- long, earnestly, and frequently! Merciful sleep finally overtook my worried mind.

When I arose on the morning of August 2nd, I followed my routine as well as I could; but nervous tension increases thirst, so I drank more water than I had planned. By the next afternoon, August 3rd, it was gone. I started dehydrating as my very dry mouth indicated. By the time I went to sleep that night I wondered how long I could last and would anyone ever find me before it was too late.

The only bright spots were that I had the sleeping bags and enough clothes to keep me toasty warm; and my dreams started getting more comforting. The latter made me wonder if my sub-conscious mind was accepting my probable fate.

As I was eating my breakfast the next morning, August 4th, I heard a strange but familiar sound. It was rain coming through the ceiling hole. My mind quickly shifted into high gear and I grabbed my plastic poncho and empty canteen and walked toward the rain. I then dug a depression under the trickling water with my hands and laid my poncho over it to trap it.

Holding my canteen upright, I soon filled it. I then lapped up plenty of water from the poncho, and there was still enough trapped in it to last several more days. I told myself, 'Poncho water first, canteen water last.' My hopes soared!

August 5th was uneventful, but when August 6th finally rolled around, my food was gone and hunger pains set in. Drinking the water was necessary, but it seemed to make my hunger worse. Time went by like a sleepy tortoise climbing a steep hill, and each hour seemed like an eternity. Then I had an idea: 'If I can capture a bat, it might solve my food problem, but how? Ah, I have it; I'll throw some stones up to their roosting place.'

On the thirteenth throw, one came fluttering down. I took my pocket knife out and skinned it. Then I ate the skimpy meat raw, because I had no way to cook it. Although it was disgusting, hunger quickly overcame the disgust. Things were looking up. I now had food and water, but could I keep my sanity?

Loneliness and almost constant darkness were taking their toll. I thought of the blind people I had known and how they had lived many years in total darkness, yet were able to find work and even raise families.

I then thought of my "Death Row" pen pal and how he overcame being locked in a small cell-- while facing death any day-- by teaching himself to draw, writing poetry and articles, taking courses by mail, and even raising money for his defense. If they could overcome their challenging situations maybe I could overcome mine!

My optimism vanished later on when the bat meat made me so sick that I threw up and my body temperature rose. I mumbled to myself, 'Just what I need, a fever! Maybe it will put me out of my misery sooner, but what an awful way to die. Would a sudden accidental death be better? It would be quicker and have less sustained pain, but very little time to review my life and all my blessings, as I had done the previous days.'

'How about a long illness like cancer, AIDS, or Alzheimer's? There would be suffering, but there would be time to review my life and visit with loved ones-- and there wouldn't be this infernal hunger and darkness! I concluded that my current situation must be one of the worst forms of death because of the loneliness, darkness, slow wasting away, and vacillating between hope and despair.

By August ninth, I was again out of water and so weak I could barely leave my bed. Fortunately, with no food or water intake, it wasn't as necessary as before. My mind was still O.K., but even it was beginning to grow fuzzy and confused. My hope of rescue had almost vanished, but a tiny bit remained. The old saying, "Hope springs eternal" was replaced with "Hope dies very slowly, and just before the body does." I mustered enough will power to say my final prayer.

"Dear Lord, I'm at the end of my life unless you intervene. But everyone dies some day, so I accept my death as your will. It should relieve me of my fear, suffering and loneliness, even if there is no hereafter. "

"But Lord, the Bible says there IS a hereafter and that true believers can enter your glorious kingdom. I hope you will overlook my past doubts and consider me a true believer. I am thankful that you have brought me to age 72, and I especially thank you for the many blessings that came my way. It has been a very good life and I hope that I have made a small contribution to mankind."

"I confess my many sins; they were small in deed but large in thought, and I am sorry that I was weak and succumbed to the temptations of the eyes and the imagination. If there is a Purgatory where we are purged of our sins, I pray that you will deduct these past days of suffering from my allotted time there."

"Above all. Lord, please comfort and guide my cherished wife, beloved children and grandchildren, and dear friends. Please stay with them until their own lives reach their inevitable conclusion, at which time I pray that we will be reunited forever."

"I ask all this in the name of your son, Jesus Christ, who suffered the agony of the cross to redeem sinners like me. Now I say "good bye" to earth, with the fond hope that you will soon say 'Welcome' as I enter Heaven! Amen." The prayer took most of my remaining strength, and I fell into a deep coma.

So now we come back to my initial question: "Tunnel to ... ?" Since I am able to write this story, with the help of my mini tape recorder, it's obvious that my time to die had not come; so how do I fill in the dots preceding the question mark. The answer depends on the viewpoint of the participants.

For Len and the others, the tunnel was used properly and led them to beautiful Paradise Lake and three fun-filled days. While still in the tunnel, one of the men had overheard Sam asking me, " Are you willing to return home so I can teach Len a lesson?"

"If you feel that strongly about it, I will, because you are my dear friend," Upon hearing my reply, he assumed that it was settled and so informed Len when they first missed us. Unfortunately, he wasn't around when I got Sam to change his mind by saying, "We'll miss a lot of good fun at Paradise Lake."

This misinformation let Len and the others stay in Hidden Valley the planned three days, where they enjoyed an earthly paradise. No one missed us until they returned home and Len called our wives. He was almost as upset as our wives to learn that we were missing, maybe more so, because he bore the responsibility as our leader.

He gathered the group to look for us as soon as possible, and notified the rangers. Our wives wanted to join them, but he persuaded them to stay home in case we returned on our own. Len and the others searched the tunnel and all the passages for a full day. Seeing no evidence of a cave- in, they concluded we weren't underground, so they searched the surrounding mountains for three days in case we had gotten lost there. Our disappearance was a real mystery to the outside world and was reported in the regional media. Futile searching and worry marred their good time at Paradise Lake, and our families went through pure hell!

For Sam and me, the tunnel was used improperly. We succumbed to the temptation of the cave passages and paid a high price. Had we waited until we returned with the group, we would have missed the huge room because no one saw the connecting passage; but we would have arrived home safe and sound like Len and the others. The result of our curiosity, impatience, and sub-conscious disregard of our leader and fellow hikers, led us to a brief adventure, followed by my many days of suffering, loneliness, despair and near death!

Sam's experience was different from mine but equally demanding. While exploring one of the passages during our huge-room circling, his flashlight flickered and he tripped over a large rock. Behind the rock, and hidden from normal view, was a deep hole, into which he plunged headfirst. Fortunately, the hole was slanted, sort of like a waterslide, so he got to the bottom without too many scrapes and bruises. But he broke his left arm and two ribs when a large out-cropping rudely stopped him.

Climbing back up was impossible because of his head first position and the steep slope, so he rested in place until he felt strong enough, both physically and mentally, to continue. He then wiggled and crawled down the narrow passage in agony until, mercifully, it grew larger. In a few more hours, he was able to stand erect and keep exploring. When he checked his wristwatch with his now functioning flashlight, he discovered the watch had been broken during the crash. He lost all track of time, and the constant darkness of the cave lost him the date. He lived several days on the water in his canteen, and suffered greatly from his hunger and broken bones,

Later on, he heard a strange noise ahead, so he moved cautiously toward it. When he got near its source, it had stopped and he was baffled. His flashlight was aimed at the ground, so when his head bumped into a soft, yielding object, he was startled. The object started screeching loudly and moving rapidly, which nearly frightened him out of his wits. Falling to the cave floor to protect himself, he quickly crawled away when he realized he had landed in a thick layer of smelly bat dung.

Yes, it was another colony of bats that had just returned from flying, hunting, feeding and whatever else bats do at night. He crawled around in the dark hoping to find a glimmer of daylight, but there were too many other passages to spot it. He then slept fitfully until he heard them flying out the next twilight, at which time he followed them and found their exit. He was barely able to squeeze through it, but he was now out of the darkness and cramped quarters.

Finding a resting place during the waning daylight, he wondered what to do. He worried about leaving me, but concluded that he could do more good by getting a good night's rest and then seeking help for both of us. The next morning he saw that the terrain around the exit was very steep and heavily wooded, so he had to "bushwhack" his way slowly and painfully.

Encouraged because he knew going down hill would lead to civilization, he became discouraged when he realized it wasn't that easy. There were several more steep up-slopes before they really went down, so it took him more days of agonized effort to hit a down slope that led somewhere.

He slept in what little shelter he could find, and when the rain came that I so welcomed, he cursed it. Not only did he get soaking wet, but he soon became very sick. Filling his canteen with rainwater and eating the few berries he scrounged helped a bit, but not enough to get him to civilization. Finally, he discovered a small trail, but he was so week and feverish that he lay there for a day and a night before two rangers found him on August 8th.

One of them went back for help while the other one stayed and gave Sam what little sustenance he could take. When help arrived a few hours later they took him to the nearest hospital, but he was too weak and mentally rambling from the fever he had acquired to tell anything of importance about my fate.

Sam's perseverance in spite of his broken arm and ribs, and later his hunger, thirst and debilitating fever, were typical of him. He is the sort of person who never gives up, as I had learned many times during our life-long friendship, beginning with his baseball exploits.

Sam's piece of the puzzle had been put in place, but the whole picture was still a mystery because no one knew my fate. It was finally assembled by chance, or so the public said, but to me it was divine intervention. Some rock climbers from Boston, who knew nothing of the tunnel or our mysterious disappearance, scaled the cliff on August 12th. One of them noticed the opening where the bats exited and saw that it led to a large room. Two of them were curious and adventurous, so they belayed down to explore, leaving two others to help extricate them later. One of them tripped over my sleeping bag, and I moaned enough for her to find me. She and her husband stayed with and nourished me until the others could contact the rangers for professional help. On August 13th, my lucky day, they pulled me up the opening and carried me to safety. It took several months of tender, loving care before I was able to resume my normal activities, including some more mountain hikes.

The rangers, who had maps of the tunnel and its many passages, spotted the cave-in of the huge-room passage, which they concluded was too slow and gradual to make a big noise, and barely noticeable. It accounted for the "muffled sound" we heard while taking photos in the side passage and why we couldn't spot the cave-in.

Eventually, they re-opened the passage and declared the cave-in a natural event, but I know better-- it was started by the ghosts of Indians seeking revenge for the early settlers "mistreatment!

I never returned to the damn tunnel and never saw Hidden Valley or Paradise Lake except via Len's photos. Sam was more daring and went with Len to Hidden Valley via the tunnel during his next outing. He tried to persuade me to go during a second trip, by saying, "Paradise Lake is aptly named," but I refused to go.

Family, friends and the other joys of life are still my earthly paradise, and I'm thankful that my journey to a heavenly one was delayed!

Author's Note: I have enjoyed caves on four continents during my 80 years, and still find them fascinating. In 1939, while I was in R.O.T.C. camp in Alabama, I had a close call. A good friend and I had explored a nearby cave one weekend and decided to explore it some more the next weekend. When we returned, it was boarded up and a sign said, "Closed until further notice due to a serious cave-in!" Previously, we had spotted a vertical entrance that we thought we could negotiate with care, and were tempted to use it to enter the cave in spite of the warning. Fortunately, we didn't, because we realized that we had missed a potential disaster by less than a week!

Caves and tunnels have also been part of my dreams. A consistent scenario is that the tunnel closes at both ends, or the cave gets smaller behind me, and I am trapped. Claustrophobia becomes so strong that my only salvation is to wake up in a cold sweat.

My experiences and dreams inspired this fictitious story. If it gave you chills and thrills, it accomplished part of its purpose. If it deepened your appreciation of your own life and good fortune, it achieved its main purpose. If it produces claustrophobia in your dreams, do what I do-- WAKE UP!

2017!
LEISURE VILLAGE'S DECISIVE YEAR?

When year 2017 rolled around, Leisure Village was in great shape. Major operational savings had been made so that monthly fees had been substantially reduced, in spite of continuing mild inflation nationally.

The board was well liked because it had a wonderful knack for accepting superior suggestions and settling disparaging disputes. Suggestors left pleased; opponents left satisfied, and some even became fast friends.

Medical research had provided healthy longevity, and insurance reforms greatly eased health-care financial burdens. Those who still had financial problems were able to use the huge appreciation of their property and the improved reverse mortgages to easily overcome them.

Yes, everything was copasetic in Leisure Village in January, 2017. It was so good that pessimists felt it couldn't prevail. Some even had a premonition that something catastrophic was bound to happen. Optimists countered by saying that the "7" in 2017 was a lucky number, and that more good things were bound to happen.

On April first, a large energy company with startling news approached the board. Their exploration experts had discovered major oil and natural gas reserves under the village. It wanted permission to slant drill off our property to recover the resources under it. One board member thought it was an April fool's joke, but the company soon convinced him that it was for real.

Another board member thought someone else owned the underlying mineral rights, but the company's legal staff had found it to be untrue. The village had 100% rights to all underlying resources. Furthermore, they were so huge that royalties would not only pay all of the village's operational and capital expenses, but greatly enrich each unit owner!

Wow! It seemed that the optimists were not only right, but had been pessimistic in their forecasts. During the next open meeting, the pessimists were skeptical. Their leader said, "Won't removing all that oil and gas do harm to the village-- maybe cause sinking, or even earthquakes?"

The company geologists patiently explained as follows: "Cold water will be pumped into the vacated spaces so there would be no sinkage. Furthermore, the earth will be cooler, so any tendency for earthquakes will be reduced. As you probably know, they are caused when increasing heat from the earth's interior expands tectonic plates, causing them to slip and create a quake. "

The pessimists' group seemed satisfied until a resident, who was an ex-financial expert, asked this question; "How will the royalties be divided? As I see it, there are five options: 1. Equally among each unit owner; 2. In proportion to the years of ownership; 3. In proportion to the present value of each unit; 4. In proportion to the initial investment; 5. In proportion to current monthly fee.

A huge hush fell over the assembled members. Old time residents figured they should get more than the newcomers; those with more current higher value units figured they should get more than owners of lower value units; newcomers liked the initial investment choice because they would get lots more than the old timers who had paid much less; hardly anyone liked the monthly fee option, since the others were more beneficial to their innate greed. Equal shares seemed inane.

Once everyone had decided what was best for their own position, turmoil broke loose. Speaker after speaker arose and made salient arguments for their case. Arguments broke out, and one old timer actually punched a newcomer, calling him "a damn young whippersnapper."

The board tried to curb the turmoil orally, but things were so out of control that security had to come in and stop it. Once order prevailed, the board decided to postpone any decision until they could get expert opinion to settle the widespread disagreement. While this was wise in view of the circumstances, it had the disadvantage of giving the various groups time to consolidate their positions and get their own expert opinion.

There was meeting after meeting, but with so many options there was never a majority vote for any one position. Things were at a standstill, and the village had never been so divided. Peace and serenity disappeared. No one even said hello when walking past, unless they knew the other person shared their position. Most of the clubs that had provided so much fun and pleasure disbanded, because the members couldn't stand their opponents.

It looked like the pessimists were right. 2017 was not a lucky year in spite of the tremendous wealth that was to come. Greed had made the village a mad house!

In December of 2017, the board called a meeting. It was the holiday season, and a time for being thankful for our many blessings: The miracle and victory of Hanukkah; the "Peace and good will among men" message of Christmas. Maybe, the board hoped, it would help the residents find a solution that would finally get a majority opinion.

A little 93-year-old woman spoke first. "I don't have many more years on earth, and I don't have any heirs left; so I will leave my house and my share of our good fortune to a charity that will help people in need."

A 70-year old man rose, saying: "Thank you mam, for your splendid example. Unlike you, I have heirs; but they are doing so well on their own that they don't need more than I had planned to give them anyway. I will do likewise."

A 65-year old woman said, "While I like the idealism of the others, I think we should be practical. I favor the current value option because it seems the fairest and has the best chance of keeping peace among my heirs. I have five, and they are a quarrelsome lot; I suspect other villagers are in a similar situation.

A 61-year old newcomer spoke next. "My neighbor and I used to be good friends, but he has lived here 28 years versus my 2 years. Naturally we had opposite positions and stopped speaking to each other. Last night we decided that our friendship was more important than getting more money than we could sensibly spend. We figure that if our heirs complained, they would be unreasonably ungrateful. Besides, we wont be here when our will is read!

We concluded that an equal division was the best way. Everyone would still have tons of money for the rest of their lives, so they could leave any surplus to their heirs or some worthwhile charity, perhaps both. Most important, we could all spend our remaining years in peace, harmony, and friendship. So I move that we act like a loving family and divide the money equally per unit--share, and share alike.

There was a second; a lengthy discussion; and a final vote. Now my question to you, dear reader, is this: "How would you vote? Would you be an optimist, and end 2017 as a lucky year by accepting the equal- share proposal? Or would you be a pessimist and support other motions until one passed after many more meetings, thus keeping 2017 the unluckiest year of our history?

2020

It is now the year 2025, and I have decided to look back to the year 2020. It was then that I celebrated my 100th birthday in January, a real milestone for those of us fortunate enough to make it. My dear wife had to wait almost two more years, but, thank God, she made it too.

We were in good health in 2020, and our health hasn't changed much since then. We celebrated my 100th birthday with my kids, grandkids, and a few great-grandkids. No great-great ones today in 2025, but we are hoping some of the newly married great ones will do the trick. Fortunately, most kids and grandkids live within driving distance, and we see them frequently. We even have friends near our age that we play bridge with, but I have to get guys and gals in their early eighties for my twice-weekly tennis game.

Now some people wonder what our longevity secret is, but it's not really a secret. You see, in 2010, we were among the few people who volunteered for a new longevity experimental program started by UCLA. My son-in-law, James, was a professor there and it was he who tipped us off to the program. And since it was an experimental program, they couldn't offer it to the public until they saw how long we guinea pigs would last. After 10 years, they offered it in 2020, and that's one of the reasons that I am looking back to that year. Our success in living those ten years made it possible for millions more to try it.

Another reason I write about 2020, is that my Children's book, "The Lonesome Little Dragon," not only reached its one millionth copy in 2020, but Disney came out with a very successful movie which followed my book reasonably well. My five other Children's books were doing well, and Disney called me on my wife's 100th birthday to offer a contract for my story called, "Jacqueline and the Magic Water," which has now been produced. With the fame from them, I got some major publishers to produce an anthology of my short stories, and to put in print some of my other e-books that I had some success with by 2009. In 2020, I became know as "Granddad Epps, Teller of Tall Tales."

But the accomplishments I am most proud of are my inventions. My most successful one was a new system that greatly reduced vehicle accidents and found and punished dangerous drivers automatically. It took almost ten years to develop and test the system before it was put in mass production, which also happened in 2020. Since then, statistics show that during the last five years 133,000 lives were saved, over a million injuries were prevented, and property damage of several billion dollars was avoided. Furthermore, state governments' revenue increased substantially due to the fines collected from the dangerous drivers they caught. I was even awarded a prize for "Inventor of the decade" in 2020.

One of the things I am most grateful for UCLA's longevity program is its ability to keep our minds clear and creative during our super-senior years, which I define as over ninety. The extra money I made was great, since I was able to make sure my heirs would be well provided for when we pass away and give a lot to some great charities. It was certainly much more than we could spend on ourselves, since people our age lead relatively simple lives.

The fame I achieved was a bit of a burden, but since I grew my beard most people don't recognize me the few times we go out in public. We moved to larger quarters and hired full time help once the dough came rolling in, so my wife no longer needs to shop or cook, except when she feels like it.

Yes, 2020 was a great year for us, and we both wonder what the future will hold. I am still writing and inventing, but am starting to slow down there and elsewhere. UCLA says living to 120 or 130 is not only possible, but probable for those on their program. And they are starting a new experimental super-longevity program, in which they want us to enroll. Our kids and grandkids are going to enroll, but my wife and I are still thinking about it.

Now if we just had 20-20 vision about the future, maybe we could make up our minds!

AN UNLIKELY HERO

Sam Perkins was a skinny kid of fifteen when we first met. He was only about five-feet, five-inches tall, wore reading glasses and was the studious type. His freckles and red hair made him the butt of many jokes and lots of teasing, and his temper sometimes flared up. People said it matched his hair-- fiery!

I was surprised when he tried out for the baseball team the next spring, as did I. I was even more surprised when he made it. He was one of those weak looking, but wiry, kids, whose strength and ability fooled you. Now when I say he made the team, I don't mean the starting line-up, like I did. I'm sorry to say it made me feel better, because if the reverse had happened, I would have been embarrassed to be outdone by someone four months younger, six inches shorter and even skinnier than I was.

By the time we both reached our senior year in high school, he was also in the starting line-up. I was number five in the batting order, he number eight. I played second base, he shortstop, so we got to know and respect each other. I even tried to get him some Saturday night dates, but the most desirable girls weren't interested, and Sam refused to compromise his high standards.

Sam was well suited for his position, because I never saw him fail to stop any ball that was within his reach, and then some. Oh, he sometimes bobbled the ball and missed getting the runner out at first or another base, but that was rare. Usually, he scooped up the hardest grounder and quickly tossed it to the proper base with unerring accuracy. Line drives in the air stuck to his glove as if opposite pole magnets were involved.

His hitting was another matter. My final batting average our senior year was .302, our best hitters were well over .400, but his was a measly .203, the reverse of mine. I learned later that those high batting averages were due more to poor pitching opponents than to native skill. We were pleased with them at the time, compared them to major league averages, and dreamed of someday joining their exalted ranks.

Sam would have been dropped from the line-up except for his stellar performance in the field. Besides, we came from Newton, a small town in western North Carolina that was a bit shy of good ball players. What we had going for us was a superb coach, Mr. Saunders, and about four really good players, two of whom later became college stars and one a minor-league player.

We also had a lot of determination, and made it to the regional championship against our archrival, Hickory. It was three times our size and had much more depth and a few more top players than we did. We were definitely the underdogs, but we were DETERMINED underdogs.

For the championship game we had to play on a neutral field, so the umpire tossed a coin for first at bat. Hickory won, and we actually felt relieved. We would be last at bat and thus have a chance to come from behind at the last minute. We figured we might need to do just that, and hoped that Hickory would grow complacent if it did happen.

We played fairly even until the fifth inning, with Hickory leading 3 to 2. I felt proud that my long fly ball gave one of our runners a chance to score, and hoped to get a real hit next time at bat. Poor Sam had struck out every time so far, and I suspected that Coach Saunders was thinking of a pinch hitter. He would have done it, too, except Sam had stopped more balls and thrown out more runners than anyone else.

Hickory drove in two runs in the fifth, but not through Sam, who was still flawless in the field. It looked bad for Newton, because the score was 5 to 2. Coach kept us from losing heart, and, when the seventh inning arrived, we made our move. I got my single, and so did the two boys who followed me. With the bases loaded, our hopes soared; but when we realized that there were two outs and skinny little Sam was the next batter, they fluttered in the breeze of uncertainty like leaves in the wind.

My feelings were mixed as I wondered if Coach would put in a pinch hitter. I wanted to win in the worst way, but I also wanted my buddy, Sam, to get his chance. As I stood at third base, I was glad the decision wasn't mine. I could see Coach walking over to him, and Sam talking vigorously with him and holding up his new pair of safety, prescription glasses. I knew that Coach had disapproved their use earlier, but with the game at stake, could Sam persuade him to let him stay in it?

Believe me, it was a tense moment, made even more so when Sam put on his spectacles, picked out his favorite bat, and approached the plate. The Hickory fans laughed and jeered at the somewhat ridiculous sight of a small, hitless player, wearing glasses. I winced a bit, then even I wondered if Sam could overcome the jeers, let alone his low average, and drive in a run or two. I feared he would leave the three of us stranded and crushed in spirit. It was one of the most stressful moments of my young life.

Baseball is a great game for keeping you in suspense. When the count got to 3 and 2, the time of decision was at hand, or so we' thought. Sam fouled the ball four times, and the Hickory first baseman damn near caught one of them. Newton fans were wild with cheers for Sam to get just a single, but became completely silent once the wind-up started. Hickory kept shouting, "Strike little four-eyes out!"

The pitcher then decided to throw a fastball right over the plate. He was tired of the foul ball routine and didn't want to walk a weak hitter and let me score. Sam was ready, so when it came zipping by he caught it squarely and used its speed to loft it way up in the air. I started for home plate at full speed, and so did all the others. It was obviously going to be a long fly ball, and if the fielder caught it we would be out anyway. But if he dropped it, several of us might score. By the time I reached home plate, I realized that a miracle had happened-- skinny little Sam had hit a grand-slam homer!

The score was now 6 to 5 and we were ahead by a run. Our side of the stands was in ecstasy. Hickory fans looked glum, but some of them shouted, "We have two more innings, so GO, HICKORY, GO!"

And go they did. When we reached the ninth inning, they were once again ahead by three runs, 9 to 6. If we could hold them at 9 to 6, our bottom of the ninth scenario might be played out. We had overcome such a lead earlier, but could we do it again? There was a mixture of doubt and determination in every member of our team. Sam made two of the throw-outs against Hickory in the top of the ninth without his glasses, which he didn't need while fielding.

Hickory didn't score, but the fans and the team were complacent, as we had hoped for earlier. They figured we were lucky as blazes to have forged ahead in the seventh, and that it was impossible to do so again. As Yogi Berra quipped later on, it was "deja vu all over again" for us. I got another single, and so did the boys that followed me. The bases were once again loaded." The only difference was there was only one out, so Coach didn't have to agonize about letting Sam bat again, or use his glasses. It was also less stressful, because when the 3-2 count came again, Sam only hit three foul balls, all safely landing in the stands. Would the pitcher try another fastball, or a change up?

Even Sam was concerned, so he prepared for the worst. When-a curve ball just missed the plate he didn't take a walk, as he could have. He swung with all the power in his wiry, little body. With only one out, we tagged up and prepared to make a dash for the next base. I watched the ball soar into the air toward right field, watched the fielder track it down and make a huge leap to catch it, and watched him miss it by inches as it barely cleared the fence. Wow! Another grand-slam homer!

We all trotted to home plate, and when Sam got there the team ran out, hugged him, slapped his back, and finally lifted him up to carry him off in triumph. The fans wanted part of the action and insisted that they, too, be allowed to carry him on their shoulders. But instead of going to the locker room, they decided to parade him around the field a time or two so everyone could join in the fun. I even saw some Hickory fans applaud as this game little player passed their side. Disappointed as they were, they recognized courage and determination when they saw them.

The newspapers all over the state wrote up the near miracle of one, low-average hitter, getting two grand-slam homers in a single game-- and a championship one at that! Sam became famous, and rightfully so. Best of all, the girls in town took a real interest in the fiery redhead, and he was never lonely on Saturday nights again.

When we went to college, neither of us made the team, so our pro dreams were not to be. Instead, we both had successful careers and happy marriages. Sam became C.E.O. of a large construction corporation and a highly respected community leader. He and his wife have four great kids. Life has been sweet for Sam, me, and our families. We both still treasure that wonderful, championship game, and it will stay in our memories until we die.

But what I treasure most is the important lesson I learned from Sam and this story, and I hope my readers will too: Never underestimate the power, determination and ability of a short, skinny, freckled, red-head kid who wears glasses-- or any other kid that looks like a loser.

Unlikely heroes can rise from the most unexpected source!

A VISIT WITH NATURE

It was a gorgeous fall afternoon when I started my walk in the New Hampshire countryside. Large, cumulous clouds drifted slowly by, morphing into different shapes in front of my eyes. With a little imagination I could see faces, animals and objects in the various formations. It made me feel like a kid in spite of my 78 years.

I wandered through green pastures filled with peaceful cows and sheep. Even the ring-nosed bull ignored my intrusion into his territory, sensing that I was no threat. All of the animals were eating the delicious grass with such gusto that I suspected they knew it may be their last chance. Soon the harsh winter chill, with its ice and snow, would once again blanket the earth with glistening white. My mind conjured up the twenty-third psalm, and I felt a Divine Presence, as if my own Good Shepherd was watching over me.

I crossed several small streams on well-placed stones, and my agile leaps to the distant ones kept my feet bone-dry. What a delightful musical sound the stream made as the crystal-clear water flowed over rocks, fallen trees, and around sharp bends. I heard a shepherd's horn in the distance, and it blended perfectly with the stream's harp-like notes. It sounded like an embryonic, classical-music composition.

The trees were full of autumnal color-- yellow, orange, red, even touches of purple. The cloud-filled sky and the dark green of the conifers, plus the light green of the few deciduous trees whose leaves were late in turning, formed a sublime background for the vivid colors. The paths through the woods were laden with similar leaves, but they were darker, dryer and somewhat drab. I surmised that they were the first to fall and that the filtered, flickering sunlight added to their drabness in a fascinating way. An occasional root made me watch my step, lest I trip and fall.

When I emerged from the woods, I discovered a grassy slope with more farm animals at its base. It exposed a view of a serene valley, a charming village, and rugged mountains fading into the distant horizon, like static waves in an ocean of color. 'Ah', I thought, 'here is a panoramic masterpiece of color and texture, composition and form, that would inspire the most gifted artist.'

I sat down to drink in its divine beauty, hoping it would last forever. It wasn't long before I realized I could lie down on the gentle slope and rest my head on a rock. With small up and down movements of my eyes, I could admire both the artistic landscape and the mobile clouds overhead. I was rapturous!

Can you guess what happened next? Yes, I fell asleep in the warm sunshine and became one with nature. Sometime later, a fierce thunderstorm woke me. Each brilliant flash of lightning was instantly followed by a loud boom, indicating that the thunderbolts were aimed at ME! Not only were they deafening and frightening, but so close together that I was frozen to my resting-place. I feared that the slightest movement would attract the bolts directly to me. I'm glad I didn't panic, because my instinct said, "Run like blazes!"

I could see rain all around me and hear the wind screeching below, but somehow I remained warm and dry. I curled up into a fetal position, covered my eyes with my hands, and waited until the storm faded away. It left with the musical rumble of distant thunder, as if some huge kettledrums were saying, "Farewell!".

Nature was again tranquil, and I remained inert to watch the brilliant hues of a spectacular sunset. The animals left their makeshift shelters for more grass, which now provided both food and drink, thanks to the rain. I wondered why the dangerous thunderstorm was necessary, but a voice inside said, "Didn't it deepen your appreciation of the miracle of creation and the power of Beethoven's Sixth Symphony, the "Pastoral"?

If you doubt the power of either, try reclining on your own sofa with a disc playing the "Pastoral" symphony. Perhaps YOUR imagination will take YOU on as wonderful a visit with nature as mine did for me.

Thanks, Beethoven, Mother Nature, and the Divine Power that created them-- and our imaginations!

VOICES IN THE NIGHT

Picture this: It is August, 1940, and a blistering heat wave has engulfed the northeastern states. To add to the misery, the great depression is reluctant to leave and Hitler's war in Europe threatens to entrap America. The future is foreboding, but faint hope and President Roosevelt sustain the nation.

You are living in a small, studio apartment on the fifth floor of a walk-up tenement on the Lower East Side of New York City. To cool off and get some much -needed sleep, you place your tattered sofa cushions on the fire escape; but voices in the night make sleep fitful and uncertain. While in your room, the voices were muffled, but your new position on the fire escape brings them surprisingly close. They seem to float upward in the darkness and reverberate off the walls of the empty warehouse on the other side of the narrow street.

As you close your eyes, a voice comes from 4-B. It is a baby crying for its mother's milk; but the mother is dry, so the baby must wait until she fixes a bottle. You have heard the sound many times before, but never so loudly, so the wait seems interminable for both the baby and you. You wonder why she doesn't soothe the baby and why it takes so long to warm milk in this damned heat? And why doesn't her lazy husband help?

Just as sleep seems near, a mature couple starts yelling at each other in 2-C. The language is foreign, but the tone convinces you that they are swear words. As the fight reaches a crescendo, you wonder if it will turn violent. Should you fetch the police? Will another tenant intercede? Will they kiss and make up? Damn these stupid decisions, and curses on people that can't seem to get along!

Later on you hear a young couple spooning on the entry stoop. He is trying to coax a kiss (or more) from his giggling, coy girl friend. You smile softly and start recalling your own high-school years with a strange mixture of joy and sadness. Yes, you had some good times, but why did you have to be thrown on your own so soon in life? Some girl classmates flash through your mind, and you visualize them enjoying the fancy colleges they now attend; but will they ever want to date the likes of you again?

Your reverie is disturbed by a radio in I-D, and you recognize the voice of a popular comedian. It sounds like Jack Benny-- yes, it is Jack, because you now pick up the gravelly voice of Rochester. The listeners laugh loudly and often, and you wish they would turn up the volume so you could hear the jokes and skits. You wonder if you should try to find a cheap, used radio to get more laughs in your struggling life and even listen to the big bands. But reality sets in, and you recognize that your low-paying job barely pays your keep.

Just as you start feeling sorry for yourself, you hear a voice in 3-C. It is a small child's innocent and sincere prayer for her missing father. You silently voice one of your own that her prayer will be answered, and, perhaps, something will happen to relieve the depressed spirit and awesome heat that fills the great city.

Your pity soon vanishes into the night air when you hear squeaking bed springs, followed by the ecstatic sounds of mutual orgasms from the young couple in 5-A. Your heart starts pounding excitedly, and you wish you could find a loving mate to share your lonely, impoverished life. You mentally dream that once you find one you might move to a small town and start a family of your own.

As the couple's passion subsides, you marvel at their ability to perform in the stifling heat. Ah, young love! It must have its day; it always finds a way! You smile at your rhymes and think, 'Maybe I should try my hand at poetry some day.'

Suddenly, the silence is broken by a 'shot' in an adjacent street. You hope it is just a backfire from a car and not another gangland killing; but cars are rare in this impoverished part of the city, even taxis, so you imagine the worst. You contemplate the fine line that separates man's ingenuity from his cruelty and wonder if old Adolph will cause you or your friends to die young, like he already has for so many in Europe.

While your thoughts are on cruelty and death, you hear an old person near life's end, moaning and groaning with pain, but reluctant to surrender the wonderful gift. It sounds like Mr. Barbarossa in 3-B, who has lung cancer from too many cigarettes. It makes you speculate about how many more years, or perhaps just months or days, you will be given, and if those night courses at C.C.N.Y will pay off.

These and more voices you hear from your improvised bed on the fire escape. You look up at the dim stars above, almost obliterated by the city lights and haze, and suddenly realize how insignificant the voices you have heard must be to the infinite cosmos. You pray that God is equally great, but not so distant, and that His compassion will mark the voices, as he does with the fall of a tiny sparrow.

The voices gradually die down and you close your eyes and fall asleep. But voices from your past and your own fertile imagination fill your wondrous dreams, and you are no longer alone.

Next morning, you wake up to the rising cacophony of the city's distant traffic and the human voices on the street below. You reflect on how precious and wonderful those voices in the night were. What a broad cross-section of humanity you have overheard, with all its pleasures and problems; promises and disappointments; achievements and failures; mortality and immortality;....

As you prepare to leave for your early morning job, you see makeshift beds on other fire escapes. You hope their occupants have been similarly blessed by hearing their own "Voices In The Night"!

Now fast forward to today: You have become old and gray, but have achieved a modest amount of wealth and have long since left the squalor of the tenements for a suburban home. . You found a wonderful mate in 1944 and raised a small, loving family. In spite of humble beginnings, you and your mate have realized "The American Dream" and now glory in your grandchildren and your life of leisure and travel. You are now living in an active retirement community, and the only "voices in the night" that you now hear are: a coyote howling; an airplane flying overhead; your own blaring TV; and your spouse's, "good night, dear!"

As you think back on those early days, you can't help but wonder: 'Is it better to be old, well off and rich with memories; or is it better to be young, poor and rich with unfilled ambitions?' But there is no answer.

The Voices In The Night Are Silent!

WORLD PEACE--AT LAST!
(Fantasy or Prediction?)

It is now 2050, and the world has been at peace since 2020. There have been no wars between nations for 30 years, and even crime and violent uprisings inside nations have almost been eliminated. Some of the wisest human minds thought it could never happen, but they were wrong. So how did it happen?

Today's historians have several reasons to explain this unexpected reversal of greed, hate, envy, conflict and violence, which have been prevalent in humans throughout history. Part of the reason was because people of enormous wealth started to contribute billions of their personal wealth to causes which would help those most in need and overcome critical world problems.

When billionaires like Ted Turner, Bill Gates and Warren Buffet made their huge gifts in the early years of our century, it started a trend. Accumulating a fortune was, and still is, a normal and desirable thing; but once personal gratification reached a certain level, the wealthy of that era wondered if the huge surplus was a blessing or a curse. Yes, it gave them more power, but it made them more vulnerable to dislike, hatred, and even dangerous deeds from disturbed people. They found that helping others not only made them more fulfilled and happy, but actually helped their remaining fortunes grow. It was like compound interest-- the more they helped, the more they made, so help compounded.

Best of all, they were such brilliant givers that they established charitable institutions that taught people in need how to help themselves, thus joining the growing mainstream of happy, productive people. When the world's needy saw hope and progress growing, they started substituting cooperation for conflict and the population explosion became manageable. Furthermore, leaders of many nations were inspired by the wealthy donors' example, and started doing more for their own people and others.

Of course there were still people with extreme ideological and religious views. The 9/11 World Trade Center disaster awoke the average citizen to the clever, but diabolic, scheme of Muslim extremists. Their number one goal was to convert the world to Islam; failing that, their number two goal was to destroy the world, even if Islam went with it!

If the entire world was destroyed, their distorted view convinced them that they would still enter Paradise, with all those sensuous and eager virgins. And if they converted everyone to Islam, their reward would be even greater, both on earth and in Paradise. It was a win-win situation to their distorted minds, and a lose-lose one for everybody else. Their method was to use civilization's great inventions and free societies to in-filter and mass kill, using tactics and strategies that would terrorize and de-stabilize governments and their citizens.

As 9/11 proved, one single incident could do a tremendous amount of damage, not only to the target site and its victims, but to the whole nation and its friends. The terrorists realized that non-Muslim nations had many more weapons of mass destruction, but figured that if they were used in quantity against Muslim nations, their number two goal would be realized.

Moderate Muslims, seeing the good trend of humanity and the evil and destructive direction of the terrorists, increased their support for the good trend. But the terrorists still had many supporters and moderate Muslims who were too frightened to oppose them, so they were still a major threat. As the historians reminded us: "People who kill and think they are fulfilling God's will are huge threats, because reason cannot prevail."

Historians gave the most credit for World Peace finally arriving to Mother Nature. Humanity's delay in fixing environmental damage started creating more and more natural disasters. Avalanches, droughts, disease, earthquakes, floods, hurricanes, insects, pestilence, polar melting, tornadoes, tsunamis, volcanoes, wild fires, and a few new ones, started growing at a rapid pace. So how did these disasters help World Peace arrive? The nations of the world became so busy coping with the disasters that thoughts and actions toward war diminished greatly.

Not only were the nations busy saving lives and rebuilding, but the international help to victims increased. That created so much good will that even the people in rogue nations rebelled against any leader who wanted to take advantage of a rival nation stricken by disaster. Furthermore, the frequency and universality of the natural disasters made it obvious that no nation was exempt. Even the most heartless leaders finally caught on, thinking: "Hmm-- if I help other nations, they will help me in return when disaster hits my country, and I can save my shaky position as leader."

Leaders of major religions attributed the favorable trend to God Almighty. Their rationale was something like this: No matter what name we give God, there is a Divine Force that created and controls the entire universe. Nature is the way God controls it, and once God saw the free will of his most gifted creatures headed for self-destruction, God took action via natural disasters and the wealthy. God's message to mankind, according to the leaders, was: "Mend your ways-- or perish!"

Most nations and religions seemed to get the message, and started fixing past mistakes. Some of the leaders even admitted they had made mistakes and repented, and the people loved them for it; especially when they followed up with sound ideas and effective actions to speed up the "fixing" process.

While all nations were hit by natural disasters, those who followed Islam seemed to be disproportionly affected. Most of their leaders felt that Allah was especially angry with them, and subsequent events strengthened that belief. Even some of the terrorists started wondering, but a large number continued their evil ways.

The natural disasters made terrorists concentrate on Europe for two reasons. First, it became too difficult to reach the United States, and second, they remembered that it was the Europeans who had done so much harm to Islam in past history. Several large European cities experienced worse attacks than had occurred on 9/11, and the situation seemed impossible to stop. Europeans started praying and there was a religious revival. Some converted to Islam, but the attacks kept coming.

In 2013, a natural disaster happened that shook the terrorists to the core. An unusually powerful earthquake hit both Mecca and Medina just before the Holy Season of Ramadan. Fortunately, no lives were lost, but some of the Muslim clerics suffered bad injuries. Unfortunately, it leveled most of the Holy sites!

The scientific community of the world was amazed at the huge improbability of <u>two, highly-concentrated quakes</u> hitting the <u>same day</u> in <u>two different special cities</u>. It was completely unprecedented, and sent them scurrying for a logical explanation. But most of the world, especially Muslims, didn't need a scientific explanation. It was clear that Allah was very, very displeased. All of the terrorists' supporters and most of the terrorists got the message. The remaining die-hard terrorists did just that. They were either killed by their past supporters or committed suicide. When 2014 arrived, the era of terrorism was finally over!

During the next six years, the world made such wonderful progress that it was unequalled in history. The United Nations ceased being disunited and started adopting sound resolutions, following them up with effective action, and quelling the human rights abuses and the few limited wars and rebellions among small nations. Rogue nations saw the wisdom of obeying the resolutions, and soon lost their "rogue" title.

Military budgets plummeted to optimum levels, and the savings went for societal improvements. Mecca and Medina were restored and spiritual additions made. The World's religions met and, after several months work, agreed to respect each other's doctrines concerning man's relationship with God. They also combined the moral values from each religion into a universal code for human relationships.

Among the many moral values in the new code were the Golden Rule, in its several forms from various religions, and those from Judaism's Ten Commandments. But the most simple and powerful one came from a Jewish Rabbi called Jesus Christ:

"LOVE ONE ANOTHER!"

EPILOGUE:

Ever since the year 2020, the world's vision became the clearest ever, and mankind excelled in fulfilling its great potential. Cooperation and healthy competition replaced conflict; intelligent charity replaced dumb greed; sound energy policies and technology fixed the environment, thereby greatly reducing natural disasters and their cost in lives, property and money; health care improved greatly and was made available to poorer nations; education became world wide and unleashed so much knowledge and creativity that most humans found a niche, where they could not only pursue happiness, but achieve it in full measure.

But the most surprising event in the first half of the 21st century was recently revealed: The Mecca and Medina earthquakes were not natural disasters, or created solely by God! They were created by German and Japanese charitable foundations as part of their atonement for the terrible death, destruction and disorder their countries made by starting World War

II.

They figured they could save the world by sending a strong "Message from God" to religious extremists, starting with the most pressing threat: Muslim extremists and terrorists. They then got their best engineers and other talented people to devise a nuclear-powered boring machine that could worm its way to Mecca and Medina thousands of feet below the earth's surface. They used a submarine to plant it secretly off the shore of Saudi Arabia. Once the boring machine wormed its way directly beneath the chosen sites, the remaining nuclear energy was unleashed to create the unusual earthquakes.

So how did the world react to this surprising news? The first reaction was shock, followed by calls to punish the participants for destroying Holy sites and injuring people. But most of them were either dead or elderly, so punishment seemed too hash. Eventually, it became clear that their bold action had not only prevented mankind's self destruction, but had triggered World Peace and all its wonderful benefits. All was forgiven and monuments erected to them.

But how about the world's religious leaders and the faithful? The leaders issued a joint statement saying: "All humans are part of God's creation, and were used as vessels to send God's message to mankind." When some questioned it, they said: "God has spoken to us many times through his prophets and the Messiah. This time they were active prophets. Besides, most people know this truth:

GOD MOVES IN MYSTERIOUS WAYS!"

Author's note: Yes, this story can be classified as extreme fantasy and unreal optimism. But suppose it got widely published and was used to make a popular movie or TV series. Would the resulting wide publicity trigger some positive thoughts among the world's leaders? Would they concoct wise policies and effective actions to minimize, or avoid, the impending disaster the world now faces? Odds are against any of the above happening during my lifetime, since I am an 86 year old man; but wouldn't it be wonderful if all of them came true? If they did, and I received royalties or fees, I would contribute heavily to worthwhile charities. Ted Turner, Bill Gates, Warren Buffet, are you interested?

I am aware that this fantasy could be offensive to some Muslims, but that is not my intent. As a Judaeo-Christian, I respect all religions and hope that the tremendous good they have done will not be undone by the evil deeds of extremists from any religion. Too many people in today's world are wondering if religion does more harm than good, and are abandoning their earlier beliefs and support. I hope that all religions, including Judaism and Christianity, will mend their own faults.

I also hope that Muslim Clerics will stop preaching anything that instills hate, violence and killing in their followers, and focus on love and forgiveness among all people, races and creeds. After all, we are all

"Allah's" children, and deserve to live in peace and harmony with each other. I especially hope that <u>most</u> Muslims will agree that extremists and terrorists distort Islamic scriptures and beliefs, and will do more to stop their evil ways and quell leaders of their nations who promote terror and destabilizing actions.

Terrorists and destabilizing national leaders are now sowing a whirlwind of hate, which, if unchecked, will reap a gigantic hurricane of death and destruction. Should that happen, it could eventually harm Islam and its followers more than the rest of the world. This is not a prophesy, just a prediction.

WORLD'S LONGEST FLYBALL
(2988 words)

Peter Kerhoulis is noted for his unusual promotions. It was he who promoted major TV shows with the number one women's tennis player's matches against men ranked between number 50 and 30 . The first one was played in the big stadium at Flushing Meadows, NY, and by golly, she beat him, just as Peter figured. Her victory led to matches with the number 40 and number 30 in other major stadiums, both of which she eked out victories. Soon to come is the number 25 man. Peter is a brilliant promoter, and plans matches with number 25, 20, 15, 10, and then 9,8,7, etc until she loses, or becomes number one!

With each victory over a man, the audience has increased and so has Peter's wealth. If she gets to the top ten ranks, he plans to pressure the tennis authorities to have unisex tournaments, thus preserving his place in history. Naturally, the men have been reluctant to compete with a woman, but the large prize money Peter offers is too tempting to let ego stand in the way. Besides, tennis is a game that doesn't depend on brute strength, as the victories of smaller men like Jimmy Connors over much larger and stronger opponents proved.

In 2006, as he was watching the World Series, he wondered how he could invade the domain of baseball. When his favorite hitter hit a homer out of the stands, he figured what he should do. Yes, it was to have a contest, using the top ten hitters, to see who could set a world's record for distance. Naturally, it would be a TV special and would be attended by fans, but where?

After a bit of pondering, he figured it should be at a major golf course. To heighten the suspense, he planed to let minor league hitters and non-professionals via a series of special events in which they might qualify. Not only would that be good publicity for the big event, but would actually fatten his purse even more.

Once the qualifying rounds were complete, two minor leaguers qualified and one non-professional. The non-professional was outstanding during the qualifying rounds, so the press started investigating his history. His name was Bruce Babcock, and he had played baseball at North Carolina State University, where he graduated five years ago with a degree in Civil Engineering. Following graduation, he joined a construction firm in a small North Carolina town and played during evenings with a local amateur baseball team. At first, he was reluctant, but his friends, and even his Mom, convinced him to "Go for it!"

The Charlotte Observer Newspaper did a bit of investigating as to why Bruce was such a long hitter, Other than an excellent physique and splendid eyesight, he seemed normal. However, there were unconfirmed rumors that his pretty mom had met Ted Williams, and that Bruce was an illegal offspring from their brief affair.

Finally, the big day arrived. Bruce was the thirteenth and last to qualify, and most everybody thought that was a bad omen. Worse yet, he didn't know any of the other players, so none of them paid any attention to him. Even the press paid little attention to him, figuring his presence was just part of Peter's publicity. However, he did get to sign all three balls he was to hit, as did the other contestants.

Peter had gotten permission to mark the course every ten yards within the projected hitting range, and stationed officials at various points to do the following: measure the exact distance; have it confirmed by the two closest officials; announce it over a microphone; mark it on the autographed balls; and deliver them to him. Once in his possession, he planned to put them up for auction within the next month, starting with the shortest distance ones. Peter was confident that the autographed balls with distances on them would make it the most financially rewarding promotion of his career, and put him in the billionaire ranks.

Each of the contestants used the same metal bat so there would not be a broken one, and the balls had been carefully selected to insure they were as identical as possible. Furthermore, a pitching machine was used, which sent each ball at the same speed, and over the exact place over home plate. To allow for different hitting preferences, the speed was 75mph on the first pitch, 80 on the second, and 85 on the third. Elevation varied three inches above and below the first pitch. The hitter stepped on a button to start the machine. It was a cloudless day, with near zero wind velocity, and the fairway was newly mowed to insure maximum rolling distance. Peter and his crew had made sure that the contest was as fair as possible.

When Bruce finally stepped up to the plate as the 13th hitter, the longest ball was hit by a Boston Red Socks outfielder, and was 823 feet. The shortest one was hit by a minor leaguer, and was 654 feet. Bruce took a deep breath, took his stance, and pressed the button. He caught the ball squarely and it arched high into the sky. The official announced, "816 feet!" There was a big gasp from the crowd, followed by applause. Bruce was in third place and won the $500,000 prize money on his first try. That would be more money than he had ever imagined, especially in such a short time.

His second hit soared even farther, and the official announced, "833 feet!!" The crowd yelled wildly, Bruce smiled and was excited that he had won first place, and the $1,500,000 prize. Once the crowd settled down, he got ready for his final swing. The other contestants looked surprised, kinda gloomy, and one said, "Who the hell is this guy? What sort of a ringer has Kerhoulis found to embarrass us this way?"

Bruce was a damn good engineer, so he had figured how to get the maximum distance by analyzing his first two hits. When the ball came over the plate, he used all his strength and knowledge, hit the ball squarely, and watched it soar even higher in the sky. Everyone gasped in awe, even the other contestants and the officials. The last official had to get help measuring the distance, because it had gone beyond the last marker, which was 900 feet. It had rolled to 947 feet, the official wrote the distance on the ball, and then held it high over his head while announcing the distance. The crowd went wild, as did the official, who would get a big bonus.

Then a very surprising thing happened. An eagle flew down from a nearby tree, grabbed the ball from the official's upraised hand and flew away with it. Peter told his crew to follow the eagle and retrieve the ball, offering $50,000 for its safe return.

Alas, all of them lost sight of the fast flying eagle. Peter then awarded the prizes, with Bruce winning $2,500,000 for first and second prize. He couldn't believe his good luck; or was it just his hidden skill? He then joined Peter and the other contestants for dinner at the clubhouse, followed by interviews by the media. Wow! He was now rich, and destined to be famous just by striking two baseballs better than anyone else.

An 18-year-old bus boy, named Alonzo Alfredo, asked Bruce for his autograph. Bruce not only gave it to him, but a $20 tip! Bruce also told him about the missing ball the eagle stole, saying, "Find it young man, and you may get a fortune of your own!"

As Alonzo biked home that night, he wondered if the eagle who stole the ball was the one he sometimes spotted when he hiked through the forest about two miles from the golf club. He knew where the eagle nested, so he decided to see if it had dropped it on its way, or maybe put it in its nest. It was too late to search for it that day, since he didn't get off work until dark. But early the next morning, he rode his bike back to the woods, hid his bike in some bushes, and, starting from the road in line with the contest hole, walked slowly toward the eagle's nest. Searching along the way, there was no sign of the ball, so he figured the eagle must have taken it to the nest. As he reached the tree, he could see the eagle feeding its chicks.

His thoughts were: "Hmm, I can climb the tree alright, but suppose the eagle attacks me. It's natural for them to protect their young, and they're pretty damn powerful. Hey, I still have my bike helmet and goggles on, so they'll protect my head and eyes, but how about the rest of me? Ah, I have it, I'll carry a big stick and use it to fight off the eagle."

His plan worked perfectly, except one of the chicks bit his hand as he grabbed the ball. He climbed down the tree and started walking back to his bike. Although he knew about the $50,000 reward for the ball, he remembered Bruce's remarks about getting rich. He was a bright young man, and decided to take the ball home and hide it in his bureau drawer. Once he got to the club restaurant, he learned that the reward had been increased to $100,000, and was tempted to get the ball and take the big reward.

Fortunately, he spotted Bruce, who had returned to the club for lunch and a TV interview. He figured he could trust Bruce, so after the interview he approached him. The conversation was as follows:

"Good afternoon, Mr. Babcock. May I have a private word with you?"

"Of course, Alonzo, lets go over here and sit on these chairs, they're out of earshot of others."

"Last night you said that if I could find the missing ball, I might get a fortune. Can you tell me how big it would be and how to go about it?"

"Did you find it, Alonzo?"

"Between you and me?"

" Of course."

"Well, I found it alright, and I have it hidden away safely. So what should I do? I'll share the money with you if you'll help me."

"That won't be necessary, Alonzo. I won $2,500,000 yesterday and already offers are pouring in for even bigger money. I'll help you just as a friend. Here's what I think you should do. Don't tell anyone about it, not even your parents or friends. Keep it hidden safely where no one will look, and wait to see what develops. I understand that the promoter, Mr. Kerhoulis, plans to raffle all the other balls to the highest bidder. With all the publicity and the rarity of the balls, I suspect they will all bring large sums, especially the winning ball. It could be worth millions! There's only one problem."

"What is it, what is it?"

"It's who is the legal owner? Mr. Kerhoulis may claim it's his, since he paid for it originally. However, there may be a law that says that anything that disappears by natural causes belong to the person who finds it. Tell you what. I'll contact a lawyer and find out. I'll stay a few extra days to do it. OK?"

"Sure, Mr. Babcock. That'll be just fine. Meantime, I'd like you to meet my mother. She's a widow and we live all alone. We don't have much money, but she works and we get by."

"Great idea. Once you finish your noontime chores, I'll drive you to her. Will she be at home or at work?"

" She'll be at home, because she works at night, and doesn't start until 4pm."

After a short drive, they approached a low-rent apartment complex. Alonzo took him to the third floor, rang the doorbell to warn his mom, and waited for her. When she opened the door, she said, "What are you doing home at this hour, and who's this gentleman? You aren't in any trouble are you?"

"This is Mr. Babcock. He's the one who won the big contest at the club yesterday. We became friends, and he wanted to meet you. And no, Mom, I'm not in trouble."

"Welcome, Mr. Babcock. I'm Maria Alfredo. Come on in and I'll fix some refreshments."

After they shook hands, Bruce turned to Alonzo and said, "I think we should tell her our secret, if you don't mind."

"I don't mind. In fact, I think it's a good idea. Why don't you tell her?"

Bruce then told her the complete story, emphasizing the need to keep it quiet until he talked with a lawyer. Maria had these wildly mixed emotions: relief that Alonzo hadn't been hurt while getting the ball from the eagles nest; happy that they might come into a lot of money; grateful for the kindness of Bruce; and concern about what the lawyer would say. Of course she promised to keep mum about the baseball, and didn't even try to find its hiding place.

After some coffee, cookies, and more conversation, Bruce drove Alonzo back to work and started searching for a reputable lawyer. After a few inquires, he found a highly respected one, Mr. Jason Cunningham, and called him on the telephone. Once Jason heard Bruce's name, he knew he was talking with the big winner, and agreed to meet early the next morning. Bruce then explained the case without giving any names, so Jason could do any necessary research.

Next morning, after the usual introductory conversation, Jason said "I have some good news for you. There are several adjudicated cases that support your case. They both involve valuable items that were lost by natural causes, and the court ruled that the finder could keep them. One involved a magpie stealing a costly necklace, and the other a valuable document being blown away by a sudden windstorm. I believe your case is similar to the magpie case, and could be won. At worse, the finder could get at least half the value of the missing baseball. Since the former owner, Mr. Kerhoulis, is very wealthy, I think the odds are very much in favor of the finder, unless he is also wealthy."

"Great", Bruce replied. "The finder is not wealthy, In fact he is only 18 and lives with his widowed mother in low rent housing. Will age be a factor?"

"Not in this state. At 18, a person is legally an adult, with all the privileges and responsibilities."

"Good, then I'll give the good news to the finder. How much do I owe you?

"Nothing for this consultation. However, I would like to represent the finder if legal services are required. I would do so on a contingency basis, charging only my usual fee and expenses if we win."

Bruce closed the meeting with, "That's very good of you, sir, and I think I can convince the finder to use your services if needed. If you win, I'll even give you a sizeable bonus. Since legal services may not be needed, I would like to pay you $1000 for this meeting. After all, I won a fortune the other day, and can easily afford it."

With some reluctance, Jason finally agreed. When Bruce returned to the clubhouse, he found Alonzo and gave him the good news. Alonzo was overjoyed. Bruce then said, "Tell you what. I would like to give you a scholarship for college. You can quit this job in the fall, and attend any university you choose that will admit you. I would also like to help your mother, if she will let me. Of course, if you come into the fortune you expect, you can use your own money and we can set up a charitable foundation to help others. Does that appeal to you?"

Alonzo broke into tears, squeezed Bruce's hand and sobbed, "Yes, yes, yes!"

Epilogue: Bruce approached Peter Kerhoulis and convinced him to let Alonzo keep the ball by telling him of the charitable foundation they hoped to establish. Peter was so impressed that he not only agreed to let Alonzo keep the ball, but wanted to join them in forming the foundation. He explained that he had now reached his billion dollar goal and had starting thinking along those lines himself.

Bruce quit his job and used his engineering skills to build housing which deserving poor people could own for the price of rent. He met a beautiful woman, and is now happily married with a kid on the way.

Alonzo will graduate from North Carolina State soon, with a degree in Civil Engineering. He plans to help Bruce on the housing and other projects.

Alonzo's mother, Maria, moved to nicer quarters and soon after married Jason, who was a widower. He now represents the foundation full time, and his new wife is on the board.

Peter decided to start a program to help unusually talented people who needed a boost. His first program was to help senior citizens who had ideas so big they didn't have the resources to accomplish them. Several major inventions are now on the market, and several seniors have become successful authors, painters, and composers. He is now starting a program to help young people with big ideas. God only knows what will come of this effort, but don't be surprised if one of them follows in Peter's footsteps and starts promoting unusual events.

This story is pure fiction, but here's hoping some wealthy person or foundation will adopt some of the ideas herein. Better yet, contact me, and I will give you more ideas than you would imagine possible from an 89 year old retired Aerospace engineer

ABOUT THE AUTHOR

L. Macon Epps grew up and finished high school in Newton, NC, following which he obtained a Bachelor of Mechanical Engineering degree from N.C. State College at age 20. He worked as an aerospace engineer for 37+ years at Grumman Aerospace Corporation, and earned a Master of Aeronautical Engineering degree from New York University's night school. He has also attended special courses given by Cornell University, Columbia University, and California Tech., plus other non-university courses.

His Grumman experience included: Shop orientation; structural design and analysis; Chief of Weights and Balance; Assistant to the Chief Technical Engineer; Assistant Director of Research and Advanced Development; Chief Value Engineer; Assistant Program Manager for the Lunar Module; and Assistant Director of Advanced Civil Systems. He retired in 1977, and was founding president of the I-Cubed Corporation, which specialized in new innovations, temporary jobs for other retirees; and sales representation for other corporation. Following his second retirement in 1986, he moved to Dover, New Hampshire.

His part time activities during his working and retirement years included: Various community and church positions; do-it yourself home improvements; tennis (a lifetime commitment); golf; water and snow skiing; sailing; oil painting; and various musical activities (He played a baritone horn in five different bands.) He and his wife have traveled extensively, visiting all continents except South America and Antarctica.

He attended several creative writing classes and it became one of his principal activities during his retirement years. In 2004, he co-authored a book "Universal Spiritual Thoughts," published by AuthorHouse, and was the originator, editor and contributor of two limited-edition anthologies titled, "The Creative Community," and "Imagination and Reality," published during the nineties by the Dover, NH Rotary Club. He was also the originator and chairman of a Rotary project to paint a large mural on a building in downtown Dover.

This collection of short stories comes from his imagination and experiences during his retirement years, mostly between the age of 68 and 88. Some were so personal to him that he used the first person; others used the third person. Readers who have a preference can make a choice, but he hopes they will try both types.

He is in good health, and hopes the genes and life style that let his mother and two of her siblings live to age 95, 95 and 96, will let him keep writing many more years.

Note: For licensing any or all of the stories herein, contact L. Macon Epps at 17236, Village 17, Camarillo, CA, 93012. Tel. # 805/389-9478.